For my babies who are growing up too fast.
I'm proud of you xx

CHAPTER ONE

I'm jolted awake by a sharp cry.

I inhale and open my eyes wide, glancing around, trying to work out where I am. My legs are cramped, curled beneath me on the sofa. I must have fallen asleep. That cry. Was it…? No, it's okay, nothing to get in a panic over. It's just the Swedish crime drama I was supposed to be watching – I can't even stay awake for my favourite programmes these days.

I stretch my legs and pause the TV, listening, just in case the noise didn't come from the television. Outside, the sky is bruising, a purplish glow spreading above the horseshoe-shaped road that forms our little cul-de-sac of six houses. A stillness seems to settle over everything, and the sky darkens further.

Another sound makes me catch my breath. Not from the TV then… There it is again – this time there's no mistake that it's a tiny whimper from the baby monitor. My little girl Daisy does that a lot, those little short cries. I bet if I were to go upstairs now, she'd be fast asleep. I try to relax, smiling to myself at the thought of her round cheeks, and those tiny fists up around her ears like a miniature boxer. I count to ten in my head, wait a moment more, then exhale in relief at the continued silence. I pull my feet up under me once more and press rewind on the remote.

Daisy is already six months old and we moved her into her own room last week. But I don't like her being so far away from us. It was comforting to have her next to me, and easier for the night feeds. Now that she's in her own room, I have to drag myself out of bed and go to her when she cries instead of reaching across and bringing her into bed with me. Moving her was more for Dominic's sake. My husband is a light sleeper and her little movements, cries and snuffles throughout the night kept him awake. He's also training for a triathlon, so a good night's sleep is important to him. That's where he is this evening – out running. I don't know how he can stand it in this heatwave, it must feel like running through treacle.

I frown at another cry, louder this time. With a sigh, I pause the TV, reach for the baby monitor and curl my hand around the chunky white plastic device, waiting to see if she wakes properly this time.

The monitor is suddenly full of static like an old radio, dots of red light flashing across its front. I wish we could invest in a new set of super-duper monitors with a video screen and thermometer and night vision and all the other extras, but money is tight at the moment. Mum got us this second-hand set from a car boot sale; they're basic, with just sound and lights, but it's better than nothing.

The static clears and the lights pulse again, and I hear a different sound through the speaker. Not a cry this time, but a cough. Not a baby's cough. An adult cough. A man's cough.

What?

No!

Fear clutches at my belly. Sweat breaks out on my upper lip and prickles my scalp. The thump, thump, thump of my heart beats in my ears. I must have been mistaken. Surely it can't have been… but there… what's that? Whispering. And then, clear as day, a man's hushed voice:

'Quick, let's just take the baby now and go.'

Terror turns my blood to ice and freezes my brain. There is someone in my house.

Daisy! *Someone's trying to take Daisy!*

My legs are concrete, but I have to move. I have to stop whoever is trying to steal my child. I lurch to my feet, a scream forming in my throat, but I press my lips together to stop it escaping.

Without any kind of plan, I race up the stairs, my mind projecting forward. I'm already imagining my scream as I discover my baby has gone. I'm already feeling the anguish and heartbreak. I'm even imagining Dominic and me on TV giving a press conference – him stoic, me in tears. I'm already imagining that my life as I know it is over. This can't be happening…

As my bare feet hit the carpeted stairs, I dismiss the fact that I'm a small, slight, thirty-five-year-old woman in a cotton sundress with no self-defence skills and no weapon to use against a dangerous intruder. I'll do whatever is necessary. I won't let them take my child! They'll have to kill me first.

The most awful thoughts crowd my mind: kidnappers, child slavery, illegal adoption, sickos… Maybe I should have called the police immediately, but there's no time, and anyway, it's too late now. I'm already approaching Daisy's bedroom, ready to tear and lunge at whoever is there. Ready to stop whoever is trying to snatch my baby. I shove open the door to the room, panting like an animal, terror clawing at my skin. I'm not scared of the intruder. I'm scared that they might harm my child. That they might take her. That I might be too late to save her.

Tensed to attack, I take in the scene.

There's no one here. The room is empty.

With a sob, I race over to my daughter's white cot. My heart jolts and lifts. She's here. My baby is here, sleeping. I drop the monitor onto her mattress and scoop her familiar shape up in my arms, stroke her dark hair with trembling fingers, drop grateful kisses onto her soft forehead, the milky scent of her helping to quell my panic. I glance over at the window, heart still knocking against my ribs. The light from a violet sunset stains the closed curtains. I draw them apart and stare out of the open window, convinced I will see two figures making their escape across the garden or the playing fields beyond. But the hazy August evening is muggy and still. Silent, apart from a slight sighing breeze through the trees and the distant growl of a car engine. As I pull the double-glazed window shut with a scrape and a thud, I notice a new blanket of windfall apples strewn by the back gate.

I stare down at Daisy's face, reassuring myself that she really is okay, she's safe. The thump of my heartbeat gradually slows, my skin cools, my breathing steadies. Did I imagine that voice in the monitor? No. I heard it clear as a bell. With a new sense of dread, I check behind the bedroom door, then fling open the wardrobe doors.

No one there.

But then I hear the unmistakable mewling cry again. The sound of my baby. Only it can't be her – my daughter is in my arms and she is quiet. The sound is coming from the monitor which I dropped in the crib. It's not the sound of *my* baby. I realise it must be someone else's child. The baby monitor must be picking up another signal.

And now I can hear the voices again – a hushed, frantic whispering, broken up by static. Are the voices coming from a neighbour's house? With a racing mind, I think about the other five houses in my cul-de-sac. There are no other babies in the road as far as I'm aware. I would know about them. Unless someone is visiting one of my neighbours. Which would mean that another child is in danger. Heart hammering, I know I have to warn my neighbours.

Daisy is a warm weight against my chest. Still sleeping, unconcerned by the drama unfolding, unaffected by my racing heartbeat. I reach into her crib and pick up the discarded monitor. Noiseless now. I turn up the volume, but there's nothing, no static, no voices or cries. Am I too late to save the other child?

I rush downstairs with Daisy in my arms and locate my phone on the arm of the sofa. One-handed, I dial 999 with my thumb before flinging open my front door and scanning the cul-de-sac. Everything looks normal: front doors shut, familiar cars parked neatly in their driveways, no visitors' cars that I can see. The ring tone in my ear stops abruptly. A woman's voice:

'*Hello, emergency services, which service do you require? Fire, police, or ambulance?*'

'Police,' I say, my voice sounding thin and hysterical. 'Please hurry.'

'*Connecting you now.*'

A man's voice comes on the line. Composed and assured. '*Hello, can I take your name please?*'

'Kirstie Rawlings.'

'*Where are you calling from, Kirstie?*'

'Magnolia Close, number four,' I pant. I repeat the address in case he didn't get it the first time. 'Four. Magnolia Close. Wimborne. Dorset.'

'*What's the nature of the emergency?*' the operator asks.

'There are intruders trying to snatch a baby.'

'*Are the intruders in your house right now?*'

'No, not my house. They're in someone else's house. A neighbour's house.'

'*What's their address?*'

'I don't know. I heard them through my baby monitor. I don't know where they are, but they said they were going to take the baby. They could be taking it right now.'

'*Please try to stay calm. We're sending someone to your address immediately. They'll be with you within a few minutes.*'

'Okay, please hurry.' I squeeze my eyes shut, praying they get here in time. I can't bear to think about what will happen to that child if they don't.

CHAPTER TWO

I'm unable to relax. Instead of pacing inside, chewing my nails, waiting for the police to arrive, I walk down the driveway carrying Daisy, with the intention of knocking on my neighbours' doors. I have to do something. I wish I could call Dominic to let him know what's going on. To tell him to come back home right now. But he never takes his phone when he's out running. *Please let him be back soon.*

It's still warm out despite the darkening sky. It's been the kind of summer you don't usually get in Britain – with a heavy, damp heat that hangs in the air even after the sun goes down. I decide to go to the house next door first. But before my feet get as far as the pavement, a police car pulls into the cul-de-sac and cruises my way.

I lift my free hand and wave them over. Daisy has woken and is staring up at me, transfixed by my face, quiet for now. Content to be in my arms. The vehicle pulls up at the bottom of my driveway and two uniformed male officers get out. I walk down to meet them.

'Kirstie Rawlings?' the taller officer asks with a warm Dorset drawl, an indulgent smile on his lips as he sees Daisy in my arms.

'Yes,' I reply shakily.

'Can we come inside?' he asks. 'Talk to you about what you heard?'

'Can you check the neighbours first?' I say. 'See if there are any babies missing.'

'We'd like to hear from you what happened.' The officer gestures to my front door, trying to guide me up the driveway, but I don't want them wasting time inside. The kidnappers could be escaping out the back of someone else's house as we speak.

'Didn't the operator tell you?' I plant myself on the driveway, 'I heard voices through my baby monitor, saying they were going to take the baby.'

'Whose baby?'

'That's the thing, I don't know. Please. We need to ask the neighbours. Check they don't have any babies staying with them.'

'What did the voice say?' the other officer asks. 'Can you remember?'

'It was something like, *quick, let's take the baby.*'

'Was the voice male or female?'

'Male. Definitely male.'

'Can we see the monitor?' the tall one asks.

I sigh and stride back up the driveway with the officers behind me. I don't feel any sense of urgency from them. Surely they should be searching the area? Don't people say that the first few minutes are vital when children go missing? These two are wasting valuable time, missing their opportunity to save a child. The thought gives me chills. What if the kidnappers had come to my house instead of a neighbour's? Daisy's window has been open all evening, they could easily have climbed in and taken her. The thought makes me momentarily dizzy. I stop walking and take a breath, the scent of next door's honeysuckle hanging in the air, thick and strong. Too sweet.

'You okay?' one of them asks, putting a hand on my shoulder.

'We need to hurry,' I say, pulling myself together and continuing up the driveway. We go in. The monitor is on the sofa where I left it, but it's silent now.

'So this monitor links to the one in your baby's room?' the shorter officer asks, taking it from me and holding it to his ear. He gives it a shake and twiddles the volume control.

'Yes. I heard a man's voice telling someone else that they should take the baby. At first I thought they were in Daisy's room trying to snatch her. I ran upstairs but there was no one there. Then I heard the voices again in the monitor. It must have somehow picked up the signal from somewhere else. But I don't know where. None of my neighbours has a baby.'

The officers both look at one another and then the taller one clears his throat. 'Right, we'll start knocking on doors, see if anyone else has a monitor which could have somehow picked up your signal.'

'Thank you,' I say, relieved they're finally going to do something. 'Do you want me to come and help? Save you some time? I know all my neighbours so I could—'

'No, you stay here. Look after your baby. She's a sweetheart, isn't she? I remember when mine were that age. Don't miss the sleepless nights, though.'

I don't reply. I just want them to stop talking and go and find those people. I want them caught.

'Okay, then,' he says. 'We'll stop by on our way back, let you know if we find anything.'

The officers leave. While they're out there, knocking on doors, I watch out of the lounge window, jiggling Daisy in my arms. She's becoming restless so I sing a lullaby to sooth her. 'Hush Little Baby Don't You Cry'. I can't remember all the words, but the tune seems to soothe her.

The police are heading over to number six – I should have told them no one's living there at the moment. It's a building site; the new owners are having work done before they move in. I contemplate going out to tell them, but they'll figure it out soon enough, what with all the scaffolding and the huge metal skip in the driveway.

I watch them knock on the door, wait a moment, peer through a window and then move on to our immediate neighbour, Martin.

A moving flash of colour catches my eye. A figure at the entrance to the cul-de-sac. Running. My breath catches in my throat before I exhale again in relief. It's Dominic back from his run, his tall, athletic figure strong and capable. Reassuring. As he approaches, he stares at the police car parked at the bottom of the drive, then he notices the officers standing on Martin's doorstep.

I rush to the front door. Open it and wave as he jogs up the drive.

'What are the police doing next door?' he asks, only ever-so-slightly out of breath.

'Come in. I'll tell you.'

Dominic plants a kiss on Daisy's forehead and then another on my lips. Even when he's tired, hot and sweaty, my husband has the power to make my heart beat faster. We've known each other since we were five years old, and started going out when we were fifteen. He's my best friend. We tell each other everything.

'I need to stretch,' he says, pulling his right leg up behind him, 'and then I need a shower.'

As he stretches out his hamstrings in the lounge, I sit on the sofa with Daisy in my arms and begin explaining what happened while he was out. When I get to the part about hearing a man's voice in the monitor, Dom stops stretching, his eyes widen.

'Wait, what?' he says. 'Someone was trying to take Daisy?'

'I thought they were, but I must have heard someone else's monitor, because when I got up there, Daisy was fine. There was no one in the room.'

Dom comes over to the sofa, sits by my side and puts his arm around us. 'That must have been terrifying. Are you okay?'

'It was awful. I really thought they were trying to take her.'

He straightens up and runs a hand through his short, dark hair. 'Are you sure you're okay?'

'It was weird. I felt like I was in a movie or something. I was so scared for Daisy.' My voice wobbles. 'I thought we were going to be like those parents you see on TV. You know, the ones who have to put out an appeal to find their missing child.'

'Hey.' Dom comes and sits next to me on the sofa. 'It's okay. Nothing happened. Our baby is here. She's safe. No one's going to take Daisy. Okay? Are you sure you heard it through the monitor?' he asks. 'Couldn't it have been on the telly?'

I shake my head. 'No, definitely not. I paused the TV and I had the monitor in my hand. The voices came from the monitor. I could see the monitor's lights flashing while they spoke.'

Dom nods thoughtfully. 'What did the police say?'

'They're going round to all the neighbours, asking if anyone has a baby staying with them.'

'Good idea.'

'What if those people are still out there?' As I voice my concerns, new worries begin to seep into my mind. 'You hear about these things, don't you? Baby-smuggling rings where they take young children and sell them to rich couples abroad. It happens.'

'Kirstie, we live in Wimborne. It's not exactly rife with international crime. I'm pretty sure there aren't any baby-smuggling rings in Dorset.' A sympathetic smile creeps onto his lips, but there's absolutely no part of this that is amusing to me.

'How do you know?' I reply. 'Maybe it would be the perfect place – a sleepy little town in England where no one suspects that anything bad could happen.'

'Let's wait and see what the police say.' He puts an arm around me and kisses the side of my head. 'I know what happened must've been scary, but try not to worry.'

I murmur agreement, but my brain is still racing with all the awful possibilities. I shudder at the thought of those whispered voices and what they were discussing. That they could have chosen *my* house and *my* baby. I'm going to have to be more careful. I'm going to have to make the house more secure. The idea of someone taking Daisy – it doesn't bear thinking about. My stomach gives a sudden lurch, and I have the sensation that something has irrevocably shifted.

That nothing in our lives will ever be quite the same again.

CHAPTER THREE

Twenty minutes later, I'm sitting on the sofa once more, having just fed Daisy. Normally it's a quiet moment, a time for us to bond, but this evening I'm on autopilot while my mind jumps back and forth from *I need to keep my baby safe* to *It'll be okay, don't panic.* Dominic strolls back into the lounge dressed in clean shorts and a T-shirt, his hair damp from the shower. I give a start as the doorbell rings.

'I'll get it,' Dominic says.

'It's probably the police,' I call after him, retying the strap of my dress and running a hand over my dark curls, making sure I look half-presentable. I glance out of the window, get to my feet and place Daisy over my shoulder, patting her back and waiting for her to burp, hoping she doesn't throw up on me – I forgot to put a cloth over my shoulder.

I hear my husband introduce himself. Seconds later he comes back into the lounge accompanied by the two officers. 'Can I make you a tea or coffee?' Dominic asks them. 'Or something cold?'

'No thanks,' the taller one says, wiping a sheen of sweat from his forehead with his fingertips. 'Just checking – you weren't in the house when your wife heard the voices in the monitor?'

'No, I was out for a run,' Dominic replies, 'but she filled me in on what happened.'

'Good. Well, we spoke to all your neighbours, and none of them have a baby in their house. It's just you with a little one.

And there aren't any other residential roads close by. You're sur-rounded by fields.'

'Could the monitor have picked up a signal from further away?' I ask.

'It's doubtful,' he replies, 'but we'll look into it.'

'Because someone, somewhere, has taken a baby – or at least they've tried to.'

'If there's an abduction or attempted abduction, I'm sure the parents will get in touch with us.'

'But what if they don't know yet?' I say, the horror of the situation dawning on me. 'What if they're sitting in their lounge watching TV thinking their baby is fast asleep upstairs, but, in reality, it's already been taken by someone? They might not check on their child for hours.' I glance out of the window once more, putting my fingers to the glass, half-expecting to see someone making off down the road with a child.

'Kirstie,' Dom says gently. 'They've spoken to all our neigh-bours. No one has a baby. I'm sure the monitor wouldn't pick up a signal from miles away. Could it have been someone else's TV programme you heard through the monitor?'

'I don't think so. No. It sounded like Daisy's cry and then someone clearly saying they wanted to take the baby. It sounded real. Not like something on TV.'

'Look,' the taller officer says with a sympathetic expression. 'Whatever you heard, it gave you a shock, understandably. But if anyone has abducted a child, we'll find out about it, and we'll act on it, okay? And, in the meantime, if you hear or see anything else that worries you, then please give us a call.'

'Thanks, Officer.' Dominic shakes his hand and the policemen turn to leave.

Is that it? I think. *Is that all they're going to do?* I could've done that myself. I could've walked around and asked the neighbours if they had any babies staying with them. Maybe they think I'm a crackpot. I know I probably look dishevelled and out of it, but I'm the mother of a six-month-old baby, for goodness sake. I turn to look at myself in the mirror above the mantelpiece. My usually glossy curls are both greasy and frizzy, and my face is pale as the moon. I bend my head to sniff my shoulder – a waft of baby milk, sweat and recent fear makes me wrinkle my nose.

Dominic sees the officers out and comes back in, his arms open wide. I step into them, still cradling Daisy. I haven't put her down since I heard the voices. Dominic smells of citrus shower gel. Of home. I feel safe in his arms. He kisses the top of my head.

'How about I make my Thai curry tonight?' he says. 'I'll put Daisy back to bed first. You go and have a shower, then sit down and put your feet up.'

'Thai curry sounds good,' I say, not really feeling at all hungry. 'But I'd rather keep Daisy down here with us after what's happened.'

Dominic steps back and stares at me. 'You're really shaken up, Kirst. You're white as a ghost.'

'I thought they'd taken her,' I say. 'It's just a shock, that's all. I'll be okay in a minute.'

'Why don't I bring Daisy's old Moses basket downstairs?' he suggests. 'It's in the spare room, isn't it? She can stay down here with us this evening.'

'Will she still fit in it?' I ask hopefully.

'She'll be fine.'

'Okay.' My shoulders relax a little. As long as we keep her with us, I'll feel better. Safer.

Half an hour later, I'm sitting at the kitchen table sipping a glass of water and Daisy is fast asleep in her old basket – her mop of dark hair pressing against the end. She barely fits, but she'll be fine in there for now. Dominic is standing at the hob, cooking away, dance tunes blaring out of the speakers. You'd think the noise would wake Daisy, but she's already used to his awful taste in music. Dom rarely cooks, and when he does it's always a Thai curry or spaghetti Bolognese, both of which he makes exceptionally well. The bifold doors are open and I'm itching to close them tight and turn the lock, but it's too hot, especially while Dom's cooking. We would roast. I'll close the doors before we eat.

'I'm going to check everything in the house is locked up,' I say, getting to my feet. 'Keep an eye on her, won't you? Don't leave her alone.'

'I'm here. She'll be fine. There's no one out there.'

But I'm not convinced. 'I won't be long.' Quickly, I move around the house, closing all the windows in each and every room, even the smaller windows that only a cat could fit through. I don't want to take any chances. I won't think about how warm the rooms will get without fresh air circulating. I can put up with the heat if it means my little girl will be safe. Lastly, I check the front door, turn the mortice lock and slide the chain across with shaking fingers.

I can't remember the last time I felt fear like this. Actual spine-tingling fear. Maybe never. No, not never. There was one time when I was about thirteen or fourteen, walking home from school one day. I was alone on a quiet suburban street and it was winter, a dark afternoon with no one else around. I heard footsteps behind me, getting closer. I was too scared to turn around, somehow convinced it was a man about to attack me, my mind conjuring up all these unthinkable scenarios. I had worked myself up into such a state of clammy terror that I couldn't think straight. I quickened my pace but didn't want to run in case he chased after me, confirming my fears. Instead, I crossed over the road and slowed my pace. It was only when I saw it was actually a woman of my mother's age that I felt a flood of foolish relief, despite my heart still battering my ribcage.

But that was a fear of my own creation. Not like this. Nothing like this.

I walk back into the kitchen, where Dom is nodding his head in time to the beat of the music from his iPod speakers while draining the water from a pan of rice. I check on Daisy, who's still asleep, and I drink in the sight of her, grateful that she's here. I could stare at her perfect face all night, but eventually I pull my gaze away, sit at the table and reach for my phone. I tap in a search for *baby monitors picking up other signals*. A whole screed of results appears – mainly old forum posts from 2010 to 2013. It seems it was quite a common occurrence with older monitors.

'Dom.'

'Everything okay?' He lowers the volume on the speakers and turns to me, one eyebrow raised.

'It says here that the older-style monitors can pick up other monitors' signals.' I turn my phone screen towards him, but he doesn't look at it.

'You're gonna drive yourself mad worrying about it,' Dom says. 'I know you heard something that creeped you out, but there could be a simple explanation.'

'Like what?' I fold my arms across my chest, starting to feel irritated by his lack of concern.

'Don't look like that,' he says. 'I'm not saying you didn't hear it. I'm just saying there could be an innocent explanation. I'm trying to reassure you.'

'Like what?' I repeat. 'What could be the innocent explanation?'

'Like... you heard someone else's TV programme. Or you misheard the actual words.'

'I know what I heard.'

'Okay, say you *did* hear what you heard. It was someone else's house. It wasn't here. No one was trying to take Daisy.'

'That doesn't make it okay.'

'No, I know. I know. Sorry. Maybe they were saying it innocently, like *let's take the baby to mum's house*, or *let's take the baby for a walk*.'

'It wasn't anything like that. It was scary.'

'What do you want to do about it?' Dom asks, setting his wooden spoon down on the worktop.

'I don't know. Be on our guard I suppose. Keep a look out. Don't let Daisy out of our sight.'

'Okay. We can do that.'

I know I sound paranoid, but he wasn't the one who heard those voices. If he had, I'm sure he would be just as frightened. That voice creeped me out. I keep hearing it in my mind over and over. *Quick, let's just take the baby now and go.* Who was it? And what did they do?

CHAPTER FOUR

I lie on my side, gazing down at Daisy in her basket. It's too dark to make out her features, but I can see her shape, and I know she's asleep by the sound of her regular breathing. Dom wasn't exactly thrilled at having her back in our bedroom. Don't get me wrong, he loves our daughter, he just has a hard time sleeping with her in the same room. But one look at my expression told him he would have to accept it. At least for tonight. Anyway, I've had to make my own compromises, as Dom refused to shut the bedroom windows. I suppose he's right – the heat would be unbearable otherwise.

So now, here I am, wide awake at 2 a.m., alert to every sound outside. Every breath of wind and distant dog bark makes me startle, setting my heart racing. I never usually mind the windows being open, but that was *before*. The rational part of my brain is telling me that if anyone were to break into our house and come into our bedroom, we would wake up, but the irrational part won't allow me to sleep. I'm also paranoid that I've missed a window. Did I lock the one in the downstairs loo? I think I did, but I can't be certain. I'm going to have to check. Maybe that's what's stopping me falling asleep. I'm sure once I've double checked the locks again, I'll be able to relax.

I slide out of bed carefully, desperate not to wake Daisy or Dominic. As I tiptoe around Daisy towards the door, Dom murmurs, 'Kirstie? What're you doing?'

'Loo,' I reply.

'Okay.' He huffs and turns over.

I can feel his annoyance. I picture him lying there, eyes wide open, cursing me for waking him up. But I can't stop thinking about the downstairs window. I need to go and check it.

Once I get there, I discover, of course, that it's locked, as are all the other downstairs doors and windows. But at least I feel a little less on edge now I know for sure that the house is secure. I creep back upstairs and decide I may as well check Daisy's room, the spare room and the bathroom. Once that's done, I slip back into bed to lie beside my wide-awake husband, worrying about him on top of everything else.

*

Sunlight blazes through the bedroom windows as I sit up in bed, giving Daisy her morning feed. I feel out of sorts. Like part of me is still asleep. Like I'm floating above reality. Anxious – as though I'm about to take a hard exam or topple off a cliff.

Dominic comes into the bedroom. He's already dressed in his suit and tie and he leans down to kiss me, the scent of his aftershave giving me a momentary feeling of normality. Everything is as it should be. Why, then, does it all feel so different?

'Sorry I woke you last night,' I say, bracing myself for him to be grumpy.

'You didn't wake me,' he says, casting his eyes around the room, looking for something.

'Yeah, when I got up to go to the bathroom, you asked me what I was doing.'

'Oh, yeah, I vaguely remember something.'

'I thought I'd ruined your night's sleep.'

'No. I slept fine. Have you seen my phone?'

Great. I tormented myself with guilt all night over nothing. 'It's on the dresser.' I point to it.

'Thanks. You're out with Mel tonight, aren't you?' he says. 'What time do you need me home?'

My stomach drops. I'd forgotten I was supposed to be going out for a meal with my old school friends this evening – my first night out since Daisy was born. I've been looking forward to it for ages, but I'm so, so tired and the thought of going out fills me with unease. How can I leave Daisy when there are possible child abductors in the area? I know Dominic will be with her, but he won't be as careful as me. He'll leave windows open, he might not be listening out for intruders.

'The taxi's supposed to be coming at seven,' I say. 'But actually, I don't think I'm going to go. After what happened yesterday—'

'What are you talking about?' Dominic says, sitting on the end of the bed. 'Of course you're going to go. It'll do you good to get out of the house for an evening. You deserve a night out with everyone. Time away from our little munchkin. You'll love it. Anyway, I've got some serious father–daughter bonding time planned for tonight. We're going to watch *Top Gear*.'

I roll my eyes and manage a half-smile. 'I don't know, Dom.'

'Kirstie, come on. You love going out with your friends.'

'Yeah, but I'm just so tired.'

'So try and put Daisy down for an hour or two and get some more sleep. Look, I'd better go. I've got a meeting first thing. I'll try and be back by six – give you an hour to get ready in peace.'

'Okay,' I say. 'Thank you. You're amazing.'

'I know,' he quips. And then he turns serious. 'Don't worry, Kirst. You'll feel better after another little sleep. I promise.'

Suddenly, the thought of Dominic leaving for work sends a tidal wave of panic through my system. 'I wish you could stay home with us today.'

'Nothing I'd like more, but someone's got to whip those sales teams into shape. Why don't you have that extra sleep then go and see your mum for an hour or two? Change of scenery. Look,

I really do have to go. See you later, Kirst. Bye, Dais.' He gives us both a kiss and a wave before leaving. I listen to the thud of his feet on the stairs, to the jingle of his keys, and finally the slam of the front door. The house falls silent.

Daisy reaches her hand up to my face, her eyes wide, fingers grabbing at my cheek. I force out a smile, but my guts are churning, my heart racing. This is crazy. I need to snap out of it.

One hour later, I'm showered and dressed and sitting on the sofa sipping tea. Daisy is lying on her mat under her play mobile, batting the hanging toys with her hands and toes. Yet unease still clings to me. This is ridiculous. I've always been comfortable in my own skin. My home is my sanctuary. The place I can relax and feel content. Yesterday's 'incident' is the first time I've felt unsettled in my own house. Things like that just aren't supposed to happen in places like this.

Wimborne Minster is a pretty market town not too far from the coast and surrounded by countryside. Everyone knows everyone and there's hardly any crime here. Even the weather is mild and sunny most days. I've lived in Wimborne all my life. So has Dominic. So have most of my friends and neighbours. It even topped one of those polls for the best place to live in Britain. One of the happiest places. And it *is*. It is a happy place. *I'm* happy. I am. Or at least I was. But now my happiness has been contaminated. I don't feel quite the same as I did this time yesterday morning. That easy contentment has curdled like cream in the sunshine. How can things change this quickly?

Am I overreacting? Hearing those voices yesterday has tipped everything off balance. Just thinking about them makes my palms sweat. But did anything actually happen? No one else seems to think so. Not Dom. Not the police. Not even my neighbours. It was only me who heard those voices. And no one actually broke into our house. No one took Daisy, or even attempted to take her. But what if they did take that other child? What if they harmed the parents? Left them for dead? I hate not knowing what happened. What if they decide to come back for Daisy?

I have to keep her safe. It's my job. My duty. I rise to my feet, scoop Daisy up into my arms and check that the bifold doors are locked. I test the handle twice. It's fine. It's secure. I think about the way I've spent most of my mornings this summer, pottering about in the garden with the doors wide open, walking inside and out while Daisy was in her crib often out of my sight. How could I do that now?

I move over to check the kitchen windows above the sink. There are three panes of glass, but only the middle one can be opened. It's closed but unlocked, and the key isn't on the sill where it should be. We never usually bother to lock any of the windows. *Never again.* I won't be so lax in future.

I head into the lounge and take the key from the front windowsill, using it to lock the kitchen window. With Daisy still in my arms, I check and lock all the other downstairs windows along with the front door. Then, I put the key in my dress pocket. I'll have to think of a safe place to stash it. Next, I head upstairs. I won't feel safe to put Daisy down until everything is secure. Maybe I'm going overboard, but she's our miracle baby. It took us four years to conceive her and I suffered three miscarriages before finally carrying her to term.

The first time I fell pregnant, I miscarried at eight weeks and the sense of loss was crushing, especially as I had excitedly told everyone I was pregnant as soon as I found out, so I then had to explain all about my loss, suffering everyone's well-intentioned sympathy. The second time I fell pregnant, Dom and I were more cautious, keeping the news a secret. But at exactly eight weeks, the same thing happened. I spent months afterwards drifting around in a daze, convinced I would never be able to carry a baby to term.

It took me a whole two years to fall pregnant again, and this time, I finally made it past the cursed eight-week mark. When I reached four months, we were cautiously optimistic and Dom wanted us to tell our parents, especially as I was starting to show. But I wouldn't let him, and it was a good job we didn't because, yet again, it wasn't to be. At my twenty-week scan, they couldn't find a heartbeat. I think, at that point, I decided that it was too painful to continue trying. The fear of hoping to have a child was too great.

However, the following year I fell pregnant again. I spent the whole time in denial, convinced I would lose the baby. Even when my twenty-week scan showed me a healthy baby girl in the monitor, and I heard her heartbeat, strong and fast, I couldn't let myself become attached or make plans, or buy any baby clothes or equipment. But my worries were unfounded. Our wish eventually came true and I gave birth to our daughter. I thought that once she was born, my fears would evaporate in a puff of smoke, but instead, they intensified.

After Daisy was born, I got to meet her, to hold her in my arms and fall in love. And I realised that even though she was here – alive – she still wasn't entirely safe. None of us are. So I consciously vowed that I would do everything in my power to protect her. And I remember my promise every day. I will not let anything or anyone threaten my little family.

Finally, with the house locked up tight, I think I can probably allow myself to relax a little. On the upstairs landing, I yawn. Tiredness tugs at my eyelids and shoulders. I really do need to lie down. Daisy should be safe next to me in the Moses basket while I crawl back into bed for a couple more hours. The thought of closing my eyes is delicious. But before I get the chance, the doorbell rings.

Maybe it's the postman. I could ignore it, but it might be important. What if it's the police back with more information? My heart begins to pound. I carry Daisy downstairs with me, starting to feel like she's permanently attached, like a baby koala. I should think about getting a baby sling.

With clammy hands and a racing pulse, I slide the chain back, turn the key and open the door.

CHAPTER FIVE

My bespectacled next-door neighbour, Martin, stands on the front path, his ashy blond hair curling below his ears like a seventies folk singer, hands clasped together in front of him like he's about to give a sermon. He's harmless enough, even if he is a bit of a fusspot, always worrying about something or other. When Dom and I first moved into the cul-de-sac, I made the mistake of asking Martin about the Neighbourhood Watch scheme, and he launched into this long rant about the lack of commitment from everyone in Magnolia Close. Not wanting to get into my new neighbour's bad books, I agreed that Dom and I would attend the next meeting.

Turns out, it was just the three of us at his house that evening. Our hearts sank when we realised that Martin had several sheets of paper listing items about neighbourhood security he wanted to discuss. It was, quite possibly, the most boring evening of our lives. When we finally managed to get out of there, two hours later, Dom wanted to throttle me for having agreed to go. I didn't blame him. But the creepiest thing about the whole evening was that when we were in Martin's lounge, Dom noticed a photo on his mantelpiece of a woman holding a baby – only it wasn't a baby, it was quite clearly a doll.

Dom asked Martin about the woman. Martin said it was his late wife. Dom then asked about the doll. Martin pursed his lips and said that he and his wife were unable to have children of their own and never adopted. He said that 'Priddy' was a comfort to his wife. Dom, not being one to beat around the bush, wanted Martin to clarify that 'Priddy' was in fact a doll. Martin said she may not have been a real baby, but Priddy was real enough to his wife.

I felt sorry for the man, but Dom thought he was a fruitcake.

Now, almost every time I leave the house, Martin tries to catch my attention so he can tell me his problems and list his complaints about this person or that person. I don't mind really. I feel sorry for him. He's recently retired, probably has far too much time on his hands. A bit like me at the moment. But I'm not in the mood to listen to his concerns. Not today.

'Hi Martin. Everything okay?'

'I'm all right. How about you and the little one?' he asks through an abundance of teeth, crammed into his mouth like yellowing piano keys. I'd really like to give Martin the name of our dentist.

'We're okay,' I reply.

'The police came to see me yesterday. They asked me if I had a baby, of all things!'

I immediately think about his wife's doll-child. 'Yes, they came here, too.' I don't have the energy to explain why they were knocking on doors. If I get into it, he'll be here for ages quizzing me about everything.

Martin huffs. 'I told them *you* were the one with the baby, not me. She's all right, isn't she, little Daisy?'

'She's fine, thanks.'

'Yes, because when they started talking about babies, I worried that something might have happened to her. But it was a bit too late to come round to your house, so I thought I'd wait until the morning. These individuals who call round in the evening when you're relaxing or eating your dinner, well it's not polite, is it?'

'Thanks, Martin. It's kind of you to pop round. But as you can see, Daisy and I are fine.'

'Good, good. Glad to hear it. Now, while I've got you here…'
My heart sinks. He's about to launch into his latest woe, I know
it. 'I wondered if you wouldn't mind just nipping next door with
me and checking the boundary wall at number six.' He pushes his
gold-rimmed glasses further up the bridge of his nose.

'The boundary wall?' He's obviously talking about the building
works going on at the house next door to him. 'I'm a little busy
at the moment. Can it wait until later?'

'It won't take a minute, Kirstie. I just need another set of eyes
on it. Make sure I'm not imagining things. Five minutes, tops.'

I sigh. May as well get it out of the way now. 'Okay. Let me
get some shoes on.' As I transfer Daisy to my other arm, she
reaches out, trying to make a grab for Martin's glasses. He steps
back and frowns.

'Daisy's hands look a little sticky, Kirstie. Maybe you could
give them a wash before coming over. I'll see you in a minute.'
He turns abruptly and leaves.

I'm used to his unusual ways. I know he doesn't mean to be
rude, but I can't help rolling my eyes as I watch him walk away
back down the path. Dominic isn't as tolerant of Martin, and calls
him 'Moaning Myrtle' after the character from Harry Potter. Not
to his face, of course.

Ignoring Martin's request to wash my daughter's hands – which
look perfectly fine to me – I slip on some flip-flops, grab the front
door key and a sunhat for Daisy, and close the door behind me,
wishing I hadn't answered it in the first place.

I stride up Martin's immaculate path, his neat front lawn turning
a coppery brown from the lack of rain. From the house next door
to Martin, the builders' radio spews out inane chatter and tinny
chart music, sporadically drowned out by the jaw-rattling sound of
a jackhammer. Martin's door opens before I have a chance to knock.

'Come in, Kirstie. But please do take your shoes off first. I don't
like to have the outside brought inside.'

I do as he asks, noting that he's now wearing a pair of tartan slippers which look odd with his shorts and shirt.

'Bring your footwear with you,' he says. 'We're going into the back garden and the ground out there is hot and very dusty from all the building works next door.'

Daisy tries to reach for Martin's glasses once more and he backs away with a look of distaste. I stifle a smile, wondering what he would do if she actually managed to grab hold of them.

'Have you seen number three's lawn?' Martin says as I follow him through his pristine hallway, my bare feet sinking into deep-pile dark-blue carpet. The stink of pine air freshener pervades every square inch, forcing me to hold my breath.

'Their lawn?' I ask, confused.

'Yes, you can't fail to notice that it's green and healthy. They're clearly ignoring the hosepipe ban. And he's a headmaster, too. It's not responsible behaviour. Not a good example to set.'

'I hadn't noticed, no.'

We're now in Martin's kitchen, a shrine to the seventies with avocado units and green and white patterned tiles on the walls. Our own back rooms were knocked through by the previous owners to open them up into one big space, enhanced by an extension. But Martin's house has the original layout, with a small kitchen and a separate dining room at the back.

'You know,' Martin persists, 'I'm in two minds whether or not to ring the Parkfields' doorbell and point out that they could be fined if they don't adhere to the hosepipe ban. Do you think I should report them? Would I have to call the council, or the police?'

'Um… what's this boundary you want me to look at?' I ask, changing the subject.

'Ah, yes. You can put your shoes back on now. I always find it handy to keep a pair of slip-on sandals by the back door.'

We step out onto the patio and I'm hit again by the racket from the builders. 'I thought the noise was bad enough at our house,'

I say, raising my voice, 'but it's deafening out here. Seems like it's been going on forever.'

'Seven weeks and four days, to be precise. Now, you see that two-storey extension they're building there on the side of the house.' Martin points next door.

I try to concentrate on what he's telling me, but Daisy's not looking happy, her bottom lip is quivering. I think the drilling noise is freaking her out. I bounce her up and down, making funny faces and kissing her cheeks, trying to distract her.

'It looks like they've built the extension too close to the boundary fence. What do you think, Kirstie?'

The extension does look quite close to the fence, but I know nothing about boundaries and building regulations. 'Why don't you check with the Land Registry or the council? They'll have the plans, won't they? Then you can see what's been agreed.'

'Yes. Yes, I was going to do that, but I wanted a second opinion before I make my complaint. I'm sure they're damaging the foundations of my property. I tried to speak to that building chappie who's supposed to be managing the site – Rob Carson, not a very forthcoming man – but he was quite rude to me. I'm not happy. Not happy at all.'

'Sorry to hear that, Martin, but, well, Daisy isn't happy either. This noise is making her cranky. I'd better get back.'

'Really?' Martin's face falls. 'I had a few other issues to discuss with you about the neighbours and about how we could—'

'It will have to be another time, Martin.' Daisy has started wailing and I feel like joining her. What am I doing in my neighbour's garden when all I want to do is curl up on my bed and fall asleep? I step back into Martin's kitchen, eager to be on my way.

'Shoes!' he calls out behind me.

I bite my tongue and slip off my flip-flops, finding it hard to bend down to retrieve them while Daisy is flailing around in my arms. As I walk back into the hall, I notice the door to the cupboard under the stairs is slightly ajar, and I'm surprised to see stairs leading downwards. Martin must have a basement in his house, which is strange because as far as I'm aware none of the other houses in our road have one. But I'm not going to ask about it now. If I do, I'll never get out of here.

CHAPTER SIX

I'm lying on my back in a dark place. I reach out to feel the space around me, and my fingertips come into contact with warm metal, rough and ridged like corrugated iron. Where the hell am I? Wherever it is, it's so hot I can barely breathe. My body is slippery with sweat. I try to sit up but my head bashes into the metal casing above me. I'm trapped inside some kind of container. Terror bubbles up inside me, but I don't have enough air in my lungs to scream. How did I get here? How will I get out? Am I going to die? Beyond my confines I hear a thin sound in the distance. The sound of crying. Screaming. It's Daisy!

My eyes fly open and I instantly close them again against the brightness flooding into my bedroom. I was dreaming. A nightmare. It was dark and hot in my dream. I'm *still* hot now, the bedsheets sticking to my body. Air. I need air. I slide out of bed and stagger over to the window but it's closed. Locked. I can't remember where I put the key.

In my dream, Daisy was crying, but she's not crying now. She's silent. I rush back to her basket in a panic, convinced she will be gone. But my baby is there. Sleeping peacefully, her cheeks a little flushed, but her forehead cool to the touch. I stretch out my fingers to stop them shaking.

The clock by my bed says 11.35 a.m. and the events of this morning rush back to me as my dream fades. I was at Martin's place, then I came back home. I soothed Daisy, checked the windows and doors, and had a nap. My head is throbbing. That bloody jackhammer is still going strong out there. Even with the windows closed I can hear it. Just when I think it's stopped, it starts up again, an instrument of torture.

I sit heavily on the side of the bed and retrieve my phone from the nightstand, trying to slow my racing brain, my speeding pulse. Trying to get a sense of where I am. That dream has thrown me off kilter. I have to keep telling myself that I'm safe. I'm home. I'm with my baby. Nothing has changed. So why do I feel like I'm in some sinister alternate universe?

I'm really not in any state to go out tonight so I tap in a quick text to my best friend, Melinda Clark, to tell her I'm not up to it. She lives over the way at number one with her two young children, James who's almost four, and Katie who's two.

My phone pings instantaneously with a reply:

Don't you dare bail on me. You're coming and that's that.

Despite my grinding headache, I can't help smiling at her bulldozer attitude. I text back:

Sorry Mel, but you'll have to manage without me.
You can't leave me to fend for myself with 'the perfect ones'.

'The perfect ones' is the name we gave to our school friends who all seem to live these untouchable, wonderful lives in sprawling houses with super-rich husbands. Saying that, they're all down-to-earth women who we still have a laugh with. Mel used to be one of the 'perfect ones' herself, until her rich and perfect husband, Chris, left her two years ago for a twenty-year-old dance student. Now she's bringing up their children on her own. Chris bought her the house and gives her a generous monthly allowance, but he rarely visits her or the children, which is sad for all of them. She could have had a much swankier house if she'd wanted it, but she said she would rather live near me than on her own in a palace.

Sometimes, in my more uncharitable moments, I'm convinced the only reason Mel moved here was so that I'd be on hand to babysit. I love her to pieces, but our relationship has always been a bit of a one-way street, with me rushing to bail her out or look after her children when disaster strikes. It's difficult to say no to her, though. Her parents died in a car crash when she was a teenager and Dominic and I are the closest thing she has to family.

I feel bad for bailing on her tonight, but not bad enough to go.

I'll come to the next one. Promise.
I'm coming over. See you in a minute.

Shit. I quickly text her back

Don't ring the bell. Daisy's asleep.

I rush to the bathroom and splash my face with cold water. By the time I get downstairs and open the door, Mel is already striding up the drive. She's gorgeous, with green eyes, glossy hair that falls in tawny waves and an hour-glass figure that most women wouldn't know what to do with. Not Mel. She celebrates her curves in style, with a wardrobe that includes figure-hugging pencil skirts, belted fifties-style dresses and Capri pants. And we've nicknamed her boobs the eighth wonder of the world.

'You look like crap, Kirstie,' she says without preamble.

'I feel it.'

We head into the kitchen.

'Fuck, it's hot in here,' she says, screwing up her face and fanning herself with her hand, blood-red fingernails waving back and forth in a crimson blur. 'Open the doors for Christ's sake. No wonder you feel rough. I'm already convinced I've got the flu and

I've only been inside your house for thirty seconds.' She strides over to the bifold doors, turns the key and yanks them all the way back. 'God, that's better.' Mel takes in a deep breath of fresh air, and I can't help doing the same.

'Hi, Mel,' I say. 'Nice to see you, as always.'

She gives my shoulder a push. 'Sarky cow. Why does it smell like an old tart's knickers in here?'

'Didn't you hear what happened yesterday?' I ask.

She shakes her head and sits at the kitchen table.

'Hang on a minute.' I nip into the lounge and retrieve the baby monitor, before returning to the kitchen where I sit opposite Mel and explain what I heard the night before.

'Weird,' she says. 'So that's why the police came round asking me about babies? They never mentioned you, or what you'd heard. Just asked if I had any babies staying with me, or if I'd seen anyone suspicious hanging around. I wondered what had happened.'

'It's scary, right?'

She waggles her head. 'Hmm, I dunno. I wouldn't worry about it. Daisy's okay, isn't she?'

'Yes, but only because I'm keeping an eye on her. I'm keeping all the doors and windows locked.'

'Ah, that explains why this place has turned into a sauna. It's thirty degrees out. You can't keep yourself sealed in. Let me open some more windows.' She moves over to the kitchen window but it's locked. 'Where's the key?'

'I think it's upstairs.'

'Go and get it. You need air in here.'

'Don't worry. It's fine.' The thought of Mel opening all the windows makes my head swim.

'Go and get it, Kirstie.'

I sigh and do as she asks, tiptoeing up the stairs so as not to wake Daisy. I think I remember stashing the key in the pocket of my dress.

Minutes later, I'm following Mel from room to room as she unlocks all the downstairs windows. I feel myself wince each time she throws another one wide open.

'Is this why you don't want to come out tonight?' she asks. 'Because of what happened last night?'

'I suppose. Partly.'

'Oh, Kirstie.' She stops what she's doing for a moment to look at me.

Annoyingly, I feel tears begin to prick at my eyes. *What is wrong with me?*

'Daisy will be fine.' Mel says. 'Dom will be with her, right?'

'Yes, but—'

'No buts. No excuses. Dom is her father and he's perfectly capable of looking after his daughter for a few hours without you. Unlike my pathetic excuse for a husband, who wouldn't know a nappy from a pillowcase.'

I manage a small smile at this. She's right – Chris is a self-centred idiot who's more concerned with the cut of his suit than the wellbeing of his family. I'm lucky to have Dominic.

'I'm actually not taking no for an answer,' she continues. 'You haven't been out for months. We planned this ages ago, Kirst. The taxi will be at my house at seven and you *will* be there… Look, I've got to pick James and Katie up from nursery now, but I'll see you later, yes?' She arches an eyebrow.

I don't reply. Don't catch her eye.

'Yes?' she repeats.

I don't know what to say. She'll only carry on giving me a hard time if I refuse. 'Okay,' I reply, wondering if I can get away with cancelling later, at the last minute.

'Good girl. Wear something saucy. It'll make you feel better.'

'How long have you known me, Mel? I don't do "saucy".'

'Well, you should.' She glares at me, laughs and heads back out into the hall. 'And open some of the upstairs windows too!' she calls out before leaving, pulling the front door behind her with a bang that reverberates throughout the house.

I cringe and hold my breath, listening. Sure enough, a couple of seconds later, a short cry comes through the baby monitor followed by a sustained wail that I can't ignore.

'Thanks, Mel,' I mutter before heading back upstairs.

Halfway up, I pause. I can't go up there with all these windows and doors still open downstairs. I turn back and make my way into the kitchen. Daisy's cries are tugging at my heart, but the need to secure my house is stronger. There are child abductors out there. They could come back at any time. I begin with the back doors – pulling them closed with a satisfying thunk. Next I close and lock all the downstairs windows, hoping Mel doesn't glance over from her house and see what I've done.

Once I'm satisfied the rooms are all secure, I realise that my hands are shaking, my breathing erratic, ragged and shallow. Daisy's cries have gone from demanding come-and-get-me-mummy cries to piercing, furious screams. How could I have left her to cry for so long? I think there might be something wrong with me. Or maybe I'm just tired. Whatever it is, I don't feel like myself. Not at all.

At 5.30 p.m. I'm crouched on the kitchen floor loading dirty washing into the machine when my phone pings. I close the machine door, straighten up and snatch my phone off the kitchen table. It's a text from Mel:

Hey gorgeous. Hope you're getting ready. Don't even think about sending me a cancellation text.

I sigh. How did she know? I should just tell her straight that I'm not going. But I can't bring myself to face her judgement. Maybe she's right. Maybe it will do me good to get out of the house. To shake away the unease that has gripped my body all day. Before having Daisy, I loved to go out with my friends, I was almost as outgoing as Mel. But after my second miscarriage, I became less sociable, more subdued. I couldn't bear the thought of people asking me about my pregnancies, or if I was okay, or when Dom and I were going to start trying for a family. All the questions and sympathetic looks were exhausting. So I found it easier to retreat into my cocoon. And somehow, despite my joy at having Daisy, those feelings of insecurity have remained.

Mel's text message pulses accusingly on my phone screen. I chew my bottom lip. If I stay home tonight, I'll only sit here worrying. Maybe a night out will take my mind off things. Taking a breath, I text her three emojis: a smiley face, a wine glass and a girl dancing.

I spend the next forty-five minutes bathing and feeding Daisy so she'll be ready for bed when Dominic gets home from work. As I hold her, staring out the bedroom window, I realise Dominic is late. With a rush of hope, I wonder if he might have had to stay on at the office. That would solve my problems. I could then apologise to Mel and say it was out of my control. She wouldn't be able to argue with that.

Almost as soon as I have that thought, my heart drops as I see Dom's Audi turn into the cul-de-sac. I watch him park in the driveway and walk up the path. Hear the click of his key in the door. Usually I'm excited to see him. Now, I feel the dark swell of anxiety in my chest.

'Hey, Kirst, it's me!'

'Hi!' I call from upstairs, injecting fake happiness into my voice.

I hear his footfalls on the stairs, and then he comes into the bedroom, loosening his tie as he walks towards us. 'Hey, I missed you both today.'

'Missed you too.' We kiss and he takes Daisy from my arms.

'It's boiling in here. Don't tell me you've had the windows closed all day.'

'Course not.' I stiffen as he sets about opening the windows with his free hand. 'You'll lock them all up again before going to bed, won't you?' I ask. 'Those people could come back at any time. They could try to break in. And you'll keep Daisy with you all—'

'Relax. I will guard her with my life. She's my daughter too, Kirst.'

'Sorry, I know. It's just... I worry.'

'Noooo. Really?'

I give him a light shove.

'Sorry I'm a bit late tonight. Roads were stupidly busy for some reason.' Dominic lifts Daisy up into the air, then swoops her back down before blowing raspberries onto her stomach. She shrieks with laughter.

'You might not want to swing her up and down like that,' I warn. 'I've just fed her. She'll throw up all over you if you're not careful.'

'We don't mind,' Dom says in a daft voice. 'We just want Mummy to ignore us and get ready for her big night out, don't we, Daisy? Yes we do.' He blows another raspberry on her tummy and I can't help laughing this time.

Things already seem better now Dominic's home. That hollow, jittery feeling is receding. Maybe I'll even enjoy tonight.

CHAPTER SEVEN

The little Wimborne restaurant is packed for a Thursday night, ringing with the clink of glasses and the scrape of silverware, the chatter and laughter of people enjoying themselves. Our glamorous group of women takes up one long table down the side. I didn't realise there would be so many of us here tonight. We all went to the same school, the majority of us in the same year. It's lovely to see everyone again, to be my old self. I feel like I've been out of the loop for ages, even though it's only been six months since I had Daisy.

My heart sinks as someone else arrives late, her sleek, auburn bob swinging as she sits opposite me and lays her purse by her feet. She turns to talk to Pia, who's sitting on her left.

I elbow Mel. 'You didn't tell me Tamsin Price would be coming,' I hiss.

'That's because I knew you wouldn't come if I said anything.'

'Too bloody right. Anyway, I thought she was living in Surrey now. Has she come back just for tonight?'

'No,' Mel says sheepishly. 'She moved back to Wimborne this year.'

'Why didn't you tell me she was back?' She's the last person I expected to see here tonight. Back when we were in our late teens, Tamsin tried to steal Dominic away from me. They had a drunken one night stand, after which she pretended to be pregnant. It took Dom over six months to win me back, but now the sight of Tamsin Price has brought all those ancient feelings rushing back.

'Just ignore her,' Mel says under her breath.

'That's a bit hard when she's sitting right opposite me.'

Mel screws up her face in sympathy. 'I know. Of all the places she could sit, that's pretty bad luck.'

'Swap places with me?'

'I would, Kirst, but Sooz wants to talk to me about something important. I think she's having marriage problems. I said we'd have a chat about it tonight, seeing as how I'm highly experienced in the area of tosser ex-husbands.' She grins.

I sigh. 'Okay. Never mind.' At that moment I catch Tamsin's eye and she gives me a disdainful nod. I give her a tight-lipped smile, and then we proceed to ignore each other.

As it turns out, most of the evening is spent reminiscing with everyone about funny incidents and awful teachers. Everyone – apart from Tamsin of course – teases me about the fact I'm now a teacher in our old school. Mel was right to make me come. I'm having a good time, even though my mind keeps straying to how Dominic and Daisy are getting on at home, trying not to check my texts every five seconds for possible news that the child abductors have returned. I need to stop worrying, and concentrate more on enjoying myself.

Another friend, Penny, sits on my left. She's also a new mum, like me. We weren't that close at school, but I always liked her. After a good twenty minutes chatting about motherhood, Penny leans back in her chair.

'We're so pathetic, Kirstie,' she says, twirling a dark strand of hair around her finger. 'All we've done all evening is talk about missing our babies. When did we get so boring?' Penny is a party planner, but she admits it's more of a hobby than anything else. Her husband is an investment banker and they're absolutely loaded, with a huge country pile, a fleet of 4x4s and staff, including a nanny.

'We're first-time mums,' I laugh. 'We're allowed to be boring and brag about our beautiful babies.'

'You're right.' She raises her glass. 'To our beautiful babies.' She clinks her glass violently against mine. 'Oops, sorry,' she giggles. 'Bit pissed. Why are you still sober, anyway?'

'Breast feeding,' I reply, sipping my mineral water.

'Ooh, you're good. I couldn't do it. Too painful and far too restricting.'

'I was lucky Daisy took to it so well. If she hadn't, I probably wouldn't have carried on. I hear it can be excruciating.'

'Yep, like little needles.'

'Ouch!'

We look at each other and start laughing.

'Must go to the loo,' she says. 'Back in a mo.'

I turn to talk to Mel, but she's deep in conversation with Sooz, who's dabbing at her eyes with a tissue. I can't interrupt what appears to be a heavy conversation.

Opposite, it looks like Tamsin is also between conversations. We catch one another's eye. She raises her chin and slides her gaze away, blatantly ignoring me. Should I pull out my phone and pretend to reply to imaginary texts? No. I've had enough of this. I don't know why she's got a problem with me. After what she did, *I* should be the one to hate *her*. I lean forward a little and address Tamsin directly, trying to be friendly. 'You've got children now, haven't you?'

She raises her eyes in surprise. I wonder if she'll blank me.

'Yeah, a boy and a girl,' she says, staring down at her French-manicured nails, her rose-gold watch glinting under the lights.

'How old are they?'

'Eli is eight and McKenna is six.' Her tone is bored, disinterested.

'I've got a six month old – Daisy.'

She raises her eyebrows again. This time in acknowledgement.

'Yeah,' I struggle on, wondering why I'm even bothering. 'I'm on maternity leave at the moment, but I'm kind of dreading going back to work after half term. It'll be so hard to leave her.'

'I can't imagine leaving my kids while I go out to work,' Tamsin says. 'Having someone else raise them. I wouldn't like that at all.'

I know she's just baiting me, but her words sting.

'Some of us don't have a choice,' I reply.

She shrugs.

'Look, Tamsin,' I say, leaning forward slightly. 'Why don't we forget about everything that's gone on in the past? It was all a long time ago. It's stupid to fall out over a boy.' I make a lame joke to try to ease the tension.

'I don't think so,' she says icily. 'It might have been in the past, Kirstie, but I'm not about to forget it all and suddenly be your best friend.'

I shake my head, unable to believe she can be so hostile towards me. Maybe she really did love Dom. Maybe she still does. 'I wasn't suggesting we be best friends,' I reply. 'I just thought we could move on, be civil, you know?'

'You might have Dom now,' she says with a sneer, 'but it doesn't mean you can have everything you want. And these are *my* friends too.'

'Fine.' I reach into my purse and pull out my phone – fake replying to fake texts will be an easy way to end this conversation. I'm done trying to mend fences with her. I must have been mad to even try. Tamsin was the one in the wrong, but it seems she doesn't care. She never apologised about any of it but tonight I had the rash thought that it might be better for us to be polite to one another. Obviously, I was wrong. Now I'm faced with the discomfort of evil looks from Queen Bitchface for the rest of the evening.

Her earlier words still bug me. I wish I could afford to stay home and be with my daughter all day, but it's out of the question.

We need my wage. Anyway, I love my job and I'm sure I'll get used to being a working mum – plenty of people do.

On the other side of me, Mel signals to the waiter to bring another bottle of wine. I push away the niggle that money is tight and try not to stress about how expensive the bill is going to be. But it's hard not to resent the fact that my friends always split the bill evenly, even when some of us aren't drinking.

The evening rolls past pleasantly enough, and at 10.30 p.m. the waiter brings the bill.

Mel taps me on the shoulder. 'Having a good time?'

'Yeah, good. You?'

She lays her head on my shoulder and I laugh at her drunken state. 'You're my best friend ever,' she says. 'I hope you know that.'

'You too,' I reply.

She waggles her finger at me. 'Best friend. Right here.' She gets to her feet and dings her glass with a spoon. Pointing down at my head with spoon, she proclaims to the table and the few other diners who are left in the restaurant, 'I want you all to know that I love you all, but Kirstie is my best friend in the whole world.'

Everyone says, 'aaah' and laughs.

Mel sits down heavily on her chair again and whispers in my ear. 'Kirst, I just realised I've left my purse at home. Can you pay for my share and I'll give it back to you tomorrow? Thanks, hon.'

My smile vanishes and I grit my teeth. 'Sure, I'll put it on my card.'

'Lifesaver.'

'You will pay me back though, Mel? It's just, Dom and I are a bit strapped at the moment.'

'Relax. Pay you back tomorrow. It's not a problem.'

Easy for you to say. I always seem to be lending Mel money, which she keeps forgetting to pay back. I love her to bits but she's terrible with finances. She's usually spent the maintenance check from her ex before she gets it. Her problem is she's a hopeless shopaholic. But I don't want to get all judgemental. I don't want this to tarnish our friendship.

'Hate to ask again,' she says, 'but could I borrow a teensy bit more for the taxi home?'

'That's okay,' I say, 'you can share a taxi with me.'

'Thing is, that hot waiter has asked me to go clubbing with him.' Mel nods in the direction of a fair-haired waiter, who looks about eighteen.

'Are you serious?' I ask.

'I know, right. Looks like I've still got it, hon.'

I shake my head and can't help grinning at her. 'Who's babysitting?'

'Jess Slater. She said not to worry if I'm late.'

'Yeah, but she's only just turned fifteen. Don't be too late, Mel, it's a school night.' Jess is the middle one of three sisters who live next door to me at number three. Her stepdad, Stephen Parkfield, is the headmaster at St George's, the school where I teach.

'Jess'll be fine,' Mel insists.

'Yeah, *Jess'll* be fine, but you know what Lorna's like. She won't be happy if you rock up at 2 a.m.' Lorna is Jess's mum. She was in the year above us at school.

'Miss hoity-toity I'm-married-to-the-headmaster,' Mel sneers.

'She's all right,' I say, sticking up for her.

'No she's not,' Mel says. 'She's a snobby cow. You know she is.'

'I dunno, I think she's just shy and a bit awkward.' Lorna and her first husband split up when their daughters were young. It can't have been easy for her with three young girls. She met Stephen Parkfield soon after, and they married almost straight away.

'Wouldn't hurt her to crack a smile every once in a while,' Mel says.

'Just try to get home by midnight.' Even as I'm saying the words, I know there's no chance Mel will be back by then.

'You're such a stresser,' she says, squeezing my hand.

'Honestly, Mel. I'm just looking out for you.'

'I know you are, hon. I know.'

I have to stop worrying about her. It's her life, not mine.

'So, can I borrow some extra cash, then?' Mel asks again.

'I've only got enough for my taxi home,' I say. 'I'll have to go to the cashpoint.'

'Thank yoooou!' She kisses my cheek and drags me to my feet. 'Let's pay the bill and go there now.'

Eventually, we all say our goodbyes, promising to meet up again soon, and I slide into my taxi, leaving Mel at the bar while her hot waiter finishes his shift. I don't know how she manages it, but men are always drawn to her. Trouble is, they never end up sticking around.

The cab journey home is smooth and quick, the driver thankfully untalkative, my mind pleasantly vacant. I stifle a yawn as we pull into Magnolia Close and I point out my house. I'm looking forward to holding Daisy in my arms and giving her a feed. It feels as though I've been away for days.

As I step out of the cab and close the door, I see the Parkfields' curtains twitch. I bet it's Lorna assuming Mel's back too. She'll probably be expecting Jess home any minute. I toy with the idea of knocking on her door, letting her know that Mel won't be home until later, but instantly dismiss the thought – I don't want to get involved in *that* drama.

The taxi has gone, and I realise I'm still standing on the driveway. I give myself a shake. But as I begin walking down the path, I notice that something is off. I frown into the dark patch of garden that lies between the porch light and the streetlight. Suddenly, I realise what it is – the plants and flowers in one of the front borders have been flattened. I take a few steps closer and peer into the flower bed. It's as though someone has stomped on all the poor plants, grinding the leaves and petals off their stalks so they're now trampled into the dry earth. Did someone do this on purpose? Why would they do such a thing? Could it have been kids?

But my questions fade as I hear a distant noise – a baby crying. Not just crying, but screaming. Daisy! She sounds hysterical. Bloody Dominic. *What's he doing?* Why isn't he comforting her? Or maybe he is trying to soothe her but she's crying with hunger and it's my fault for staying out too late.

I run down the drive and along the path, fumble with my keys in the lock and stagger into the hallway. The lounge door is open and the TV is on. I see the back of Dom's head. Why is he sitting in there, when Daisy is screaming her lungs out?

'Dom!' I march into the lounge.

He opens his eyes. 'Eh?'

'Were you asleep?' I snap, noting the open windows.

'Yeah, must've nodded off.'

'Your daughter is screaming her head off up there.'

'What?' He jumps to his feet and frowns. 'No she's not.'

I tilt my head to listen. Sure enough, she's quieted down. 'Well, she was a second ago.' I glare at him, stomp out of the room and race up the stairs, hoping to God she's okay, wishing I had never gone out. I stride into our darkened bedroom and peer into the Moses basket, ready to scoop Daisy into my arms.

But it's empty. Daisy isn't there.

CHAPTER EIGHT

'Dom!' I yell. 'Dom, come quickly!

'What is it?' He switches on the light and stares at me, bemused.

'Where's Daisy?' I ask, on the verge of panic. 'Why isn't she in her basket?' I see that our bedroom window is open and I suddenly remember the trampled flowers in the front garden. My skin goes cold.

'It's okay, Kirstie.' Putting his fingers to his lips, he leads me into Daisy's room and over to the cot where our daughter lies on her back, fast asleep.

As I stare down at my baby, relief swamps me. My hands tremble as I reach down to stroke her hair, marvelling that she really is here. That she's safe. That my fear was unfounded.

'I moved her back into her own room,' Dominic quietly explains. 'I thought it would be best.'

'For a minute, I thought… I thought…'

'I'm sorry,' Dom whispers. 'I should've told you. I didn't think.'

'It's okay.' I push my fingertips into my forehead, and take deep, steadying breaths. 'But I heard her screaming. When I was outside, she was yelling so loudly. I thought she must be hungry.'

'She's fine,' Dom says. 'Good as gold. No tears all evening.' He puts his arms around me and brings me close to his chest. 'I'm sorry, Kirst. I can't imagine how you must have felt seeing the empty basket.'

'It's not your fault,' I say. 'I'm sorry I panicked.'

'It's fine, don't worry about it.'

I lean back and stare at him, trying to discern his expression, but I can't see him clearly in the gloom. 'If it wasn't Daisy scream-ing, then whose baby did I hear?'

'It was probably just foxes,' Dom says.

'It wasn't foxes. I know the difference between foxes and babies.'

Dominic sighs. 'The main thing is that Daisy's safe.'

'Yes,' I say. 'Yes, you're right. She's safe. She's here. But there *is* something strange going on.'

'Strange?'

'Someone trampled all the flowers in our garden.'

'What are you talking about?' Dom frowns.

I lead him out of Daisy's room and down the stairs.

'Kirstie?'

I open the front door and walk across to the decimated flower bed. Dom follows behind and I point at the mess of earth and leaves, breathing in the heavy scent of crushed flower petals.

'Who did that?' he asks.

I shrug. 'It was like this when I got home.'

'Must be kids,' he says. 'Little shits.'

'It looks deliberate, though.' I wrap my arms around myself. 'Why would kids walk down our drive and do something so horrible?'

'Could it be one of your pupils?' Dom asks. 'Maybe you gave them a low mark or something, and they thought they'd get back at you by doing this.'

I give a small shiver and Dom puts an arm around me. 'Come on,' he says, 'let's go back in. Whoever did it is an idiot, but I doubt they'll be back.'

I let myself be guided back inside the house, still disquieted by the flower bed, but also haunted by the ghost of that screaming baby I heard earlier. I briefly wonder if I could have been hearing things. Could it have been foxes like Dom said? No. Definitely not. Maybe there is another baby nearby? But our road is isolated. And there are no other babies on this street. These thoughts circle my brain as I check that the front door is locked properly. I don't want to think about all this now. I'm suddenly exhausted. All I know is that Daisy is okay. She's upstairs in her cot and I won't be leaving her side tonight. Though I know she's safe, the nagging suspicion that someone is trying to take her won't leave me alone. And the thought I'm losing my mind keeps growing.

I bring Daisy into bed with me. She's hungry and contented as she lies in my arms, her fingers stroking my face as she feeds. My earlier panic is finally receding. There's no way Daisy will be sleeping in her own room tonight and Dominic knows better than to try and persuade me. He comes into our bedroom.

'I'm so sorry about before, Dom. About overreacting like that when I thought Daisy was crying, and then when I thought she was missing.'

'Don't worry. It's fine.'

'It's not fine. I completely panicked. This whole baby-monitor thing yesterday, it spooked me. I'm a nervous wreck.'

'Forget it.' He shakes his head and gives me a small smile.

'I'm sorry,' I repeat.

'You were worried, that's all. Let's get some sleep. Things will seem better in the morning.' He yawns and scratches the back of his head.

'I don't know how I'm ever going to sleep tonight.'

'Look, the main thing is that we're all okay. You're fine, I'm fine, Daisy's fine, so let's just forget about it, okay?'

'Okay.'

But it's not okay. Everything is off-balance.

Once Daisy has finished feeding, I wind her and change her nappy, chatting to her and dropping kisses onto the soft skin of her shoulders and cheeks. The thought of anyone trying to snatch her makes me ill with anxiety. I try to push the thoughts out of my head. To clear my mind of troublesome thoughts. I lay my daughter down in the Moses basket and climb back into bed.

'Anyway, how was your evening?' Dominic asks, getting in beside me.

'My evening?'

'Yeah, your evening with Mel and the girls, how was it?'

I'd almost forgotten about my night out. 'It was good,' I murmur.

'Who was there?'

'The usual. You know.' I think about Tamsin Price's sneering face, but I don't mention her name to Dom. It took the two of us long enough to get over that particular episode. The last thing I want is to dredge it all up again.

'Mel behave herself?'

'Ha. She pulled a twelve-year-old waiter.'

'No!'

'Yep. Honestly, I don't reckon he could've been more than nineteen.'

'That girl,' he says through a yawn. 'Tell me all the gory details tomorrow. Can't keep my eyes open any longer.'

Dom falls asleep almost instantly. Once his breathing deepens, I slip out of bed to check that all the doors and windows in the house are closed and locked. Reluctantly, I decide to leave the windows in our room open, as I know Dom will wake up if he gets too hot. Eventually, I return to bed and fall asleep, but when I wake a short while later, in the early hours of the morning, I feel the urge to check the house again. I can't help myself. It's like an itch I have to scratch. A compulsion.

As I'm checking the back doors I hear a dull bump outside. I catch my breath and peer into the garden. There's nothing but blackness. No movement. The rational side of my brain says that this is nothing more than a cat jumping from the fence onto the shed roof, a sound I've heard a million times before. But I don't think I am in my rational mind. What if it's *them* lurking around outside, checking our defences?

I picture the door handles moving up and down as though someone is testing the locks. In reality, the handles are unmoving, but I can't shake the image of a person pulling at them, trying to get in. My heart thumps and I think about grabbing a knife from the kitchen drawer for protection. But that's ridiculous. There's no one out there – I saw as much with my own eyes. I need to stop this. I need to go back to bed.

But as I plod back up the stairs with the image of the moving door handles lodged in my brain, I realise there will be no sleep for me tonight.

*

My brain is still wired as the sky begins to lighten. Dominic and Daisy are sleeping, safe and sound. I rub at my eyes, noting that the clock reads 6.25 a.m. I think this is the longest she's slept through without a feed. Finally, I allow my eyes to close, my body to relax.

Through a fog of sleep, I hear the beeps of Dominic's alarm. It's easy to ignore. I curl my legs up into my body and sink deeper into the mattress. But almost as soon as sleep takes me again, Daisy's cry cuts into my consciousness. I can't block her out. She needs me.

'I'll change her,' Dom whispers in my ear. 'Sleep a while longer.'

I give a murmur of thanks and relax once more.

Too soon, Dominic is back in the room, Daisy fussing in his arms. I know she's hungry. I prop myself up in bed and Dom passes her to me. As she feeds, I close my eyes again and try to doze. My mouth tastes sour and my head is fuzzy. It must be the lack of sleep.

Memories of last night return – not my night out with friends, but what happened when I got home: discovering the trampled flowerbeds, shouting at Dominic, frantically checking the locks, viewing my distorted reflection in the bifold doors and the darkness beyond, imagining the door handles moving. It seems crazy that I let myself get carried away like that, allowing myself to imagine such terrible scenarios. I'm not that person. I'm Kirstie Rawlings, wife, mother, teacher, always calm and rational, happy. I push the disturbing images away as though they are an unwelcome nightmare, not an actual memory. Last night was an aberration. I won't let it happen again. I'll catch up on my sleep and get back to my normal self.

'I'm going now, Kirst.'

I force open my eyes and give my husband what I hope is a nice, wifely smile. 'Have a good day.'

'It's Friday, so I should be home a bit earlier tonight. Shall I pick up some ready meals from M&S?'

'Sounds good. Thanks.'

'Any preference?'

'You choose.'

'Okay. See you later.' I manage to stop myself from begging him to stay home today. It wouldn't be fair. He'd only worry. But as I listen to his disappearing footsteps followed by the bang of the front door and the car starting up, it's all I can do to stop myself running after him. As the sound of his car engine recedes, the newly familiar hollow lump of dread takes up residence behind my sternum. A crushing anxiety that I have no idea how to dispel.

I should sleep. If I'm not awake, these thoughts can't plague me.

Once I've finished feeding Daisy, I take her with me to the bathroom while I clean my teeth and swallow down two paracetamol. She's quite content, so I place her back in her basket and climb back into bed. Almost as soon as I let myself drift, I'm dragged awake by the juddering roar of a pneumatic drill and the whine of some kind of electric saw. The builders at number six must be out in force.

It's okay, I tell myself, *I can tune it out*. I'm sure I can. But instead of fading into background noise, each sound seems to grow louder and sharper – the blaring radio, the raucous shouted instructions, the beeping of a reversing truck… Anger builds in my gut. I grind my teeth and ball my fists. This disruption has been going on all summer and I've had enough. Surely they can give it a rest for one morning. *Surely.*

I fling the sheets back and stomp around the bedroom, throwing on a sundress and dragging my fingers through my tangled black curls. Daisy is cooing contentedly in her cot, not at all bothered by the racket outside.

'Come on, little one,' I say, picking her up, eliciting a wide grin, 'let's go and tell those naughty builders to shut up. They're doing Mummy's head in.'

Downstairs, I open the front door and screw up my eyes against the sun. What will I say to the builders? Will they become angry? Abusive, even? But my craving for silence overrides my nerves. I'll draw on my teaching experience and pretend they're a bunch of unruly teenagers.

I'm about to step outside when I see a puddle of something white beneath my raised foot. It has oozed down the front step and onto the path, gloopy tentacles splayed out in all directions. *What the hell?* I teeter in the doorframe for a moment before bringing my foot back inside. A second later I register the unmistakable stink of paint. My heart begins to thump uncomfortably. Why is there spilt paint on my doorstep? I take a giant stride over the puddle and glance left and right in case whoever did it is still hanging around. I can't see anyone. I can't believe this! First the flower bed and now paint everywhere. *What is going on?*

CHAPTER NINE

Spying something else white under one of the bushes, I walk over and pull back a leafy branch, while Daisy tries to wriggle out of my arms. There, tipped onto its side beneath the bush, lies a paint can leaking more of the toxic stuff into the ground. A few yards away the lid lies glinting on the trampled flower bed. This is getting ridiculous. What's going on around here? I bite my lip, unsure of what to do.

Perhaps the paint can is from the building site. I may as well go over there – I can ask them about the paint as well as asking them to keep the noise down. That drill feels like it's boring into my brain. I reach over the puddle to close the front door, before walking back to retrieve the paint can, its handle warm and sticky.

I take a breath and walk over to number six. The noise has already spooked Daisy, whose happy nonsense-chatter stops as the drilling gets louder. A burly man in his forties, dressed in a plaster-splattered T-shirt and shorts, paces on the driveway, shouting into a mobile phone clamped to his ear. I pay no attention to his words, concentrating instead on what I'm going to say to him. He looks up and catches my eye, holds a forefinger up to indicate he'll be a minute. I wait, unsmiling.

Finally, he ends the call and raises an eyebrow.

'Hi,' I say. 'I'm Kirstie Rawlings. I live at number four.'

'Speak up, love! Can't hear you.'

'I live at number four!' I point to my house.

'Oh yeah?'

'I'm Kirstie.'

'Rob. Rob Carson, site manager. How can I help?'

I vaguely recognise the name.

He glances behind him at a young guy pushing a wheelbarrow down the drive, then barks some instructions at him before turning back to me. 'What's it you want?'

'Is this yours?' I hold out the dripping paint can.

'Careful, love, you're getting paint all over your dress, not to mention the drive. Gloss paint is a bugger to get out.'

'Yes, well, it's all over my front step. Does it belong to you?'

Carson holds his hands up. 'Nothing to do with me. We haven't even started the plastering yet, let alone the painting, and we wouldn't be using that stuff anyway.'

I don't suppose he'd admit to it even if it was from their site.

'All over your front step?' he adds. 'I don't envy you, cleaning all that lot up.'

'Thanks,' I reply drily. 'So you don't know how the paint ended up on my step?'

He gives me a hard stare.

'I'm not accusing you,' I say. 'Just asking, that's all.'

He softens his gaze a little and shrugs. 'Haven't got a clue, love.'

'Well, if you hear anything, can you let me know? I've had a couple of incidents now – trampled flower bed, spilt paint.'

'Sounds like kids.'

'Yeah, well. Don't suppose you know how to get gloss paint off a stone step?'

'Paint stripper and a scrubbing brush.' He tuts and shakes his head. 'Bloody kids. I can chuck that paint can in our skip if you like?' Carson reaches across to take it from me.

I pause for a moment, wondering if I might need it as evidence. But it's a sticky mess – I don't want to keep it – so I hand it over. 'Thanks.'

'Well, sorry about the paint and all that, but I'd better get back to it.' He turns away.

'Also,' I say, 'I was wondering… if there's any chance you could stop the drilling and sawing? Just for an hour or two. It's just, I've got a baby and it's so loud that I can't—'

'You want me to stop work?' He raises his eyebrows. 'Mmm, I'd love to have the day off, but I don't think the owners would be very happy if I got the lads to down tools.'

'Just the noisy tools,' I clarify.

'They're all noisy – it's a building site, isn't it.'

'Just the drilling, then?'

'Sorry, love. No can do.' He goes on to explain why my request is impossible, but I only catch odd snatches of his words. He speaks quickly, dismissively, with no eye contact, like he's already finished the conversation, his attention caught by cement mixers and spirit levels, suppliers and late deliveries. I am a nuisance, a distraction, hardly worth bothering with. I'm not sure why I even thought he would listen to me. Wishful thinking, I suppose.

I turn away from Carson with a muttered goodbye and head back home, shifting Daisy to my other side to give my left arm a break. Going over there has made my headache worse, and talking to that condescending builder has made me irritable. There's no point going back to bed now. I'll never get to sleep.

I should make a start on cleaning up all that paint, but I can't face it. Not right now. Besides, I don't have all the right equipment. I'll do it later. Maybe I'll fetch Daisy's pram and we'll go for a walk – get away from the cul-de-sac for a while. That might be nice. Take my mind off things.

I glance up the road at the sound of a car. It's Mel in her cherry-red Mercedes. Back from dropping the kids off at nursery no doubt. At least she made it home last night. I decide to head over there to find out what happened with her waiter, and also to see if maybe I can get my cash back.

As I approach, Mel gets out of her car, her hair tied up in a swinging ponytail, Jackie O sunglasses covering half her face. She's wearing a slightly creased cotton skirt, a plunging halter top and strappy sandals.

'Nursery run,' she croaks. 'At least I can go back to bed now. Although, what the bloody fuck are they doing over at number six? Sounds like they're sawing the house in half.'

'I've just been over there to ask them to keep the noise down.'

'Ha! Bet that went down well.'

'Actually, they're more likely to listen to *you* than me,' I say, 'if you ask them especially nicely while wearing that top. And yes, I *am* prepared for you to stoop that low for a bit of blessed peace and quiet.'

'Maybe later,' she drawls, and shakes her head. 'Got time for a coffee? A quick one, though, and decaf for me – I need sleep.'

'Good luck getting to sleep with that lot going on.'

'You know me, I could sleep through the apocalypse.'

I'm envious of her ability to sleep through the noise.

'You didn't happen to see anyone in our front garden this morning, did you?' I ask.

'Your garden? No.' She squints. 'Come inside. It's far too bright for civilised people out here.'

I follow her into her immaculate house. When she first moved in, she made everything ultra-modern, with sleek surfaces and glossy worktops. But she got bored of that last year and now it's done out in a New England style, with painted wood and tasteful pastel colours.

'Someone sloshed paint all over our front step,' I say.

'What? *Paint?*'

'White gloss paint. A great big puddle of the stuff. I almost stepped right in it.'

'That's…'

'I know, right.'

'Any idea who did it?'

I sit on the sofa with Daisy on my knee. 'Not a clue. The builder at number six said it's not their paint.'

'Iced coffee?' Mel asks.

'Please. Although gin would be good about now.'

She gives me a sympathetic look. 'Don't worry. Sounds like it's just kids mucking about.' She walks over to one of the kitchen cupboards and takes out two tall glasses.

'I guess so.'

'Bit weird though, *paint*.'

I shake my head. 'Really weird. Anyway, enough about my boring life. Tell me how last night went with your hot waiter.'

'It was fun.' Her eyes sparkle. '*Alfie* and I went dancing.'

'*Alfie?*'

'I know. Isn't that just the last name you'd think of when you look at that baby face of his.'

'And?'

'And nothing. That's it. We danced, had a smoochy kiss and then he dropped me home at one thirty.'

'Really? Are you going to see him again?'

'No.' Mel rolls her eyes. 'He was sweet, but way too young. I must have had my wine goggles on last night. You should've told me I was hooking up with a minor.'

'*No!* He's not, is he?'

'Joking! He's twenty-two. Still, that's bad enough.' She brings our drinks over and sits on the sofa opposite. 'So, did you have a good night? Are you glad I made you go?'

'Yes, I'm glad. It was good to talk to other grown-ups for a change. Apart from Tamsin, that is,' I mutter.

'She's not that bad, is she?' Mel says, raising an eyebrow. 'I know she was awful to you back then, but that was years ago. Surely she's moved on.'

'You'd think so,' I huff. 'But no. She pretty much said she hates me.'

'Wow. Okay. Well, give her time. Now she's back, I'm sure she'll get over it.'

I want to snap that Tamsin actually has nothing to 'get over'. She slept with my boyfriend. She should be the one apologising and begging my forgiveness. But that all sounds so petty, so I tell myself I'm better off forgetting about the woman. I need to take the high road and act like it doesn't bother me. 'You're right,' I say, biting back my feelings. 'It's all ancient history. I shouldn't get so hung up on what she thinks.'

It's a relief to change the subject. Mel fills me in on Sooz's marriage problems, and then we chat some more about our other friends' lives and what they're all up to. I'm hoping Mel is going to bring up the matter of the cash she owes me, but from past experience I know that's not likely, so I decide to be brave. 'Hey, Mel, don't suppose you're able to pay back that money I lent you last night?'

'Money?' Her face tightens.

'You forgot your purse, remember? I lent you eighty quid.'

'Oh, yeah.' She takes a sip of coffee. 'I haven't got any cash on me at the moment, Kirst. I had to pay the nursery some overdue fees this morning. They got all snooty with me – I really could've done without their attitude this morning. Honestly, I've got a mind to find somewhere else for the kiddiwinks to go. I'll be glad when James starts school next year and I don't have to pay such exorbitant fees.'

'It's just,' I say, ploughing on, 'I really need it or I'm going to go overdrawn. I've got a direct debit going out of my account today.' It annoys me that I'm having to explain myself. It feels like I'm the one in the wrong. 'It doesn't have to be cash, you can transfer it into my account if that's easier?'

'Today might be tricky, hon. But I can probably sort it for you next week?'

'Mel, you promised. Last night you said you'd pay it back today.' I take a breath. 'The thing is, I won't be able to lend you any more until you've paid back what you owe me. It comes to over seven hundred pounds now.' I didn't mean for it to come out so bluntly, but I guess there really is no nice way to ask for money.

Her mouth drops open, and then she snaps it shut again.

My heart is pounding and my face has gone all hot and clammy. I feel terrible, but I won't apologise... And then I go and do just that. 'Sorry,' I say. 'I'm just tired – new baby, late night, spilt paint, noisy builders. I didn't mean to snap. It's just, money's tight, you know?'

She bites her lip, subdued.

'Look, I'd better go.' I take a last sip of my drink and rise to my feet.

'I'm sorry about the money, Kirst,' she says. 'I didn't realise how much I'd borrowed. Are you sure it's that much? Never mind. Whatever. It's just...' She heaves an enormous sigh. 'It's so hard being a single mum. You have no idea the strain it puts on everything. A fat tear rolls down her cheek. 'I'll get the money somehow. I will, I promise.'

'Don't cry, Mel.' Now I feel terrible. 'Of course it's hard. Of course it is. Just... pay me back whenever you're able to, okay. No pressure at all.' I know as I say these words that I'll never see that money again, but it's fine. I'd rather keep our friendship than let a few hundred quid get between us. 'Forget I asked, okay?'

Mel sniffs and wipes her eyes. 'Thanks, hon.' She stands up and we hug. 'God, the state of us, both blubbing away. That'll teach us to get pissed on a school night.'

I don't bother to remind her that she's the only one of us who was drinking last night. We say goodbye and I head back to my house. My earlier burst of energy has evaporated and I don't think I could face going for a walk now. Maybe I'll slob out on the sofa and watch some crappy TV with the sound turned up loud to drown out the drilling, see if that will take my mind off things.

I realise I'll have to tell Dominic about the money. He won't be at all pleased. As I walk back across the road, my annoyance grows. Once again, I've let myself be duped by Mel. She always does this. Gives me a sob story and I fall for it. I'd be happy to help out if she really needed the money, but the reality is, her monthly maintenance cheques are more than double what Dominic and I earn jointly. She has money to remodel her kitchen, but not for nursery fees. Money to spend on new clothes, but somehow the electric bill becomes overdue and then I have to bail her out. Mel always comes up with some excuse not to pay me, and every time I fall for it.

I hate feeling like this; bitter and angry. It's not who I am. But the hard knot in my chest is saying otherwise. Do I even know who I am any more?

CHAPTER TEN

Incredibly, the builders haven't turned up to number six today. Granted, it is a Saturday, but that's never stopped them before in the two months they've been working there. Whatever the reason, it's a welcome relief to wake up to relative silence. And, even better, I only checked the locks once last night and then managed to sleep right though. I almost feel like I'm back to normal.

With Dominic at home this morning and the sun shining, my worries for Daisy's safety have shifted to the back-burner. I even feel semi-okay having the back doors open, although I can't help scanning the fences every few minutes. Dom helped me tackle the paint spill yesterday evening and we managed to get most of it up. But there's still a massive white stain over the step and the pathway. It doesn't look like we'll ever get rid of it properly.

'Cup of tea in the garden?' Dom asks.

'Sounds good,' I reply, my voice sounding more upbeat. I take Daisy outside and lay her on the grass on her play mat under the faded green sun umbrella. Then I plonk myself down on one of the garden chairs. When we first bought the wooden patio set, we had good intentions about oiling the wood every year to keep it looking nice. Of course, that never happened and now the wood is grey and flaky with neglect.

Dom brings out two mugs of tea and places them on the table before sitting across from me. 'Did you see the Parkfields have got a "sold" sign on their house?' he says.

'Really?' I sit up a bit straighter. I knew number three was for sale, but hadn't thought much about it.

'So, looks like we'll be having new neighbours,' Dom adds.

'I hope they're nice. I wonder where the Parkfields are moving to.' Dom and I don't have much to do with them socially, what with him being the headmaster of my school and Lorna being stand-offish. I suppose Stephen Parkfield likes to keep work and pleasure separate, which is fine by me.

'No idea,' Dom replies, taking a sip of his tea.

'I wonder if that means Parkfield will be leaving St George's,' I muse.

'Maybe,' Dom says.

'They'll probably know about it at work.' Since being on maternity leave, I've been out of the loop. I make a mental note to text Tim, my head of department, for any gossip. 'And if Parkfield leaves, maybe that means their girls will be leaving St George's too.'

'Mmm,' Dom replies. I can tell he's not really listening, with his face turned up towards the sun, eyes closed.

I've taught all of Parkfield's stepdaughters at one time or another. 'Jess and Lydia are sweet girls,' I continue, 'but I won't miss Hannah. She's got a real mouth on her.'

'That the eldest?' Dom asks.

'Yeah.'

'They've been on holiday all summer.' I pick at a splinter of flaking wood, peeling it back from the top of the patio table. 'They only got back this week.'

'All right for some,' Dom murmurs.

'To be honest, I'm relieved they're moving. It's always been a bit weird, living next door to my boss.'

'Yeah.'

'As long as whoever moves in doesn't start knocking walls down,' I say. 'I don't think I could cope with building work on both sides.'

'No. That would *not* be cool.'

I take a sip of tea and look down at Daisy who's cooing and smiling under her play mat, tugging at the scrunchy giraffe that's hanging above her.

'Dom, I need to tell you something.'

'Uh oh,' he says, opening his eyes. 'Sounds ominous.'

I wrench my gaze away from Daisy and turn to look at my husband. 'Not really. Well, sort of. I'll just come out and say it. It's about Mel.'

'What about her?' He leans forward.

'The thing is, I've been lending her money.'

'Ri-ight.'

'Quite a lot of money.'

'How much?' Dom asks.

I wince. 'About seven hundred pounds.'

'Bloody hell.' He rocks back in his chair, so it's on two legs. I worry he'll fall back and crack his head on the patio flagstones, but I don't tell him to stop.

'I know,' I say. 'It wasn't all at once. It was bits here and there. But it's kind of added up. And the thing is, each time I lent her some she promised she'd pay me back, but she never has.'

'Ah, it's okay,' Dom says, bringing his chair back onto four legs. 'She's our friend. I don't mind helping her out if she's struggling.'

'Really?' I say, eying him suspiciously. He doesn't seem to be batting an eyelid. I thought he'd go ballistic. He's always so careful with money. 'I told her I wouldn't lend her any more until she pays the rest back. I had a bit of a go at her, actually.'

He frowns. 'Did you fall out?'

'To be honest, I'm not exactly sure. I did lose my cool a bit. She got a bit upset, and she cried.'

'You made her cry? That's not like you, Kirst.'

'It was just one tear, but I think it was more for sympathy. She started telling me how hard it was being a single mum…'

'I suppose it *is* hard though, Kirst. Maybe you were a bit harsh? I'm sure she'll pay it back when she can.'

'Dom, I don't want to be mean but I'm pretty sure we'll never see that money again. And we can't really afford it. I've already gone overdrawn because she didn't pay me back yesterday like she said she would.'

'Want me to transfer some money to your account?' he asks.

'Would you? Thank you.'

'I feel sorry for her,' Dom says. 'It can't be easy.'

I don't point out that her ex-husband is loaded and pays Mel a hefty amount of maintenance. I don't want to come across as churlish. Mel always manages to make me feel guilt, even when she's not here. 'Well we can't lend her any more money. And I've told her that, so hopefully she won't ask again.'

'Well, if we're getting things off our chests,' Dom says, 'there's something I need to tell you, too.' He has that hesitant, apologetic tone in his voice, the one where he knows I won't like what he's going to say. He takes a swig of his tea.

'What? What is it?' I reply. Maybe that's why he was fine with me lending Mel money. Maybe what he's about to tell me is far worse.

'I need to go out training today,' he says.

'Oh.' My heart plummets. I thought he might. It's not the end of the world, but my anxiety is already kicking in. It's lonely enough during the week with him at work all day, but leaving us on a Saturday too makes my heart twist.

'The thing is,' he says. 'I really need to train tomorrow, too.'

'What! Both days?'

'I know, I'm sorry. It's only for the next six weeks. Once the triathlon's finished I'll be home earlier after work and my training won't be so full on. But if I want to do well, I need to train. Otherwise there's no point competing.'

'You want to train at weekends for the next six weeks?'

'If that's okay with you.'

I sigh at the thought of endless lonely weeks rolling out in front of me, suddenly feeling a renewed sympathy for Mel, who's on her own all the time. 'Look,' I say, 'I don't want to stop you doing something you love. It's just... I get lonely. And what about Daisy? She loves having you at home too. It's just the two of us here by ourselves all day, every day. We so look forward to having you home at the weekends.'

'I know. I'm sorry. But you can hang out with Mel, can't you? Or your mum and dad... they love having you over.'

'Yeah, I can. But you're my husband. I married you to spend time with *you*, not Mel or my parents.'

'I know, I know.' He stares down at his mug of tea.

'Don't you like spending time with us?' I ask, knowing that's an awful question to ask.

'Of course I do!' His face goes scarlet. 'I *love* spending time with my girls, you know I do.' He frowns and shakes his head. 'Look, do you want me to knock it on the head, cancel the triathlon?'

'No, of course not,' I reply. Sport is his passion. When he was younger, he wanted to be a footballer, but he wasn't quite good enough to go professional. Now he's got his fitness back he's become almost fanatical about training and competing again. It's all amateur stuff, but he takes it as seriously as he used to take his football. I never minded when I was working, but now that I'm home all day with Daisy, I feel his absence more keenly. I hate feeling like this: needy, lonely. It's not me. It's not who I am. But I can't shake the feeling that he'd rather be training than spending time with us. I guess I feel rejected. Although maybe that's me being melodramatic.

I take another sip of my tea. 'It's fine,' I say with a sigh. 'Of course you need to train. I know it's only short term.'

'Are you sure?' He doesn't wait for me to reply. 'Thank you, Kirstie. I'll make it up to you once the race is over. I promise.'

I don't reply. What can I say? I try to push down any lingering stabs of resentment. Before having Daisy, there wasn't any other pull on his time – I never minded him spending a lot of time on his outside interests. I've always been quite independent and enjoyed my own company, so it was never an issue. But since being on maternity leave, away from the company of other adults, I feel more isolated, adrift. It doesn't help that Dom's mother has always spoiled him, cherishing him like a prince. I suppose I've mimicked her example and continued to treat him the same way, always happy for him to do what he wants, when he wants, going along with whatever plans he makes. So now, when I need him to be a little less self-obsessed, he can't understand it. Can't see why I suddenly need him to look after me for a change. He's not trying to be difficult – he simply doesn't understand how I'm feeling.

Now I wonder if my need for him is pushing him away. If he's going off me. Things have been different between us lately. We've hardly touched one another since Daisy was born. We're less romantic and more like friends. Yet isn't that to be expected? Isn't that how it is with all couples after they have a baby?

Maybe I need to make more of an effort again. I just wish Dominic would look at me more. See the girl he fell in love with. Think about *me*, rather than his precious triathlon. I feel like everything is slipping out of my grasp. My perfect life is sliding into the mud and I don't know how to pull it back. The sunshine suddenly feels too bright, the sky too blue, the birdsong jarring.

'Are you okay, Kirst?' he asks.

I shrug, knowing my body language is laying a guilt trip on him, but I can't pretend I'm happy about this.

He sighs. 'How about if I just do one day at the weekend?'

'Could you?' I feel my whole body lighten. 'That would be so much better.'

Dom's face drops. 'Okay,' he replies, tight-lipped.

'What's the matter?' I ask, suddenly realising he expected me to say, *No, that's okay, you go ahead and train all weekend.*

'Nothing,' he replies. 'It's fine.'

'It's obviously not fine,' I snap.

'It's just… oh never mind.'

'What?' I say. 'It's just what?'

'Well, it's just that it's only two half-days at the weekends. Six weeks will go by really quickly.'

'Look, Dom, I already said it was fine to do both days. Then you suggested doing one day and I said yes that would be great. So don't make me out to be the bad guy, okay?' My voice has become shrill and I'm guessing the neighbours can hear our pathetic argument, but I'm too annoyed to be embarrassed about it.

'So you're okay with me doing the two days then?'

'Dom, do what you want. It's fine.'

'I'm sorry,' he says, tipping the dregs of his tea onto the grass.

I shake my head, not trusting myself to speak. This morning started out so positively, but now it's all gone to shit again. And Dominic will be gone for the rest of the day, leaving me to stew over everything. I want to scream with frustration. Instead I sip my tea and stare at the table, avoiding my husband's bewildered gaze.

CHAPTER ELEVEN

It's Sunday, and Dominic has gone out again, leaving me and Daisy alone. He was back by three thirty yesterday afternoon, so at least we got to spend some of the day together, but the hours in between dragged terribly. I'm in a no-win situation. If I tell him I don't want him to train, I come across as a nagging, clingy wife; if I give him my blessing, I'm left on my own every day for six weeks. And I'm pretty sure this won't be the last event he'll enter. There will be more triathlons, more training. Am I being unreasonable? I honestly don't know. All I do know is there's a chasm of emptiness opening up before me, and I'm falling into it, spinning over and over, down and down and down.

Daisy has started making little frustrated noises, she's hot and bothered, irritable, so I take her out onto the lawn with some of her toys and we sit under the sun umbrella, taking advantage of the half-hearted breeze. I pull her onto my lap so she's facing me, managing to find a little comfort in her wide-eyed smile. I bounce her up and down but my heart isn't in it. All I want to do is go back to bed. To sleep away my loneliness. How can I be feeling such despair when on the surface of things I have everything I ever wanted? What has changed?

A Greek philosopher once said that *the only thing that is constant is change*. Well, I don't want things to change. I want what Dom and I have to remain the same. Our strong relationship, the safety and comfort of our house. I realise that since I heard those voices in the monitor four days ago, I no longer feel comfortable in my own home. I'm scared to be here alone. Maybe that's why I'm resentful of Dom's training. I don't know. I don't trust what I'm feeling. I don't understand it.

It's as if outside influences have moved in and taken over. Made me uncertain of everything. Made me suspicious, untrusting. I look at the sky, at the distant trees, at the grass, and instead of filling me with calm, they mock me with their other-ness. An imperceptible change that only I can sense. The blue of the sky has turned harder, colder, more remote. The leaves on the trees whisper treachery and wickedness. The green of the grass appears an unnatural hue, as though it isn't real. I shake my head to dislodge these thoughts. There must be something wrong with me. Maybe I'm ill, or maybe I'm simply suffering with an overactive imagination, the heat of the sun addling my brain.

The doorbell snaps my thoughts back to reality. Whoever it is can go away. I don't trust myself to have a normal conversation with anyone right now. I bring Daisy close to my chest, inhaling the milky scent of her hair. My whole body tenses as the doorbell chimes once more. I want to scream at it to shut up. To tell whoever it is to leave me alone. But it rings again. They'll have to give up eventually, surely. I begin counting, silently mouthing the numbers. When I reach sixty and there have been no further doorbell chimes, I exhale in relief. Whoever it is must have gone.

I need to go inside to check the locks. As I rise to my feet a voice makes me jump so violently I almost drop Daisy.

I shriek.

'Kirstie, I do apologise if I startled you.'

I glance across to the fence, where I see Martin's bespectacled face peering over at me.

'Jesus Christ, Martin, you scared the life out of me.'

'I did try ringing the doorbell, but no one answered. I presumed you must be in the garden, unable to hear it.'

'What do you want?' I ask through clenched teeth, letting out a silent scream in my head that echoes through every fibre of my body.

'Apologies for disturbing you on a Sunday morning. But I wondered if I could call on you to accompany me next door. It won't take long.'

'Again?' I ask. 'You want me to come over to your house?'

'Actually, no.' His face flushes and he lowers his voice. 'I was hoping we could pop into number six's garden while the builders are away. I want to check the extension measurements against the plans which I managed to acquire from the council yesterday.'

'Isn't that trespassing on private property?' I say.

'You're right, Kirstie,' Martin replies, the crimson hue in his cheeks deepening even further. 'But, if what I suspect is correct, then those builders are flouting planning permission by building closer to my boundary wall than has been permitted.'

I don't reply, frantically trying to think of an excuse. If only I hadn't come outside, he wouldn't have had the opportunity to ask me.

'So you'll pop round, Kirstie? You and the little one?'

Annoyingly, no excuses are coming to mind.

'Actually, if you come to mine first we can look at it from my garden. Then we'll nip to number six to take the measurements.'

'Okay,' I say, furious with myself for not saying no.

'Wonderful. See you in a minute, Kirstie.'

Once his face has disappeared from view, I roll my eyes and haul myself to my feet, silently cursing my neighbour.

On the way over to his place, I remember the fact that Martin has a basement in his house. It's stupid and paranoid of me to worry about this. Martin has lived there for years and we've been his neighbours for as long as we've lived here and never had reason to suspect anything untoward. But the fact remains that I never knew about the basement until this week. Was it built at the same time as the house? Or did he have it constructed after he moved in?

The silence out here today is unnerving. Ironically, I wish the builders were back, shouting and hammering and drilling. I can't even hear any birds singing, just the swish of my dress as I walk and the dull thump of my heartbeats.

I begin to speculate about what is down in that basement. Is it used for storage? Is it an extra living room? I can't help more sinister thoughts creeping in. Maybe it's some sort of torture chamber or prison cell? Does he keep girls prisoner like in all those news stories? I shudder and tell myself not to be so silly.

Martin opens his front door as Daisy and I walk up the path. 'Remember; shoes.' Martin says.

I want to take them off and lob them at his head, but instead I dutifully remove them before walking into his claustrophobic house, its stink of pine air freshener making me want to gag.

'It's a shame about that young couple,' Martin says, shaking his head. 'You know, the Cliffords at number two.'

I follow him into the kitchen and through to his back garden, refusing to be drawn into the conversation, but he carries on anyway, even without a prompt from me.

'Have you noticed, they're always having people round? And their visitors park extremely inconsiderately up on the kerb or over the neighbours' driveways. I've seen them park over *your* drive, Kirstie. You should let them know it's not acceptable.'

'I've never noticed,' I reply.

'Well I have,' he says sagely. 'I leave notes on their windscreens but they don't seem to pay any attention.'

I blow air out through my mouth, trying to tune out his moaning. It doesn't normally bother me, but today it's winding me up to the point where I want to yell at him to shut up.

'Also,' Martin continues, lowering his voice, 'I don't want to poke my nose in where it's not wanted, but I thought you should know your husband is spending a lot of time at the Cliffords' house.'

'What are you talking about?' Dom and I are always friendly towards the young couple who live at number two, but I wouldn't necessarily say we were actual friends. And Dom's never mentioned going over there.

'Well, I don't like to tell tales out of school,' Martin says with an apologetic shrug, 'but I've seen young Dominic coming in and out of their house quite a lot.'

'What do you mean by quite a lot?' I snap.

'Maybe four or five times. It's usually just after he gets home from work. But I've seen him there at weekends, too.'

I want to tell Martin to mind his own bloody business, but I also want to find out what he's talking about. 'How long does he spend over there?' I ask, hating myself for digging up gossip about my own husband from Martin, of all people.

'Hmm, I'm not sure. Not long. It's not as though I'm timing him or anything.' He gives a low chortle and I think to myself that, actually, Martin probably is the type of person who would time him. 'A few minutes or so would be my guess,' he adds.

'Well, I'm sure Dom was just being neighbourly,' I say, wanting to erase the gleam in Martin's eye. He must be aware that he's unsettled me with his revelation.

'Well I don't trust those two,' he says. 'You want to tell young Dominic to watch himself. They're a noisy, flighty pair and there's something shifty about them.'

'They're just a… carefree, fun-loving couple, like most people in their twenties,' I say.

'Hmm.' Martin crosses his arms over his chest.

'Anyway,' I say, keen to get this visit over with, 'what is it you want me to look at here?'

'Ah, yes. I have the plans this time, so we can prove my theory is correct.' He waves a sheet of paper triumphantly in the air. 'Like I said before, I'm worried that the underpinning for next door's extension is having an effect on my foundation. I think they've built it too close to the boundary line.' Martin drones on for several more minutes, pointing out heights and elevations and jabbing his finger onto various areas on the plan.

I cut him off. 'Shall we go next door and measure up?'

'Good idea, Kirstie. Let's get hard evidence.'

I shift Daisy to my other hip and follow him back through the house towards the front door. As we pass through the hall, Martin stops to push the open cellar door shut, but not before I catch a glimpse of carrier bags piled up at the top of the basement steps. I recognise the logo – they were Toy Shack carrier bags. Why would Martin have bags from a toy shop?

My heart begins to thump uncomfortably. Martin doesn't have any children or grandchildren, unless you count that creepy doll that belonged to his late wife. I stop where I am. I have a bad feeling.

'Come on, Kirstie,' Martin says, turning back to face me. 'Why have you stopped there? Something the matter?' He smiles, showing those yellow teeth, and a sudden wave of nausea sweeps across me. Who is this man, my neighbour? I don't really know him, yet here I am alone in his house with my baby. No one else even knows I'm here.

With a start, I realise that the Toy Shack also sells baby stuff – formula, nappies.

What if he's got a real baby down there?

That could have been the crying I heard the other day. Oh my God! Our neighbour could be a psycho. *Get out of here*, screams a voice in my head. Get Daisy away from him.

'I'm sorry, Martin,' I say, my voice strangely calm and steady, 'I've just remembered something really important. I've got to go.'

'What? Now? But we haven't—'

'Sorry.' I cut him off.

'You can't go,' he says. 'You said you'd help me.'

My gaze is now locked on the front door ahead of us. I should have waited until we were outside to give my excuses. In here, he can bar my exit. I tamp down the terror in my throat and take a step towards him, wondering if he is going to try and physically stop us from leaving his house.

I sidle past him, holding my breath and trying not to cry. Then, I pull open the front door and pray he doesn't try to grab at us.

'I need you to come with me, Kirstie,' he says, his hand coming down to rest on my bare shoulder.

With a squeal, I shrug him off and stumble outside. I begin to run down his driveway without stopping to put my shoes back on, praying he doesn't follow us but too scared to turn around and check. I must have been mad to go round there on my own. What was I thinking? I need to get home. I need to lock all the doors and windows, to close the curtains so we're safe from prying eyes. I'll have to leave everything out in the garden – Daisy's toys, my mug of half-finished tea. It's not safe for me to go out there even for a moment. Martin could easily climb the fence. He could take my daughter and put her in his basement. My body is hot and cold, I can barely breathe. Can it be true? Can I be living next door to a psychopath?

CHAPTER TWELVE

Back home, I slam the front door behind me, slide the chain across and sink down onto the floor with Daisy on my lap. She must have picked up on my fear because she's fussing and squirming in my arms. I had always thought of Martin as a harmless busybody. But what if he's not? What if there's something sinister going on next door? You hear about these things on the news, where the neighbours had no idea they were living next door to a nutjob. Is he? Is Martin dangerous?

Footsteps outside. They're getting closer. I try to quieten Daisy with kisses and forced smiles, but she's not having any of it. The doorbell rings and my heart pounds.

'Kirstie? It's me, Martin!'

He's followed me home. What's he doing here? What if he knows I'm onto him? What if he's come to drag us over there, into his basement? Can he get in here? Did I close all the windows? Did I lock the back door? I can't remember. The doorbell rings again, an echoing chime through my body, setting my teeth on edge. My thoughts skitter all over the place. I ease myself up, away from the door, and start to tiptoe away down the hall towards the kitchen. As I do so, the sound of his voice, clear and loud, makes me give a stifled squeal.

'Kirstie, are you all right?' He's calling through the letterbox. I'm sure he can see me creeping away, but I daren't turn back around. 'You seemed a little scared back there,' he calls out. 'Did something happen? I can see you, Kirstie.'

I freeze. I don't know what to do. I can't reply. Can't move.

'What are you doing?' he calls out. 'Why did you run away like that? Aren't you coming back?'

I stand rigid. Daisy has started wailing, her face red and angry.

'All right. Well, I'm going now,' he says. 'But I'll call back later – check you're okay.'

'I'm fine,' I croak. 'Just feel a bit sick. No need to come back.'

'Sick? Okay. Well, I hope it isn't contagious. I suppose I'll have to measure next door on my own.'

'Okay, bye, Martin.' I hear the letterbox rattle closed, and I pray he's really going. That it isn't a ruse. That he won't try and come to the back door instead. I still haven't turned around. That saying 'frozen in terror' is a real thing. I can barely breathe, let alone move.

But Daisy's displeasure finally forces me into action. Breathing heavily, I carry her into the kitchen and place her in her high chair and put her favourite set of plastic keys on her tray. She instantly stops crying and shoves one of the oversized keys into her mouth. I stumble over to the back doors, relieved to find them closed and locked. I wish we had blinds or curtains that I could pull across to block the vast expanse of glass. Next, I check the kitchen windows, my fingers shaking as I test each handle in turn. But I won't be able to leave it there. I'm going to have to check the whole house, top to bottom. For a brief second, I toy with leaving Daisy in her high chair while I check, but I dismiss the thought straight away. I'll have to bring her with me.

As I make my way from room to room, I try to marshal my thoughts. To think logically about what I just saw at Martin's house combined with everything else. Fact: I heard a baby crying the other night. Fact: it wasn't Daisy who was crying. Fact: Martin has several Toy Shack carrier bags in his house. Possibility: they could contain baby paraphernalia. Fact: Martin has a basement in his house. Possibility: the crying could have come from Martin's basement – maybe there are windows or vents down there. Or maybe Martin brought the baby into the main part of the house during the evening, which is how I heard it crying.

Why would he have a baby in his house and then lie about it to the police? Could he be keeping the baby's mother down there against her will? Worse still, is the baby his offspring, the result of keeping a woman prisoner down there, like some Dorset version of Josef Fritzl?

Having finished my checks, I stand at Daisy's bedroom window, staring out across the fields at the back of the house. I realise that I have no proof of anything. Just a gut feeling that something is terribly off. But can I trust my gut? With all the doors and windows finally secured, I should be able to relax, safe in the knowledge that no one can get in. Instead, I feel more terrified than ever. Like a prisoner. Like the outside world is pushing up against the boundaries of our house, closing in, squeezing the air from the rooms, from my lungs. I can't see anyone out there. Just a distant dog-walker at the far treeline. I glance across to Martin's garden, but I can't see him out there either. Maybe he's gone next door to number six. Or maybe he had no intention of going over there in the first place. The whole thing could have been a ruse to get us over to his house. I shudder.

If only Dominic were here with me. If only he hadn't gone off for the day. I don't even know what time he's coming back. *No.* I don't want to be this pathetic woman, desperate for the support and comfort of her husband. I'm stronger than that, aren't I? I want to be a good role model for my daughter. To teach her independence and self-reliance. I've always been proud of my career, of the fact that I have a strong mind, separate to Dominic's. I'm not meek and mild. So why am I desperate for my husband to be here right now? Why am I this quivering mess when he's not home?

I can't call my parents; they would only worry and fuss. I don't want to tell Mel; she would dismiss it as me having an overactive imagination. She would tease me about it, and I couldn't bear that. My mind is too fragile for teasing today. And anyway, we're still not on the best of terms after the other day. No. I'll have to deal with this on my own. I won't be able to relax until I know exactly what is down in that cellar.

A movement outside makes me start. There's someone leaning over the Parkfields' back fence. A man. Not Stephen Parkfield, not Martin either – someone slimmer, younger, with dark hair. I press my nose up to the window and try to see if I recognise who it is, but there are too many trees and bushes in the way. I can't get a clear enough look at their face. What if they're trying to break in?

I can't stand here and do nothing. Am I brave enough to go out there? Not really. The thought makes my palms sweat and my head swim, but I can't ignore it. I could call the police, but I'm hesitant to do so after last time. If I can just summon up the courage to go into the garden, maybe I can scare off whoever it is.

Before I can talk myself out of it, I hurry down the stairs and into the kitchen with Daisy and open the bifold doors. The warm air and openness makes me instantly regret my decision. I feel as though I'm about to pass out. I pull the doors closed again and stand for a moment, trying to calm my panic.

What am I scared of? Martin? What if his face appears over the fence again? But what can he do? He can't drag me over the fence. Not without a fight. Not without me kicking and screaming. He's not a big, strapping man. He could snatch Daisy. But he would have to come into my garden to do that. And then he would have to climb back over the fence with her in his arms. That's not likely. I decide to lock Daisy in the house. At least she will be safe inside. I strap her into her high chair, and place several of her toys on the tray. I won't be outside for long. Just a few minutes at most.

I slide open the doors once again and remove the key. I take a deep breath, feeling unsteady as I place my foot over the threshold. Then I slide the doors closed behind me and turn the key in the lock. The air is still and sweet. Birds sing and a dog barks in the distance, setting off a volley of other dog barks. A bluebottle buzzes around my head but I barely register it as I walk across the yellowing grass, dislodging puffs of dusty earth. Maybe whoever it was has gone. I hope they're not already in the Parkfields' garden, sizing up the house. Maybe if they can't break in next door, they'll try my house. The thought stops me in my tracks for a moment. But I can't just wait around inside to be burgled or worse.

Once I reach the back fence, I peer over, instantly shrinking back down. The man is still out there, his arms resting on next door's back fence. It looks like he's just staring up at the house. Maybe he's casing it. Checking for weaknesses. I need to scare him away.

'Hey!' I call out in my sternest voice, even though I'm still hidden behind the fence. 'What are you doing out there? This is private property.'

I cock my ear, but there's no reply, no sound or movement. Maybe he's gone. I peer over the fence once more and find myself staring directly into a familiar pair of eyes, and a face framed by chocolate-brown curls. I give a start, almost crying out in shock.

'Hi, miss,' the boy says, his voice deep and scratchy. Although, I guess he's more of a young man than a boy. A name surfaces from my memory. It's Callum Carson. He used to be one of my students, but he left school at the end of last term. He was a promising artist but he didn't want to pursue it. He said there was no way he was going to art college, that he wanted to start earning money, not racking up debt. I don't suppose I can blame him, but it's a shame when talent isn't allowed to blossom due to a lack of funding.

'You scared me, Callum. What on earth are you doing back here?'

His eyes dart away to the ground before he looks back up at me. He kicks at the grass with the toe of his trainer. 'My football went into their garden. I was just looking for it.'

'Do you want me to go and ask them for you?' I offer.

'Nah, that's okay. I'm gonna head off.'

Something occurs to me. 'Callum…'

'Yeah?'

'Your second name is Carson, isn't it? Is your dad Rob Carson, the site manager at number six?'

'Yeah. I started working with him over the summer.'

'Do you like it?'

'S'all right I suppose.'

'Day off today?'

'Yeah, Dad's a bit of a slave driver, but even *he* lets me have Sundays off. Just thought I'd have a kick about on the field.'

'Okay, well, nice to see you again.'

'You too, miss.' He turns and walks away, his hands stuck in his jeans' pockets, shoulders hunched.

Strangely, after talking to Callum, I feel much calmer. Less panicky. Almost back to my normal self. I decide I'm going to go next door and get his ball back for him. I can give it to him on Monday when he's back on site. First, I'd better check on Daisy, make sure she's still okay in her high chair. I stride back towards the house feeling altogether lighter. Seeing Callum reminded me of school. Of work. Of normality. Earlier, my mind had conjured up something sinister, when all along it was a teenage boy playing an innocent game of football. Maybe I over-reacted back at Martin's place. I think I must have had some kind of panic attack. Even if there is something dodgy about Martin, he's not about to grab me in broad daylight.

Daisy's face lights up as I slide open the doors and walk over to her. She reaches out her arms to be picked up, and I undo the straps and lift her out.

'Soon be time for your lunchtime sleep, Daisy Doo.'

She gives a happy gurgle in reply. I lock up the back and head out the front door before my nerve deserts me. I feel like I'm pushing myself out of my comfort zone, but it feels good. Like I'm spitting in the eye of my fears. And Callum is a good kid. I'm glad to be getting his football back, to be doing something nice for him.

I walk past the sold sign in the Parkfields' front garden, stand on the doorstep and ring the bell. A few seconds later, a very flustered Lorna opens the door. She's wearing shorts and an old T-shirt, her normally perfect blonde hair scraped off her face in a messy bun. Her face is flushed and she scowls at me like I'm the last person she wants to see.

'Hi, Lorna. Err, sorry, is this a bad time?'

'No, it's okay. I'm just trying to get stuff packed up. It's all a bit chaotic in there.'

I move back as she steps outside onto the pathway and closes the door behind her.

'I don't envy you,' I reply. 'Packing is a nightmare.'

'Try it with three kids,' she says, no trace of a smile on her lips.

My request is probably not going to go down too well. 'Well, sorry to disturb you, but a young lad I used to teach has accidentally kicked his football into your back garden. I was wondering if I could get it back for him.'

'A football?' she says. 'What young lad?'

'His name's Callum.'

She heaves a sigh and shakes her head. 'No,' she says. 'He most certainly cannot have his ball back. Now, if you'll excuse me.'

'Oh.' I'm taken aback by the venom in her voice.

'Look, Kirstie. There probably is no football. That boy has a crush on Hannah and he keeps hanging around our house. Is he still out there? If he is I'm going to tell him to piss off.'

'He's already gone.'

'Good job. Where was he exactly?'

'On the playing field behind your house. But he's a nice lad, honestly. He's harmless.'

'How would you know?' she snaps.

'I used to be his art teacher.' With anybody else, I'd put her rudeness down to moving stress, but Lorna has always been an uppity madam – and that's a nice way of putting it. I bite back a rude retort and instead decide to ask her something else. 'I don't suppose you've heard a baby crying in our road? Apart from Daisy, that is?'

'A baby?' She frowns. 'No.'

'It's just that I could've sworn I heard a baby crying the other day, and I'm worried about Mart—'

'Look, Kirstie, like I said before, I'm a bit busy and I really haven't got time to stand around chatting. Some other time, okay?'

Yeah, like the twelfth of never. 'Sure, sorry, I'll leave you in peace.' I turn to go.

'Kirstie…'

I turn around, wondering if she's going to apologise.

No such luck. Lorna is back inside her hallway, a scowl etched onto her face. 'If you see Callum Carson hanging around here again, tell him if I see him I'll call the police.'

'Why? What's he done?'

'Oh, just mind your own business, Kirstie.' She turns away and slams the door.

I stand there for a moment, unable to believe her cheek. I was only trying to help someone out. Well, that was a complete waste of time. I'll be glad when the Parkfields have finally left Magnolia Close.

CHAPTER THIRTEEN

By the time Dominic gets back from his swim training, it's almost six o'clock. He walks in bearing flowers and chocolates by way of an apology, as he went for a quick drink with his mates afterwards. I'm so pleased to see him that I don't give him any hassle for being late back. Anyway, I spent the rest of this afternoon moving Daisy's cot back into our room and I know Dom won't be happy about it. She's outgrown the Moses basket and it's not fair to make her sleep in it with her head wedged up against the end. But Dom won't want her back in our room permanently.

Five minutes later, he's standing in our bedroom with his arms folded across his chest as he frowns at the cot. 'Kirst, I'm sorry, but I can't do it.'

'She's our daughter,' I reply.

'Yes, and I love her, but I also need to get a good night's sleep. I've got work tomorrow. She was perfectly happy sleeping in her own room before. If she wasn't happy, I'd have her in with us like a shot, you know I would.'

'What about *my* happiness?' I ask, sitting on the bed with a whump.

'Kirstie, you're worried after what happened with the baby monitor. But everything is fine. She's only in the next room. Daisy is completely safe in there.'

'You hope.' I have a sudden thought. 'We should get an alarm installed.'

'An alarm?' He raises his eyebrows. 'How much would that cost? We don't need an alarm. This isn't exactly a high-crime area. Anyway, who needs an alarm when we've got Martin, King of the Neighbourhood Watch, living next door? It's like having our own personal guard dog – granted, he's probably more of a Chihuahua than a Rottweiler, but you get my point.'

'He's part of the reason I want an alarm.'

'Martin? He's boring, but harmless.'

'I'm not so sure. He came round again today.'

'Oh yeah?'

'Wanted me to check some measurements at number six. But that's not the reason I'm worried. When I went into his house, I saw something weird – did you know he's got a basement?'

'*No.* But what's that got to do with anything?'

'None of the other houses in our close has got a basement.'

'How do you know?'

'Well, *ours* hasn't, *Mel's* hasn't.'

'So? Have you got basement envy or something?'

I roll my eyes. 'Don't you think it's odd? I wonder why his house has got one and ours hasn't. Weren't all these houses built at the same time? Do you think he might have built the basement himself?'

'Dunno.' He grins and lowers his voice. 'Maybe he's got a red room down there.'

'A what?'

'You know,' he says in an exaggerated whisper. 'Maybe he's got sex slaves.'

'Ugh! Don't say that!' Is it weird that Dom has mentioned exactly what I had been thinking?

'It's always the quiet ones you have to watch.' Dom winks.

'The thing is,' I say, picking a stray hair off the bed and letting it fall onto the carpet, 'I also noticed some Toy Shack carrier bags in his house, but he doesn't have any kids.'

'So?'

'So, what if he's got a baby down there? What if that baby I heard the other night is in his house right now? Remember that fake baby his wife had? That doll? Maybe he's got a real one down there now. He really creeped me out today, and I'm not kidding, I'm worried for Daisy's safety.'

'Did he say something to you?' Dom's eyes narrow. 'Threaten you?'

'No, not really.'

'So he didn't do or say anything to you?'

'No. It's just… it's just a feeling I had.'

'Want me to have a word with him?' Dom says, his expression still serious.

'Maybe. No. I don't know. What would you say?'

'I dunno, something like, *Hi Martin, can I have a look in your cellar to check for missing babies?*' Dom smiles.

'It's not funny.'

'I know, but really, what do you want me to do about it? The man hasn't actually done anything.'

'Don't you believe me?'

'Of course I believe you, but if he's got some hidden torture chamber he's keeping secret, don't you think he'd have hidden the entrance, not had a door for everyone to see?'

I guess Dom has a point, but it seemed to me like Martin pushed that door shut a little too quickly. 'Martin also said something else…'

'What?'

'He said he's seen you at the Cliffords' place a few times.' I study Dom's face for his reaction.

Dom frowns briefly and then gives a laugh. 'Moaning Myrtle's been spying on me? Hilarious. Yeah, I've been over to Jimmy's – he's invited me over for a quick beer a couple of times after work.'

'Really? You never mentioned it.'

'That's because it wasn't a big deal. Also, I felt a bit guilty, you know, not coming straight home.' His cheeks redden.

'Since when have I ever minded you having a beer with friends?' I'm a bit taken aback by his reply. But I suppose I'm satisfied that he's telling the truth.

'Bloody Martin, snooping around and stirring things up,' Dom says, frowning. 'But apart from being a gossip, he's pretty harmless, Kirst. Anyway, I don't see what any of this has got to do with having Daisy to sleep in our room. Sure, our neighbour is a bit of an oddball, but we've lived next door to him for four years. You've never been worried about him before.'

'We've never had a baby before.'

Dominic comes and sits next to me on the bed, puts his arm around my shoulder and kisses the side of my head. 'I think it's natural to worry about our daughter, but I honestly don't believe Martin is dangerous.'

'How would you know that? You can't see inside his head, or inside his house. I think I should call the police.'

'And say what?'

'I could tell them about the basement, and the toy shop bags.'

'Really?' Dom tilts his head. 'Last time I checked, neither of those things is illegal.'

'But if you add that to the baby-monitor thing, and the doll, and the fact I heard a baby crying the other night…' As I say it out loud, I realise that the police would never take me seriously. It's not enough to go on. I need solid evidence.

'Call them if you like, Kirstie, but I honestly don't think they'll do anything.'

I shrug Dom's arm off my shoulders and get to my feet. 'Fine. Forget it. I need to give Daisy her bath.'

'I'll do it,' he replies.

'It's okay, I can do it,' I say, hearing the martyred tone in my voice.

'Let me do the bath,' Dom insists. 'I haven't seen her all day.'

And whose fault is that, I think uncharitably. 'Okay,' I agree.

'And, Kirstie,' he adds. 'I'm going to move the cot back into her room. We need to get back to normality.'

'Fine. Do what you want.' I'd been looking forward to me and Dom spending a nice evening together, but we're already at each other's throats. I know he thinks I'm over-anxious and paranoid – I mean, I already think that about myself – but I'm not about to take any chances with our daughter's safety. 'Dom, if you move her cot back, then I'm going to sleep in there with her.'

'Really?' he says, his voice full of dismay.

'I'm not leaving Daisy on her own.'

'Okay,' he agrees. 'You stay with her for a night or two, just until you feel better about things. Look, why don't you go downstairs and chill out. I'll bath Daisy and sort out the sleeping arrangements.'

I leave him to it, wishing I could untie this tight knot of anger in my chest.

*

It feels strange to be lying on the futon in Daisy's room, and not just because it's so low to the ground. It's odd without Dominic by my side. But what choice do I have? Leaving Daisy alone all night just isn't a possibility. Thankfully, things between me and Dom improved after our earlier disagreement. Neither of us mentioned Martin, or Daisy's sleeping arrangements, for the rest of the evening, and we managed to relax and not fall out over anything else. Dom didn't try to persuade me back into our bedroom, for which I'm grateful, but if he thinks this arrangement is just for one or two nights, then he's mistaken. I won't move back until I'm certain she's no longer in any danger.

I lie awake for a while, listening to my daughter's quiet move-ments and murmurs, mulling over the day's events. My quiet life seems to have been taken over by strange occurrences. Magnolia Close has always been a sleepy little cul-de-sac where everyone minds their own business, except, of course, for Martin, but he's just a harmless old busybody – or so I thought. Now, it's as though a strange new world has converged on my doorstep, threatening my peaceful, contented existence. Or am I being paranoid? Imagining things where there is nothing. Even Lorna was rude to me today. And, okay, she's always been stand-offish, but that was more in a keeping-to-herself kind of way, not a slam-the-door-in-my-face way. The stress of moving house must be getting to her.

I turn onto my side and close my eyes, trying to let sleep take me. I've already checked the doors and windows twice since coming to bed. I desperately want to check them again, but I know I shouldn't. I keep imagining that Martin is out there trying the handles on the back door. I picture him in my mind's eye – his yellowing teeth, his ashy hair. A sudden, terrifying thought flies at me. What if Martin swiped a key from our house? He could have done that, couldn't he? I think back to when he's called round here on past occasions. I don't think he's ever got further than the front doorstep. But he could easily have climbed our back fence and crept in through the back doors while we were in another room. If he has a key, then it won't matter if the doors are locked. He could get in any time he wanted. The thought makes me go cold. I wish I could get the locks changed, but Dom wouldn't understand, and besides, we can't afford it. I'll have to try to work something out.

I peel the sheet off and get to my feet. I've thought of a temporary solution – a warning system. First, I pad over to the cot to check on Daisy. Faint moonlight highlights her rounded face. Love swells in my chest and it's all I can do to not reach down and gather her up in my arms. But I can't risk her crying out and waking Dom. I gaze at her for a few more seconds before creeping downstairs.

We keep half of Daisy's toys in a basket in the back room. In her short life, she's already amassed quite a collection – the usual cuddly creatures and plastic offerings, along with some more environmentally friendly wooden toys. I pull out a random handful from the basket, cringing as they clatter together. Then, I line them up in front of the back door. I lay a few more outside the kitchen and place the rest by the front door. Now, if anyone breaks in, hopefully the scattered toys will form a noisy trip hazard, alerting me and Dom. Before returning upstairs, I check all the locks and test the handles once more, although if Martin *does* have a key, a locked door won't make any difference.

Back upstairs, I check on Daisy, lie back down on the hard futon and close my eyes, more relaxed now that my warning system is in place. I really think I might actually manage to get to sleep…

CHAPTER FOURTEEN

I wake, but my mind is woolly and slow, my mouth dry, temples pulsing with tiredness. My brain trawls through the events of yesterday. My disagreement with Dom. My broken night's sleep. Perhaps that's why I have such a terrible headache today. I curse the hardness of this futon, roll onto my back and crack open one eyelid, then another, cringing against another bright morning.

The house feels quiet. Either it's extremely early and Dom is still asleep, or it's really late and he's already left for work. I don't usually sleep late. Maybe I needed it.

I sit up and roll my shoulders. My boobs are throbbing with milk. I need to feed Daisy. Hauling myself to my feet, I shuffle across to her cot. She's not there. Must be downstairs with Dom. Maybe he's defrosted some milk and fed her already to give me a little lie in. I smile to myself. Dom is probably trying to make things up to me.

I take the opportunity to go to the loo, brush my teeth and have a quick shower. My head is still pounding though. I hope we've got another pack of painkillers somewhere. I jog downstairs and into the kitchen ready to thank my husband for being so thoughtful, but I stop dead in my tracks when I see the wall clock. It says the time is 9.20. Maybe it stopped last night. I turn to look at the cooker clock. The luminous blue numbers tell me it's 9.18. So that must be the correct time.

It's Monday today. Dom will be at work by now. So where the hell is Daisy? I notice that all the toys I laid out last night as a warning system have been moved aside. I meant to get up early and put them away. Did Dom move them? Or could it have been someone else?

Don't jump to conclusions.

'Dom!' I cry, racing out of the kitchen and throwing open the lounge door – empty. 'DOM!' I yell, staggering to the downstairs cloakroom. Again, it's empty. *Check upstairs*, I think. Maybe he took Daisy back to bed with him and he fell asleep with her by mistake. Yes, that's what will have happened. Almost sobbing with the relief of a plausible explanation, I take the stairs two at a time, yelling my husband's name. I push open the bedroom door, ready to break the news to Dom that he has overslept.

But our bedroom is empty. Our bed is unmade.

'DOM! I scream. The room expands outwards like a concertina and then closes in again, squeezing the air from my lungs.

No, no, no. Calm down. I go back into Daisy's room to check her cot once more – maybe she was in there all along and I just didn't see her. I know I'm grasping at straws and it's no surprise when I see the cot is empty.

Is this real? Could I be having a nightmare? I pinch myself on the arm, hard, like they do in the movies, but all it does is hurt. I'm still here, still awake, still don't know where my daughter is.

Ring Dom. Find out if he saw her before he went to work. No. Ring the police first.

I do a sweeping check of the upstairs rooms once more before running downstairs and checking all those rooms again, too. I unlock the back doors and slide them back, scanning the garden, but it's empty. No Dom. No Daisy. Where is she? *Where is she?*

I switch my mobile on but it's taking an age to boot up. I haven't got time to wait. Every second is precious, so I snatch up the landline handset and dial 999.

The operator takes forever to go through his questions and I want to scream at him to find my child, but I know they have to take this information down, so I give them my details, trying not to hyperventilate.

'Please stay where you are. The police are on their way,' he finally says.

I throw down the handset, snatch up my mobile and call my husband.

It goes straight to voicemail. 'No!' I call again. Straight to voicemail again. 'Dom, it's me. Was Daisy in her cot this morning before you left for work? Because she's not there now. She's not fucking there, Dom. She's gone. Someone's taken her.' I pace up and down the length of the back room, bashing against furniture, sounding like a crazy person, sobbing and gulping and gasping. 'Call me back, Dom, as soon as you get this and then come straight home. I've called the police. They're on their way.' I end the call.

I should have let Dom go round to Martin's yesterday. We should have gone over there together to confront him. Why didn't we? I'm going there now. I'll kill that man if he has harmed a hair on Daisy's head.

Without bothering to close up the back doors, I snatch up my keys and leave the house. Rather than walk the long way around – up the path, down the drive and along the pavement – I cut straight across Martin's front lawn, risking his wrath. When I reach his door, I ring the doorbell and then I make a fist and hammer on the wood. 'Martin! Open the door!' I ring the bell again, keep my finger on it so it repeats itself over and over. *Ding dong, ding dong, ding dong, ding dong.* I bash on the door again. 'Martin! MARTIN!' I go to the lounge window, cup my hands over the glass and peer in, but the net curtains make it doubly difficult to see into the dingy front room. I bash on the double glazing, rattling the windows in their panes. 'Martin! Open up!'

What if he's down in the basement and can't hear me? I march across the rest of his front garden and down the other side of his house. But there's a wooden gate blocking my way. I rap on the gate, grazing my knuckles. 'Martin!' I yell.

I need to get around the back, so I clamber up onto a low brick wall and lever myself over the gate. I land awkwardly and my ankle twists. I wince and pause for a moment, testing my weight, Thankfully, it's not that bad, just a slight twinge, so I keep going, checking the base of Martin's house to see if I can spot any low air-vents or windows that might belong to his basement. But all I can see are regular air bricks. I call through them, anyway, screaming out to Martin. But he doesn't reply. If he *is* down there, he either can't hear or he's choosing to ignore me. I sweep around the exterior of his house, banging on every window and door, yelling my lungs out. But I know it's useless. He's not coming out.

Back at the front of the house, I try his doorbell one more time, my hands shaking uncontrollably now. As I check my phone to see if Dom has called me back, I swing around, startled by a voice.

'Everything okay over here?' It's Callum's dad, Rob Carson. My shouts must have brought him over.

'My daughter's missing,' I cry. 'Daisy. She's only six months old. I was trying to get hold of Martin—'

'Looks like he might be out,' Rob says. 'His car's not in the drive.'

Sure enough, I see that Rob is right. Martin's car isn't there. It's *always* there. Where has he gone? Maybe he's never coming back. Maybe he has Daisy and he's fleeing the country.

Despite the rising temperature out here, my teeth are chattering and my fingers feel icy.

'Have you called the police?' Carson asks, his eyes filling with concern.

I nod. 'They're on their way.'

'Sit tight. I'll go and ask the lads on site if they've seen anything.'

'Thank you,' I reply with a wavering voice. 'I'll go across to my friend at number one. Ask her if she knows anything.'

'Okay,' he says. 'I'll come and find you if I hear anything.'

'Thanks.' We part ways and I run across to Mel's house, my right ankle protesting every time I put weight on it. I can hardly feel the ground below my feet. It's as though my whole body is numb. My ears are ringing yet everything feels loud and quiet at the same time. Where is my daughter? What if I never see my daughter again? What if she's gone? *Don't think like that. Stay positive.*

I ring Mel's doorbell, trying to restrain myself from bashing down her door. We haven't spoken since our disagreement about money last week, but that all seems so trivial now. After what feels like forever, but must only have been a few seconds, Mel opens the door. A sheepish smile creeps onto her lips, but once she takes in my dishevelled appearance and shuddering body, her expression drops.

'What is it?' she asks.

'Daisy's missing.'

'What?'

I gabble out a condensed version of events and she instantly takes charge. 'Right,' she says. 'Are the police on their way?'

I nod.

'All right – you go back home and wait for them. My two are at nursery, so I'll go round all the neighbours and ask if they've seen anything suspicious. And then I'll organise a search party.'

My mind is wandering over all the awful possibilities. How have I found myself in this situation? I've been so careful, so vigilant. How could someone snatch my daughter right out from under my nose? It's my fault – I should never have slept so late.

'Kirstie?' she says.

'Sorry, what?' I give myself a shake and try to force my mind back to the present, to concentrate on what Mel is saying.

'I'm going to organise a search party,' she says.

'A search party?' I picture rows of people combing the fields for a dead body and I feel like I'm going to throw up. 'Thanks, Mel,' I manage to say, 'I appreciate that, I really do, but it's not like Daisy can wander off by herself. Somebody's taken her. She'll either be in someone's house, or…' I blow air out through my mouth and put my hands on my waist to steady myself, trying not to collapse onto Mel's front step.

'Kirstie,' she says sternly. 'A search party is a good idea. Someone might have noticed something – we'll go and ask people in the area if they've seen anyone with a baby, or anyone acting suspiciously, okay? It might help. You go home and wait for the police.'

I nod. 'You're right, of course you're right. I'm sorry. Thank you.'

'Don't worry, it's not a problem.' She takes my cold hand in her warm one. 'Daisy will be fine, hon. We'll find her, okay?'

'Okay,' I squeak.

But Mel can afford to be positive. It's not her child who's gone missing.

CHAPTER FIFTEEN

I'm standing on the pavement in front of my house with Dom's number on redial. I must have left him a dozen hysterical messages. I've only been waiting about ten minutes for the police to arrive, but it feels like hours, and I want to *do* something – drive around and search for my baby, break into Martin's house, *something*. But instead I'm doing nothing, waiting helplessly.

True to her word, Mel is gathering up the neighbours. Jimmy and Rosa Clifford from number two are talking to her at the moment – I didn't think they'd even be in at this hour. I guess they must work from home, although I don't know exactly what it is they do. Something lucrative, if their brand-new cars are anything to go by. *Why am I thinking about that now?* I must be slightly delirious. This is all becoming scarily real, all my fears over the past few days coming true. I should get down on my knees and pray.

Rob Carson is striding back towards me, a serious expression on his face. What if he has bad news?

'Hi,' he says. 'The lads haven't seen or heard anything out of the ordinary, but if there's anything we can do to help—'

'Are you sure they didn't see anything?' I check. 'Did you ask everyone there? Did you ask them if they saw any strange cars? Any people hanging around?' I know I sound crazed, frantic, not even pausing for breath, my words running into each other.

'Hey, hey, calm down,' Carson says. 'I spoke to all the lads. They understand how serious this is.'

'My neighbour, Mel, she's organising a search party over there.' I point towards her. 'But I know you're probably too busy—'

'Good idea,' he says, cutting me off. 'We'll all join in. There are half a dozen of my lot here today. The more of us there are, the more ground we can cover.'

When he says these words, when he talks about covering ground, I think about someone running across fields with my baby in their arms while she screams, terrified to be with a stranger. But then I tell myself that it's more likely that she's closer to home. That hardly any ground has been crossed at all…

'I think my neighbour might have taken her!' I blurt out, even though I have no real proof and I'm accusing Martin simply on a hunch. But I can't afford to be delicate about it. If Martin's got Daisy, then I need to act fast. I run back along the pavement towards Martin's house.

'Which neighbour?' Carson calls out from behind me.

'Down here,' I cry, turning down into Martin's driveway. Behind me, the thuds of Carson's footsteps match my own.

'The miserable old git who lives here?' he asks, catching up to me. 'You think he's got something to do with it?'

'Yes, Martin Lynham,' I say, panting. 'He's got a basement, and I think he might have my daughter down there.'

'Bloody hell,' Carson says, stopping halfway down the drive. I stop too for a moment and glance back to see the builder rake a hand through his greying hair. 'Are you sure about that?' he says, staring at me with what looks like suspicion in his eyes. 'His car's not in the drive, so he's probably just out shopping or something. I mean, I know he's a bit of an oddball, but to take someone's child…'

'I know, I know it sounds mad, but please trust me. We have to break in and see. Will you help me?'

Carson holds up his hands. 'You're better off leaving that to the police. I can't break into someone's house.'

'What if it was your baby? Wouldn't you do everything you could to keep your child safe?'

Carson scratches his chin. 'Let's give the boys in blue a few more minutes to get here. If they don't show up by ten o'clock, I'll jimmy the back door, okay?'

I check my watch. It's 9.45. 'That's fifteen minutes away! Can't you do it now?' *Where the hell are the police?* Just as I'm having this thought, I hear the single blip of a siren and see the whirr of a blue light up ahead. *They're here.* Ignoring Carson, I run back the way I've just come.

As two police cars pull into the cul-de-sac, my stomach swirls, but at the same time my heart lifts ever so slightly. Maybe they will suggest something I haven't thought of. Maybe they've already found my baby.

The cars pull up outside my house, blocking the drive. The first vehicle is a marked car, the second is an unmarked Audi. As I reach the pavement, with Carson not far behind me, two plain-clothes officers get out of the unmarked vehicle – a woman with short, mousy hair and a young sandy-haired man. I jog over to them, out of breath and panicky as a third vehicle approaches – an estate car.

'Hello,' the woman says to me, 'Kirstie Rawlings?'

'Yes, I'm Kirstie.'

'You called us to say your child is missing?'

'Yes, Daisy. She's been taken.' I clasp my hands together in front of my face. 'She's just a baby, six months old. She was missing from her cot when I woke up this morning.' Saying the words out loud again increases my panic.

'That must be very distressing for you,' she says calmly. 'I'm Detective Sergeant Lisa Callaghan, and this is my colleague Detective Constable Whitmore.' She turns to Carson. 'And are you Mr Rawlings?'

'Who?' Carson replies. 'Err, no, I'm Rob Carson, project manager of the work going on at number six.' He points to the house at the end. 'Me and the lads will join in the search party if you need us.'

'Do you mind if we talk to Mrs Rawlings alone for a minute?' Callaghan asks Carson. 'We'll want to speak to you too, so please don't go anywhere.'

'Oh. Yeah, sure.' He gives me an encouraging smile and walks off, but I wish he could have stayed. I notice that there are two dogs in the back of the estate car – a German Shepherd and a spaniel. With a jolt of understanding, I realise that they must be sniffer dogs. My throat constricts. How can this be happening? I have to focus. The detective is speaking to me again, but my legs are giving way.

'Are you all right, Mrs Rawlings?' DS Callaghan asks. 'Do you need to sit down?' She takes my arm and leads me over to our front wall, which is just about low enough for me to lean my backside on, the rough brickwork scraping the backs of my legs.

'Sorry. Sorry. I'm freaking out,' I say, trying to calm my breathing.

'It's okay,' she says. 'Can you tell us when you last saw your baby?'

'I'm sleeping in Daisy's room at the moment. She had her last feed at around half eleven, as usual.' At the mention of Daisy's feed, I realise my breasts are throbbing and painful, so swollen with milk that they're rock solid. But I can't worry about that now. 'I remember finding it hard to get to sleep,' I continue, omitting to tell the officer about my obsession with security, or how I scattered Daisy's toys alongside each of the doors and windows as a warning system. 'I checked on her again just after midnight and then I must have eventually fallen asleep. When I saw she wasn't in her cot first thing this morning, I assumed Dom, my husband, had taken her downstairs, so I didn't worry – just got showered and dressed. But when I got down there I saw that it was after 9 a.m. – way after the time Dom goes to work, so I checked the whole house again, and that's when I realised Daisy was missing and I called you.'

'Have you told your husband she's missing?' Callaghan asks.

'I've left loads of messages on his mobile but he must be in a meeting, because he hasn't got back to me.'

'Okay, we'll send someone round to his workplace, if you can give me the address. Maybe he knows something about it. Could he have taken her?'

'To work?' I shake my head. 'Dom would never take Daisy without telling me.'

'Even so,' she replies. 'We'll need to speak to him.'

'Are those sniffer dogs?' I ask, pointing to the estate car.

Callaghan nods. 'We'll see if they can pick up a scent. But if she's been taken in a vehicle then—'

'Can you get the dogs to check my neighbour's house?' I interrupt.

'Your neighbour?'

'Sarge!' one of the uniformed officers from the squad car calls out and Callaghan turns to look.

I follow her line of sight, annoyed to have been interrupted. But then I see the reason why. I was so busy talking to the police that I hadn't noticed my husband pull up behind the squad car. I hadn't noticed him get out of the car and walk towards us… with Daisy in his arms.

'What's going on?' Dom calls out. 'Everything okay?'

'You've found her!' I cry. I rush over to him and scoop Daisy out of his arms, bringing her up to my face to inhale her scent and kiss her forehead. Tears spill down my cheeks and I can barely stand upright. 'How did you know she was missing? Where was she?'

'Kirstie! Tell me what's happened,' Dom says, his face turning grey with concern.

'Is this your daughter?' Callaghan asks, coming up behind me.

'Yes! Yes, my husband's found her. You got my messages, Dom. Where was she?'

'What messages?' he asks, confusion spreading across his face.

And then I notice he's wearing shorts and a T-shirt, not his usual work suit. 'What day is it?' I ask, confused.

'Monday,' he replies.

'Is it a bank holiday or something?'

'Don't think so, no.'

'So why are you dressed like that? Why have you got Daisy?'

His cheeks redden. 'Why are the police here?' he hisses, so only I can hear.

'I woke up and Daisy was missing! I was frantic with worry – I thought someone had taken her!'

'She wasn't missing,' Dom says firmly. 'I told you last night I was taking the day off so you could take it easy this morning.'

'You didn't tell me that!' My heart thumps uncomfortably at the drama I now realise I've caused.

'Yes, I did,' Dom insists. 'Last night, while you were feeding Daisy, I came in and told you I'd take today off so you could relax. I told you to have a lie in this morning while I took Daisy to the supermarket.'

'No,' I murmur, shaking my head. Why don't I remember that conversation?

'Do I take it there's been a misunderstanding?' Callaghan asks. 'Can you confirm that this child is the one you reported missing?'

'Yes, this is Daisy. I'm so sorry.' I hang my head. 'I didn't realise my husband had taken her out.'

Dom's nostrils flare and he holds out his hands. 'I *did* tell you, Kirst. I was trying to do something nice for you – give you a break. You seemed so stressed yesterday.'

'As long as she's back safely,' Callaghan says, 'that's what matters, eh?'

I nod and bend my head to kiss the tip of Daisy's nose. To hold my daughter in my arms once more is so sweet, so unexpected, so utterly joyful. But my relief is swiftly overlaid by something else – humiliation.

I can't wait to take my daughter back into the house, away from everyone. Away from their bemused stares. Rob Carson is outside Martin's house with the other builders, and they're all looking over at me. Mel and the Cliffords are standing in the road, eavesdropping on our conversation. And I'll bet Lorna is peering out of her window to see what's going on.

I'm mortified. They must all think I've got a screw loose. But I honestly don't remember Dom telling me he was going take the day off. How can I have blanked something like that out? Could I really be so stressed that I would forget an entire conversation? I don't know, but right now all I want to do is get back inside, away from everyone's incredulous stares.

I murmur more apologies to the police officers before taking Daisy back into the house, my heart hammering against my ribcage. I leave the door open for Dom to follow me, even though I feel like slamming it in his face. How could he have taken her without telling me? He knows how worried I've been about her safety.

I carry Daisy into the living room and peer out of the window. Dom is still talking to the detective, no doubt apologising on my behalf, making excuses for his unhinged wife. But it wasn't my fault. What the hell was I supposed to think, waking up and finding my daughter gone?

The detective must have said something amusing, because Dom laughs in response. I can't believe it. He's actually laughing, while I'm in here feeling like shit. My blood heats up; all my earlier terror and humiliation swelling together into a seething rage.

The police leave and Dom works his way around the neighbours – from Mel and the Cliffords to the builders at number six, charming them, explaining, apologising. Finally, he comes up the driveway and into the house. He walks into the lounge with an expression that's halfway between apology and condescension.

'How could you!' I cry.

'What!'

'How could you take her without telling me?'

'I *did* tell you. I told you last night!' Dom throws up his hands.

'I don't remember you telling me anything like that. I would have remembered.'

'I did. I swear I did.' His face darkens. 'Are you saying I'm lying?'

'Maybe you meant to tell me, but you forgot?'

'I didn't forget. I came into Daisy's room and told you. Believe me or don't believe me, but I'm telling the truth. Why would I lie? And how could you have forgotten?'

Daisy begins to fret in my arms. She doesn't like the atmosphere in the room and neither do I. 'Just... Just don't *ever* do anything like that again,' I say through gritted teeth, before marching past him and up the stairs, hot tears dripping down my cheeks.

'Like what?' Dom calls after me. 'Like going shopping and giving you a lie in? Okay, I won't ever do that again!'

I reach the bedroom and slam the door behind me, making my poor baby jump out of her skin. I'm trembling with rage and shock and humiliation. Ten seconds later, the whole house shakes as the front door slams too. I stare out the window and watch my husband stride up the pathway, get into his car, reverse noisily and drive away.

CHAPTER SIXTEEN

Dom comes back home just before lunch, but things are strained between us. I'm barely speaking to him. Not that he's made much of an effort to speak to me either. We're kind of deadlocked, neither of us backing down over who was in the wrong this morning. Mel calls round but I hide upstairs, pretending to be asleep, in no mood to talk to anyone. I'm relieved when Dom says he's going back to work this afternoon. Maybe by the time he gets home this evening, we'll have calmed down and be on speaking terms again. Maybe.

The fact that Daisy wasn't snatched by Martin or anyone else hasn't stopped me feeling nervous. And it's made me more determined than ever to keep her safe. I will never allow something like that to happen again. Sure, it was only Dominic who took her out of the bedroom this morning, but that's not the point. The point is, I slept right through it. Anyone could have come in and lifted her out of her cot and I did nothing but lie there, out of it, oblivious.

It hasn't allayed my suspicions about Martin. Far from it. His car is still missing from the driveway, so either he's away or he's at home and his car is in the garage. I know what I need to do, but I feel dizzy at the thought of it, so I won't let myself think about that right now. Instead, I potter about the house trying to distract myself from the heavy feeling in my gut. From the thought that all the neighbours must think I'm crazy. From the fact that Dom and I are growing further apart. And all the while, someone out there wants my baby.

*

I awake to the sound of a dull thud. My eyes spring open, my pulse ticking. Was that a sound from my dreams, or from reality? A shaft of moonlight throws the unfamiliar ceiling into relief. Where am I? It takes me a few moments to work out that it's the middle of the night and I'm on the futon in Daisy's room. I sit up and tilt my head, listening hard for any sound other than my frantic heartbeats. Another thud and what sounds like the scraping of wood. Definitely coming from outside. With the blood whooshing in my ears, I get to my feet to check on my daughter. I lean over the cot and exhale when I see her lying there, safe. Next, I edge over to the window, twitching the curtains aside a fraction.

The garden appears to be deserted. My eyes stray to my neighbours' gardens but I can't see every angle from here. I give a small gasp as I notice it – a dark figure just beyond our garden. Too far away to make out if they're male or female, if they're old or young. Just a hulking shape standing in the field behind the house. I release the breath I was holding. Was that person in here? Did they break in? Are they about to break in?

My breathing is shallow, my vest top sticking to my back as I check the bedroom window locks and test the handles once, twice, three times before I'm satisfied that they're secure. I check Daisy once more and then head downstairs. The toys are all where I left them late last night, strewn along the doors and windowsills – my warning system. The other doors and windows are still secure. It doesn't look like anyone's been inside. But what if they came in, noticed the toys and stepped over them? What if that person out there is the same man I heard on the monitor the other day? Or could it be Martin? But why would he be standing in the field in the middle of the night? Unless… what if it was someone visiting Martin's basement? An accomplice.

Should I go back upstairs and wake Dom? I only consider this for a brief moment before dismissing the idea. When he got home from work earlier, it was awkward. Neither of us mentioned the incident with Daisy. He stuck around for a measly half-hour before disappearing off for a bike ride. By the time he got home again, it was dark and I was in bed in Daisy's room, fuming. So, no, I'm not going to wake Dom up now, no matter how terrified I feel.

In the stillness of the kitchen, my heart is beating out of my chest, but I have to go outside. I have to see if anyone is out there. With a wildly shaking hand, I unlock the back door and step out beneath the violet sky into the moonlit garden, closing the door behind me. The air is damp, almost cool, and I stay with my back to the glass for a moment, gathering my courage. I take a breath, tiptoe across the patio, and step down onto the grass, scratchy beneath my bare feet. I cross the garden quickly, my heart still thumping. I check the back gate. It's locked, but whoever is out there could easily have scaled the fence. I should have checked the grass for footprints, but I'm no expert and if there were any prints, I've probably already obscured them with my own.

I peer over the fence and suddenly wonder if it could have been Callum coming back for his football. That seems likely. Or maybe Lorna is right, maybe Callum does have a crush on Hannah Slater and it was him hoping to get a glimpse. She is a stunner, but he shouldn't be hanging around – especially not at night – he could get into trouble. I hold my breath and gaze across the dark fields, but there's no one in sight. Whoever it was has gone. Unless they're hiding… *watching*.

I shiver and turn around, convinced whoever I saw is staring at me right now. What the hell am I doing out here on my own at night? I must be mad. I march back across the garden trying not to panic, focusing on the back of our house – brick and tile, unremarkable, built in the 1950s, like all the other houses in our road. My home. But it looks alien in the pre-dawn morning, looming forward as though it's tilting, about to fall forward and squash me. I start to run, my body hot, my breaths shallow. Any minute now, someone is going to grab me from behind, tackle me to the ground. It's all I can do to stop myself from squealing aloud.

Finally, I slide open the back door, my hands slippery with sweat, and stagger back into the kitchen, stumbling over Daisy's toys and pulling the door closed behind me. I lock it, check it and check it again, my breath ragged, a thin film of cold sweat on my forehead.

I'm tempted to race upstairs to tell Dom about the person I saw out there. A glance at the luminous blue figures on the cooker clock tells me it's 3.25 a.m. Dom wouldn't thank me for waking him at this time of night. And all I saw was a figure in the field. It's a public place – nothing illegal about someone being out there. What about the thump I heard? Dom would tell me it was nothing but a cat or a fox. Maybe it *was* a cat or a fox. But I have a strong suspicion that those noises were made by that figure out there scaling one of the garden fences. *Our* garden fence.

Wired, I stand by the back door, chewing the skin around my thumbnail, wondering exactly what it is that's going on around here. I'm also wondering if there's nothing going on, and whether I might actually be going a little bit crazy.

*

My eyes fly open at the sound of a crash. Sunlight makes me squint and blink.

'What the hell, Kirstie!' A yell from downstairs. Then footsteps on the stairs.

I groan and close my eyes again, remembering the toys strewn around the floor down there. I meant to get up early and put them all back in the basket, but I've overslept again. I stagger upright and peer into Daisy's cot. She's still in her sleeping bag but is attempting to grab at her toes. Her eyes light up when she sees me and my heart lifts.

'What's with all the mess downstairs, Kirst?' Dom says, throwing open the door and marching into Daisy's room. 'This is the second morning I've found Daisy's toys all over the floor. I almost broke my neck on that bloody xylophone. What's going on?'

I turn to face him, but I can't bring myself to tell him why I put the toys there. In this sunny suburban bedroom, my fears will sound unreasonable. He'll think I've lost the plot even more than yesterday.

'Kirstie?'

'I'm sorry. I haven't been sleeping well so I decided to have a sort out.'

'A sort out? But they're everywhere. Nothing looks sorted out to me.'

'I know, I got distracted. There was someone out there last night.' I grip the top of Daisy's cot with my left hand.

Dom frowns. 'Out where.'

'In the field at the back.'

'Whereabouts? Are you sure you weren't... dreaming or something?'

'No. They were staring up at our house,' I exaggerate a little, so he won't think I'm losing my mind. 'Dom, I think whoever it was might have been in our garden. Or they might have been coming from Martin's place.'

'What time was this?'

'Early hours. Three-ish.'

'God, Kirst. You were sorting out Daisy's toys at three in the morning?' He runs a hand over the top of his head and blows air out through pursed lips.

'I told you, I couldn't sleep.'

He sighs and his shoulders sag. 'You should come back into our bed tonight,' he says softly. 'I miss you. No wonder you can't sleep on that futon thing. It's hard as a rock.'

I realise this is Dom's way of calling a truce, but I don't respond to his request. 'Who do you think it could have been out there?' I ask instead.

'Probably just kids. Did they come into the garden?'

'I don't know. I just saw them in the field.' I chew my lip.

'Don't worry about it then. There are always kids hanging out in the fields, especially this time of year.'

'I suppose so.'

'Anyway, look, I better get going.'

'Sorry about the toys,' I say, hanging my head. 'I hope you didn't hurt yourself.'

'I'll live.' He pulls me into a hug. 'Are we okay now, Kirst?'

'Yeah,' I say, suddenly feeling a renewed warmth towards my husband. 'Course we are. Yesterday was just a stupid misunderstanding.'

'Good. I hate it when we fight.' Dominic releases his hold on me and I feel instantly colder, more alone. He's leaving for work, and once again I have this sinking, twisting feeling in my belly about Daisy and I being left on our own. I need to get a grip. I lift Daisy out of her cot. I need to change her nappy, but we'll do it in a minute. For now, we follow Dom down the stairs and kiss him goodbye. I stand in the doorway and watch as he walks away.

'Okay, Daisy Doo, I better get you changed.' I turn and close the door, about to head back up the stairs, when there's a loud knocking at the front door behind me, like someone's using their fists. Dom is shouting for me to open the door. I turn back and pull it open. His face is red, confused, angry.

'Dom? What is it?'

'Some bastard keyed my car!' he cries.

'What?'

'Yeah, there's a huge great gash running all the way down the driver's side. I can't believe it!'

'Who did that?'

'I have no idea. But I'll bloody kill them if I find out.'

'Could it be the same person who did the flowers and the paint?' I ask.

But Dom is already striding away down the path. Still in my pyjamas, with Daisy balanced on my hip, I follow him towards his gleaming, dark-blue Audi. Daisy's eyes widen as she looks around, enjoying being outside.

'It must have been kids,' I add. 'Or…'

'What?' he says. 'Or what?' He stops and turns to me.

'That person I saw in the fields last night, it could have been them. It probably *was* them.'

'Of course! I forgot about that. What did they look like? Did you see their face?'

I bite back a retort. *Now* he's interested in who it was. Now that his precious car has been damaged. But that's not fair of me. I'd be pissed off too if it was my little Golf. 'I told you I didn't get a good look at them. It was dark. I couldn't see them properly.' I think about mentioning the fact that Callum has been hanging around the Parkfields' house, but I honestly don't think it was anything to do with him. What possible reason would he have to scratch Dom's car? He was never a troublemaker at school. I can't imagine it would have been him. And if I tell Dom, he'll mention it to the police and Callum might get in serious trouble. I don't want to be the cause of that.

We continue on down the path until we reach Dom's Audi and I walk around to the driver's side. At once, I'm both fascinated and repelled by the previously immaculate paintwork now scarred by a thin, uneven metallic line from front to back. For a strange moment, my cheek throbs in sympathy, like someone has scored the skin across my face. I put my free hand to my cheek, gently touching it with my fingertips. But, of course, it's smooth, unhurt.

'I wonder if *my* car's okay.' I glance over at my silver Golf.

'It's fine,' Dom says. 'I already checked.'

'You better call the police,' I say.

He sighs and rolls his neck from side to side. 'You're right. I'll call them when I get to work. Otherwise I'll be late.'

'Do you think it's just *your* car?' I ask. 'Maybe the neighbours' cars got—'

'Good point,' he interrupts, and strides off in the direction of the Parkfields' driveway. He scans Stephen's BMW and Lorna's Honda CRV. Next, he heads over to the Cliffords' drive. While he's checking Rosa Clifford's cream VW Beetle, she steps out of her house, a flimsy white dressing gown wrapped around her willowy figure. Even from here I can tell she doesn't have much else on underneath. Her dark hair is tousled and she shades her eyes against the morning sun as Dom points my way. But then I realise he's pointing to his car, explaining. Rosa's hand flies to her mouth. They check her Beetle together, walking all the way around it. Next, they check her husband Jimmy's black VW California.

Dom says something and Rosa laughs, lightly pushing his shoulder. They seem very pally. I think back to what Dominic told me, about visiting their house to have a beer with Jimmy. I wonder if Rosa was there at the time. And if she was, why didn't they ask if I wanted to join them? Is Dom ashamed of the post-baby me? Does he have a better time when I'm not around?

My husband eventually heads over to Mel's place to check on her Mercedes. Rosa gives me a short wave before disappearing back into her house. I wave back, thinking uncharitable thoughts.

Finally, Dom heads back to me, jogging across the road, handsome in his suit, his tanned face creased in a frown. He slows down once he reaches the pavement, and shakes his head. 'Their cars are all fine. It's just mine. Typical.'

'What about Martin's car? Is it back in his drive?' I suppose I could have checked it myself, but I can't bring myself to go over there.

'Oh, yeah. Hang on.' Dom disappears from view for a few moments.

Martin's house is screened by laurel hedges and leylandii. Despite the rising heat, I give a shiver. For a Tuesday morning, our close is very quiet. The builders haven't arrived yet.

Dom returns, a scowl plastered across his face. 'Of course they don't touch Martin's twelve-year-old Corsa, no, they have to vandalise my brand-new Audi. Wankers.'

'Martin's car's back then?'

'What? Yeah, it's in his drive.'

'Don't worry,' I say, putting a hand on his arm, and trying not to think about the fact that Martin has now returned from wherever he was yesterday. 'Work will get it fixed for you. It's covered by insurance, isn't it?'

'I bloody hope so. It's not just that, though. It's the hassle. Explaining what happened, calling the police, filling in forms. I could do without it, Kirst.'

'I know.' It's not actually Dom's car, it's a company car. But he loves that thing like it's our second child.

He gives me and Daisy a distracted kiss each before sliding into the disfigured vehicle and closing the door. He buzzes down the window. 'I might be late tonight.'

'Late?' I cry, trying not to overreact. 'How come? You're working really long hours at the moment.'

'Tell me about it.'

'They shouldn't expect you to stay late every night. They know you've got a new baby.'

'Look, I don't want to worry you,' he says, which has the effect of instantly making me feel worried, 'but there have been a few rumours at work. Some people are saying that the company might be taken over.'

'Taken over?' I don't like the sound of that. 'What does that mean?'

'They're saying an American company is interested in buying us out. Hopefully they're just rumours. But, even if it's true, I'm pretty sure my job will be safe.'

'Pretty sure?' My mind starts to rush ahead. Without Dom's income we're screwed. We'd have to sell up, downsize. We'd probably have to leave Wimborne. It's not exactly a cheap place to live. 'Why didn't you tell me this before?'

'I didn't want to worry you. But that's the reason I've been staying later than usual.'

'What will we do if you're made redundant?' I ask, even though I know now is not the time to talk about it.

'Don't worry,' he says reaching out a hand through the window and taking mine. 'As long as I work my butt off and make myself indispensable, there's no way they'll lay me off. But I have to put the hours in, okay? I don't want to give them any excuse to get rid of me.'

'Okay,' I reply. I don't suppose he has any choice.

'I'll call you later. Let you know what time I'll be back.'

'Good luck with the police,' I say.

'Thanks. Love you. See you later.' He lets go of my hand and closes the window.

I watch him drive away, plumes of dust swirling in his wake, my whole body churning with anxiety.

CHAPTER SEVENTEEN

As I head back inside the house, I feel an overwhelming sense of loneliness. A whole, empty day stretching out in front of me with no company or conversation other than baby talk. I don't think I can do it. I close the front door behind me and bite my lip. Calling friends or family to stave off my loneliness feels like such a cop out. Like I'm giving in. Like I can't cope. I never used to feel like this. I used to relish my own company and enjoy getting together with other people. Now, I loathe my own company and feel guilty when I call on others. What's all that about?

This is ridiculous. I march into the kitchen, strap Daisy into her high chair and unplug my mobile phone from its charger. I scroll through my contacts and press the call button. It rings twice.

'Kirstie, darling! How are you?'

'Hi, Mum.' My voice wobbles and I sniff back an impending flow of tears.

'Dad and I were getting worried; we haven't heard from you in a while. Everything okay, love?'

'I wondered if you were busy today. Do you fancy coming over for lunch?' I picture the warm comforting presence of my parents and already feel my spirits rising.

'Today?' There's a pause.

'Only if you're not too busy,' I add, steeling myself for the fact that they might be.

'Oh, Kirstie, I would have loved to, but your dad and I have invited Derek and Marjory over for a late lunch. You know Derek, from Dad's old office. Actually, no, I don't think you've met them. Anyway, it's been booked for a while so I can't really cancel. We could pop over to yours later, though. Probably around seven-ish. Sorry that's quite late, not sure what time they'll leave. Marjory is a terrible talker. Sometimes I swear I wouldn't even have to be in the room, she can carry on an hour-long conversation on her own.'

'That's okay, Mum. Don't worry.' I bite back tears of disappointment. 'You have a lovely lunch. Seven's a bit too late. It's Daisy's bath and bed time and Dom will be coming home around then. But we'll do it another day.'

'Absolutely, darling. Give me a ring when you're next free. I'd better go – the house is a bit of a mess and it'll take me all morning to prepare lunch. I'm doing that Moroccan recipe of Nigella's that Dom liked that time, do you rememb—'

'Okay, Mum, sounds great, but you're busy, I'll let you go.' I press the end call button, feeling awful that I've just cut my mother off, but I've actually started crying now, and I didn't want her to hear the tears or she would have asked me what's wrong and it would turn into a whole *thing*. And I couldn't cope with that.

I need to snap out of this mood. Since when do I cry because my mum can't meet up with me? Not since I was about ten years old.

I suddenly realise that today is the first day of the school term. If I wasn't on maternity leave, I'd be returning to work this morning, seeing my work colleagues, getting to know a new intake of eleven and twelve year olds. As much as I adore being with Daisy, I also miss the bustle of school, the smell of the art studio – that familiar chalky scent of clay, turpentine and paint. Sure, it can be frustrating and exhausting, but it's also fun and rewarding. I love my students, and have a good relationship with most of the teachers.

A couple of them messaged me last week to see how I was doing and to ask me to bring Daisy into school to say hello. I hadn't really thought much about it, but right now I feel a sudden, desperate urge to get away from the house, to leave Magnolia Close and become part of the outside world for a while. I think I might go in today. I know the first day of term isn't an ideal time to go, but I'm sure it'll be fine. If I get dressed now I can be there by break time – have coffee and cakes with everyone and show off my beautiful little girl. It will give me a few hours to forget my anxieties. Put aside all thoughts of loneliness, intruders, basements and possible redundancies. The darkness lifts a little as I get ready.

*

St George's is a large comprehensive school set on the edge of town. Originally an unexciting brick building, it was given a facelift a few years ago with huge glass panels, light wooden cladding, and strips of bright colour. Everyone declared the makeover to be a success. Aside from the look of the place, it's a good school, and I like to think that most of our pupils are happy here.

I pull up in the visitors' car park, with butterflies at the thought of seeing everyone again. I haven't been here since before February half term when my maternity leave kicked in. Normally when I arrive in the morning the car park is gridlocked and there are children everywhere. Today the place is quiet, or as quiet as any school can be when there are fifteen hundred pupils inside. I check my watch – a quarter of an hour until the bell goes for break. I spend a couple of minutes getting Daisy out of the Golf and then we make our way over to reception.

The school receptionist, Moira, is on the desk as usual and she fusses over Daisy while I sign in. She waves me inside the main building, but not before I give her one of the cupcakes I picked up from my favourite bakery on the way here.

I walk down the silent corridor, my shoes click-clacking on the polished concrete floor. Daisy's eyes are wide, drawn this way and that, fascinated by the paintings on the wall, bewildered by the unfamiliar echoing brightness. My feet take me automatically to the staff room. I'm not expecting anyone to be in there yet, but I smile when I see who's sitting at a table at the far end of the room. It's my head of department, Tim Barnes. He's writing in his planner, a look of fierce concentration on his face.

'What are you doing skulking in here, Mr Barnes?' I say in my most serious voice.

He looks up with a frown before his face melts into a smile. 'Kirstie! And… is this the new sprog?' His familiar Scottish lilt warms my heart.

'No! Never call her that. She's my angel is what she is.' I give him a mock glare.

He laughs. 'She's a bonny wee thing, I'll give you that.' He pushes his reading glasses up onto his head, gets to his feet and makes his way over to us. Tim looks like the stereotypical image everyone has of a school teacher – brown corduroy trousers, tweed jacket with leather elbow patches, greying hair, sardonic expression. But he once told me that his partner, Sebastian, bought him a set of 'teacher-ish' clothes as an ironic present when he first qualified. Tim thought it was hilarious and wore them on his first day as a dare. He ended up liking them so much, he thought it would be fun to keep up the teacherly image.

'So this is Daisy,' he says, putting a finger under her chin and staring at her in fascination.

'You remembered her name, then.'

'Well, if I can remember the names of over a thousand teenagers, I think I can remember the name of my favourite person's first born.'

'Aw, I'm your favourite person?'

'You might be.' He winks. 'She looks just like you.'

'D'you think so?'

'She's your mini-me.'

I grin like an idiot. 'Everyone else thinks she looks like Dominic, so I'm happy she got a few of my genes, too.'

'Sorry we haven't been over to see you yet,' Tim says.

'No problem. You and Seb should definitely come over for dinner one evening.'

'Sounds good.'

'But it'll probably be a takeaway,' I add. 'My multi-tasking skills seem to have deserted me since having this one. I can't cope with cooking anything more complicated than ready-made pasta or jacket potatoes.' This was a good idea. I'm already beginning to feel like my old self again. The funny, smart woman I've always been. Not the paranoid, anxious, wretched creature I've been impersonating for the past week. Where has the real me been hiding?

I spend the next fifteen minutes showing Daisy off to all my colleagues. She's handed around like a parcel, but she doesn't seem to mind. She'll probably be exhausted for the rest of the day. So will I. I've got out of the habit of talking this much.

Tim clears his throat and nudges me in the ribs with his elbow as Stephen Parkfield comes into the staff room. Like the subjects of an emperor, we all cower a little under Parkfield's all-encompassing gaze, his tall frame taking up more than just physical space.

'Kirstie,' Parkfield says, smoothing down his tie. 'Nice to see you here with, ah, your little one.'

He's obviously forgotten her name. I give him an awkward smile. 'Just brought Daisy in to say hello to everyone. I won't stay long.'

'Very good, very good.' His eyes sweep the room again, like he's bored of us already.

'Would you like a cupcake?' I proffer the cardboard box.

He peers in the carton at the remaining cakes. 'Yes, thank you. I'll take it into my office.' He chooses a chocolate one and makes a swift exit. I know he's not happy about the disruption I've caused by bringing my daughter in. He probably wanted to give his usual back-to-school staff room pep talk, but I've scuppered his plan.

I scan the room and see that Daisy is currently being cooed over by Madame Cambron, the head of languages, and Danielle, the drama teacher. Tim murmurs something in my ear.

'Hmm?'

'I said, you know this is Parkfield's last term here?'

'Really?' I can't hide my pleasure at the news. 'I was going to ask you about that actually. His house has just sold so I did wonder if he was leaving.'

'No more living next door to the boss.'

'I know, right.' I grin.

'Caroline's taking over until they can find a replacement.' Caroline is the deputy head, a far more approachable member of staff than our present leader.

'Where's he going?' I ask, my eyes trying to ascertain Daisy's whereabouts.

'Not sure,' Tim replies. 'The latest rumour is he's got a job at a school in Yorkshire, but no one's actually asked him outright, and he hasn't volunteered the information.'

My mind isn't on the conversation any more, I've lost sight of Daisy. Madame Cambron is pouring herself a cup of tea, and Danielle is rummaging around in her handbag. Neither of them has her. A tight, panicky sensation begins to claw at my throat.

'Are you okay?' Tim asks. 'You've gone a bit pale.'

'Can you see Daisy anywhere?' My vision has begun to blur and I hear the wobble in my voice, betraying my fears. I can't overreact. Not after what happened yesterday. I force myself to take a breath and try not to panic. But it's not working. I feel as though I'm being sucked into a deep, dark tunnel.

Tim narrows his eyes at me. 'Kirstie? Are you okay?' he repeats.

'I can't see my daughter anywhere.' I stumble away from him and begin weaving my way through the crowded staff room, shouldering my way past my oblivious colleagues, who are happily eating cake and laughing, with no idea of my increasing fear. I'm such an idiot. How could I have let her out of my sight for a second?

'Kirstie,' Tim calls out from behind me.

But I ignore him. I have to find Daisy. Anyone could have snuck in here and taken her. They could have followed me all the way from my house, waiting for my back to turn for a moment before snatching her away. After yesterday's scare, I should have been more careful. Everyone's faces blur and I have to stop myself from yelling at all of them to stop what they're doing and help me find my child.

'Kirstie!' Tim grabs my shoulder, but I shrug him off. I'm losing it. My breaths are shallow gasps and sweat is forming in my armpits, on my top lip, sliding down my back and breastbone. I'm going to scream or faint any minute.

CHAPTER EIGHTEEN

'Kirstie, stop.'

I try to shake Tim off once more, but this time he has hold of my arm, stopping my manic progression through the staff room.

'Daisy's over there,' he says gently.

At his words, I whirl around, hardly able to dare believe it.

'She's there,' he says, 'look, by the window with Caroline.'

I follow his line of sight to see my daughter sitting contentedly on the deputy head's knee while she chats away to her. I realise some of my colleagues are already beginning to stare at me with bewildered looks on their faces, but I couldn't care less what they think. I make my way over to my daughter and have to force myself not to snatch Daisy out of Caroline's arms.

'She's adorable Kirstie. I just want to kidnap her and take her home with me,' she jokes.

But it's not a joke that I find amusing. Thankfully the bell goes and everyone begins to gather their things. Caroline stands and reluctantly hands Daisy back to me while talking about something to do with GCSE results. I nod and fake smile without hearing what she's saying, but I manage to squeeze out a strangled goodbye before turning my attention back to my daughter.

'Kirstie,' Tim says with a frown, 'what just happened?'

'I think I need to sit down for a sec.' I plonk myself down on the battered sofa. I attempt to pull myself together, get my breathing under control. Tim must think I'm some kind of madwoman.

He sits next to me. 'Are you okay?'

'Fine,' I lie. 'Just a bit over-protective, and tired. New baby, no sleep.' I roll my eyes in an attempt to be light-hearted. 'Hadn't you better get going? You'll be late for your next lesson.'

'It's Year Twelve. They'll be fine for a couple of minutes. I'm more concerned about *you*. Tell me what's up. What made you panic like that?'

I take a breath. I can't tell him about all my paranoia. About the voice in the monitor, my odd neighbour Martin, my obsessive checking that the house is secure. My terror that someone out there wants to take Daisy. And even if I did feel comfortable enough to say anything, now is not the time. Tim has to go to his class. I force myself to my feet. 'Honestly, Tim, I'm absolutely fine. Must have been an allergic reaction to the crap instant coffee.' I plaster a grin to my face.

'It is pretty bad coffee,' Tim replies. 'But you can always tell me if there's something going on. I'm a good listener.'

'I know you are.' I drag my gaze from Daisy's face to give Tim what I hope is a reassuring smile. 'But I'm fine.'

'Okay, well as long as you're all right…'

'I'm great. Honestly. Go.'

'Okay, I'm going. It was lovely to see you both. Daisy is beautiful.' I rise to my feet and he gives me a hug. 'Call me any time.' Finally he leaves.

Standing in the empty staffroom, clutching a newly grizzling Daisy, I'm relieved to have her back in my arms. So why then am I trembling? Why is my heart still thumping out of my chest? A wave of something else sweeps across me – is it fear? Loneliness? I'm not sure. It's a sense of being *apart* from everyone else. Of feeling different. Separate. I don't want to be here any more, but I don't want to go home either.

I try to think of any other places I could go for the rest of the day until Dom gets home. I would have visited my parents, but they've got Marjory and whatshisface over for lunch. I wish my brother lived closer. I always used to get on with him, but Rory left home as soon as he was eighteen. Wimborne was never enough for him. He couldn't wait to get away. He lives in London now, an eternal bachelor, still pubbing and clubbing in his thirties, showing no signs of wanting to settle down with a family. It pains me to realise it, but we've grown apart.

I could mooch around the shops in town, but it would be too busy, too exposed, too risky. Normally, a walk in the countryside would lift my spirits, but if there's some nutter out there who wants to take Daisy, then we would be alone, vulnerable. I can't go to Mel's, as I'm still unsure how things are between us after the money thing. And I'm mortified about throwing her and all the neighbours into a panic yesterday when I thought Daisy had been snatched. I guess there are other friends I could call on, but I feel too out of sorts to be good company.

No. I have no choice but to go home. And the thought fills me with dread.

*

As I pull into the cul-de-sac, I see Mel's car parked in her driveway. Guilt needles me. I really should thank her for organising the search party yesterday. I don't even bother to drive over to my house. Instead, I pull up on the road outside her house, behind someone's brand-new BMW X5.

I ring the doorbell, Daisy in my arms. The clip-clop of Mel's footsteps make me smile, but when she opens the door and sees me, her face drops a little. Is she still mad at me about the money? A flare of anger sparks in my chest.

'Kirstie,' she says. 'How are you?'

'Fine,' I lie.

'And how is this little troublemaker?' She touches Daisy's nose with her forefinger.

'Daisy's fine. It's her mummy who's been losing the plot.'

'Don't be daft. You're not losing the plot.'

'So you don't think I overreacted yesterday?'

'Of course I don't think you overreacted. I told Dom he was a prat for not leaving you a note.'

'Did you?'

'Yeah, when you went back inside with Daisy, Dom came round and apologised to everyone for the misunderstanding. I had a go at him for putting you through all that worry.'

I'd been imagining them gossiping about how unreasonably I'd acted. It's a relief to hear that Mel doesn't think I did anything wrong.

'I came round, and left you voice messages,' she says, giving me a fake glare, 'and texts, to tell you not to worry. When you didn't answer, I thought you were mad at me.'

'Sorry, Mel. I'm not mad at you. I just felt like an idiot. All I've wanted to do is hide away from the neighbours in shame.'

'Daft cow.' She kisses Daisy. 'Your mummy is a silly billy. What shall we do with her?'

'Just wondered if you fancied a bit of company?'

'Oh, uh…'

'Don't worry if you're busy. I just popped in on the off-chance.'

'I would have *loved* that.' She squeezes my forearm. 'But I've got someone round at the moment.'

'Ooh,' I say, suddenly intrigued. 'New man?' I mouth. 'That his BMW outside?'

She shakes her head, red-faced.

Mel doesn't 'do' embarrassed, so now I'm *really* intrigued.

'If you must know,' she says in a low voice, 'it's Tamsin.'

I'm not sure if I'd heard her correctly. 'Tamsin?'

She nods and grimaces.

'As in, Tamsin-who-slept-with-Dom Tamsin?' I ask, narrowing my eyes.

'I know, I know. She got my number off Penny and asked if we could meet for a coffee.'

'So you said *yes*?' I hear the accusing tone in my voice, but honestly, it feels like a betrayal.

'Sorry, Kirst. I couldn't think of an excuse quick enough.'

'She's only doing it because she knows you're my best friend. She wants to piss me off.'

'We're not at school any more, Kirst.'

'Feels that way sometimes.'

'It's just a coffee. Why don't you come and join us? Never know, it might be fun.' Her eyes twinkle.

'Thanks, but I don't think so.' I can picture Tamsin's face if I walked in right now. She'd be smug and condescending and I just don't have the strength for that kind of confrontation. Not after everything else that's gone on this week.

'Okay,' Mel says, her eyes softening, 'well, we'll get together soon, yeah?'

I try to smile, but the lump in my throat is too big, so it comes out like a weird wide-eyed inhalation.

Mel gives me an awkward hug and I turn away as she closes the door. I guess I'll just have to go home.

*

Daisy and I spend all afternoon and evening locked up tight inside our house. I'm trying not to think about my best friend and my arch-enemy over the road chatting together, but the thought of them is making me insecure. Will Tamsin try to turn Mel against me? Probably. Tamsin has made it quite clear she hates me. While Daisy naps, I plonk myself on the sofa and open Facebook on my phone. I go onto Mel's page and see that she's friends with Tamsin Price – of course she is.

I click on Tamsin's name and it takes me to her page, where I see a photo of a smiling Tamsin on a tropical beach drinking cocktails with friends. I get an uncomfortable jolt as I notice that her status says 'single'. Scrolling down, I see that she's friends with all my school friends. All except me. I scroll further and see various posts where she's out with friends in various wine bars and coffee shops. Going back further, she posts about her divorce, saying she's 'finally free'.

Tamsin Price seemed a lot less threatening when I thought she was still happily married. Now that she's newly single, does that mean she could be a threat to my marriage? Could she be after Dom again?

I don't even know why I'm looking at this stuff. I should just ignore Tamsin bloody Price. But it's hard when she's back in Wimborne and in contact with our group of friends, but purposely excluding me. It's even worse that she isn't with her husband any more. But just because she's single doesn't mean she's a marriage wrecker, does it? I wonder if Mel knows that Tamsin has split up from her husband. She must know. So why didn't she tell me?

This is ridiculous. I shouldn't give Tamsin another moment's thought. She's just some annoying woman I used to be friends with, that's all. I close Facebook and check my messages instead. I have a new WhatsApp notification. Looks like Penny is organising a Christmas dinner for all of us. It seems a bit early to be arranging Christmas already, but like she says at the top of the page, all the good places get booked up early. I realise I'm looking forward to it. Scrolling through the group chat, I see that Mel has already replied:

MEL: Yay, am having a cheeky lunchtime prosecco with Tamsin and we'll both be there. Can't wait!
TAMSIN: Mel's a bad influence, girls. Just saying ☺
PENNY: You two are a nightmare. We'll have to seat you at opposite ends of the table.
MEL: Noooo! We're twinnies. Me n Tam were separated at birth.

My heart sinks at their posts. I know it's just friendly banter, but I feel so excluded, like I'm already on the outside of my own friendship circle. How can I reply to the chat now? I'll have to wait until a few other people chime in, so it doesn't look like I'm trying to gatecrash Tamsin and Mel's lovefest. This is exactly what I was afraid of. And part of me believes that Tamsin is doing it on purpose. Although, I guess they're her friends, too.

With a sick feeling in my throat, I spend the rest of the day trying to distract myself from thoughts of Tamsin and Mel. From thoughts of Martin, and all my worries for Daisy. I attempt to make the time pass more quickly by dozing and watching crappy daytime TV. But the minutes drag, the hours are endless. Daisy fusses, frets and grizzles. I thought she would have a lovely deep sleep after her busy morning, but she is overtired and cranky. I can't get her to settle. Not with rocking or singing or feeding or any bloody thing.

Dominic eventually arrives home at quarter past seven, by which time I'm hot and frazzled and slightly delirious with exhaustion.

'Hey,' he says, coming into the lounge and planting a kiss on my lips. 'How are my two favourite people?'

I can't tell him about this morning's episode at school – not after yesterday's debacle. And I can't mention that I'm upset at the fact that Tamsin was round at Mel's, because mentioning Tamsin's name will only dredge up uncomfortable memories between us. 'Your daughter's been a pickle,' I say instead. 'She won't sleep and she's not happy.'

Dom takes her from me and I watch her face break into the first smile she's cracked since this morning. 'She seems okay to me,' he says.

'Yeah, sure, *now* she's okay.' I try not to sound bitter and moody, but I don't think I'm doing a good job of concealing my irritation. 'How was work?'

'Good, yeah.'

'Did you get a chance to call the police about your car?' I ask.

'Yeah, I called them.' He scowls and kisses the top of Daisy's head.

'And?'

'And nothing. They said it was unlikely they'd find out who did it, but that I should tell the neighbours to be vigilant.'

I roll my eyes and sigh. 'Sorry, that's crap.'

'Work said they'll book one of those mobile car repairers to come into the office car park, so at least it won't cause me any more hassle. But they have to go through insurance so it won't be done for at least a couple of weeks.'

'Well, at least it'll get it done.'

'Yeah. Just means I'll be driving around with that bloody great scratch on the side. It doesn't look good when I'm turning up to see clients.'

I give him a sympathetic smile.

'Any more news about the takeover?' I ask.

'It's only a rumour, Kirst. I probably shouldn't even have said anything to you. I hope you haven't been worrying about it.'

'I'm *glad* you told me. And I want to know if you hear anything else, okay?'

'Okay, course. I'm going for a quick cycle now, if that's all right? Clear my head.'

I don't know why he bothers asking. I can't exactly say that it isn't all right. I don't even feel like I can ask him how long he'll be gone for, as it will only come across as nagging.

'Kirst? That okay?'

'Sure. Have you eaten?'

'Had something at work. I won't be too long. An hour tops. Gotta make the most of these light evenings.'

In my opinion, an hour is not a quick bike ride. But I don't comment.

'Want me to try and put Daisy down first?' he asks, obviously sensing that I'm not thrilled about him disappearing so soon after getting home.

'Would you?' I say. 'Every time I lay her down, she screams her head off. I don't know what's wrong with her.'

'Come on, Mrs Daisy Doo,' Dom says, taking our daughter into his arms. 'Let's get you to bed.'

As he leaves the room, the doorbell rings. All my senses shift into overdrive. Who could it be at this time of the evening?

'I'll get it!' Dom calls out.

A few seconds later, I hear the front door open and the sound of voices, of laughter. It sounds like there's more than one person at the door. I get to my feet, wondering if it's anyone we know, if Dom is going to invite them in. My dress is a crumpled rag, my hair's a mess, and my face is probably a red, blotchy disaster. I glance around at the toys and clothes strewn around the room, the hot, stuffy, smelly atmosphere. Please don't let him invite whoever's out there into our hovel.

'Come in,' I hear him say. 'Kirstie's in the lounge.'

Great. I smooth down my dress ineffectively and try to corral my face into a welcoming expression.

Dom swaggers into the lounge. 'It's Rosa and Jimmy,' he says, handing Daisy back to me.

The neighbours from number two. What the hell are they doing here?

CHAPTER NINETEEN

'Hi,' Rosa says, immaculate in a bottle-green maxi dress and gold sandals, her eyes taking in the state of the place, the state of *me*, but she's too polite to let her features betray her.

'Hey,' Jimmy says. 'Nice to see you, Kirstie.' His hands are jammed into crisp beige shorts, an expensive looking watch on his wrist. Short and stocky, the man only comes up to Rosa's nose, but there's an infectious vitality about him. He radiates charisma.

'Nice to see you too,' I say with forced brightness.

'Can I get you guys a drink?' Dom asks. 'Iced water, beer, glass of wine?'

'No,' Rosa says, 'that's okay, we're not staying. Just wondered if you're around on Saturday the sixteenth.'

'Yeah,' Jimmy adds, 'that's not this Saturday, it's the one after.'

Dominic looks at me briefly, but I can't think that far ahead so I shrug my shoulders. He turns back to the couple. 'Yeah, pretty sure we're free, aren't we, Kirst?'

'Great,' Jimmy replies. 'We're having a barbecue. From three o'clock onwards. Thought we'd better invite all the neighbours – stop you guys from complaining about the noise.' He and Rosa laugh.

'Sounds awesome,' Dom says.

Sounds awful, I think. That means banging music until all hours of the night. 'What about your triathlon training?' I ask Dom. 'I thought weekends were important.'

'I'll do an early one,' he replies. 'Make sure I'm home in time.'

'Brilliant,' Rosa says. 'We'll see you then.'

'Sure you won't stay for a drink?' Dom says. 'I've got a nice bottle of Sauvignon Blanc in the fridge.'

What about your cycle ride? I want to ask him. *What about your vitally important training schedule?* I guess it's top priority until our glamorous neighbours come round.

'No, that's okay,' Rosa says with a twinkly smile. 'Don't want to disturb your evening.'

'It's no trouble,' Dom insists.

I feel a twinge of embarrassment for my husband. They obviously want to leave, but he's not taking the hint.

'Another time, mate,' Jimmy says, clapping Dom on the back.

I think about Dom going round to the Cliffords' place without me. I do sometimes worry that Dom yearns to be back in his twenties, like Jimmy and Rosa, free from family life, free from the ties of having a child. Is my husband tired of me?

At least the Cliffords are tactful enough to not mention the drama yesterday. Dom finally lets them leave, then he comes back into the living room to reclaim Daisy. 'I'll put her to bed and then I'm off for my bike ride.'

'Okay.' I sink down onto the sofa.

'That was nice of them to invite us,' Dom says. 'Should be fun.'

'I probably won't go,' I say, hating how I sound like such a miserable cow. 'I'll stay home with Daisy. You go though.'

'What are you talking about?' Dom says. 'Of course you're coming. We'll get the grandparents to babysit.' He notes my horrified expression at that suggestion. 'Or we'll bring Daisy with us. It'll be a laugh.'

'We won't know anyone there,' I say, thinking about the fact that it'll be rammed with a load of skinny twenty-somethings with shiny hair and glowing skin.

'It'll be good for us, Kirst. We need to get back to having fun again.'

He's probably right. I just wish we could have fun with our own age group. 'Okay,' I reply grudgingly.

He gives me a loud, approving kiss and bounds away and up the stairs to put Daisy to bed. I hope he has better luck at settling her down than I've had.

I snatch up a hair elastic from the coffee table and tie my hair back. What's wrong with me? I'm feeling less and less like myself. And I can't stop thinking about Mel and Tamsin getting all buddy-buddy. I know Tamsin is doing it to upset me. It's like she's stuck at age fifteen or something. Why can't she just leave me alone? If I voiced these thoughts I would sound so unreasonable and paranoid – she has as much right to be friends with Mel as I do. It's just that I know she's not doing it for the friendship. She's doing it to mess with my happiness, through some twisted sense of revenge or jealousy. And if I'm honest, I'm disappointed in Mel. I'd have thought she'd have understood my feelings more. If someone had slept with one of Mel's boyfriends, I wouldn't be inviting them over for coffee.

It's funny, this morning at school I had a brief glimpse of my old confidence and humour. I was the Kirstie that everyone knows, until I got back home again. Everything is shifting around me, and it feels like I can't trust even those closest to me. Nothing seems solid and real any more. How can everything change so much in such a short space of time? And how can I get back to being me?

*

I lie on the futon, aware of every lump and bump beneath me. Whose idea was it to sew buttons onto the mattress? One of them has come loose and keeps digging into my hip. I have to shift over to the edge to get more comfortable. I've checked the locks twice tonight. That's an improvement on last night, but even the thought of it makes me want to get up and check them again. I will myself to stay where I am, to not give in to the temptation.

I squeeze my fists so tightly that my nails dig painfully into my palms. The doors are locked, the windows are closed. I know they are, so why am I torturing myself imagining they've somehow popped open again?

Martin wouldn't try to break in, would he? Not while Dominic's here. I should try to think about something else, something nice and non-threatening. Daisy, think about Daisy. I picture her chubby cheeks and gummy smile, her mop of dark hair and dark eyes. But the problem with thinking about my daughter is that all my thoughts inevitably turn to her safety. To the fact that someone out there wants to take her. And it *is* a fact, I'm sure of it. I don't care that there's no hard evidence. Don't they say that a mother's intuition is always right? Well my intuition has gone into overdrive. I know something is wrong.

The random thought comes to me that it's bin-collection day tomorrow. I wonder if Dom remembered to put them out. The bins are full to the brim, so we can't afford to miss a collection. Especially not in this heat. Ugh, I'm going to have to get up and check. I inhale and sit up, a beat of relief in my chest – checking on the bins will give me a legitimate excuse to check the locks again.

First, I lean over the cot and check on Daisy. She's sleeping peacefully. I could so easily watch her all night, but I manage to tear my gaze away before tiptoeing down the stairs. In the lounge, I head over to the windows, cup my hands around my face and peer out through the glass. I'm relieved to see that both bins are sitting out there at the end of the driveway under the flickering streetlamp. Dom remembered to do it. Now that worry is out of the way, I begin testing the window handles, tugging each one down several times before moving onto the next. As I head into the hall to check the front door, I pause mid-step as an idea comes to me. Something that could possibly get me the proof against Martin that I'm looking for.

I realise I'm only wearing thin cotton shorts and a vest top, so I toy with the idea of going upstairs to get my dressing gown, but

I won't be out there for long. Before I can talk myself out of it, I unlock the front door and step out into the silent night, the fresh air cool against my bare arms and legs, the road quiet and still, just the faint hum of the streetlamps and the whisper of a breeze. I shiver and pick my way, barefoot, down the pathway, wincing as I step on a sharp piece of gravel.

Going out in the early hours of the morning seems to have become something of a habit. Before last week, I had never had problems sleeping and I would never dream of going outside at this time of night. But if I'm going to keep my family safe, these are the things I must do. Nevertheless, my blood zings through my body, all my nerve endings buzzing with energy, my muscles taut, senses alert.

I turn left out of our drive and stay close to Martin's hedge, fairly confident he wouldn't be able to catch sight of me if he were looking out of any of his windows. I keep tossing surreptitious glances up to his house, the top strips of his dark windows like blank-eyed stares. The only other residents who would be able to see me from this angle would be Mel or the Cliffords. Hopefully they're tucked up in their beds.

Martin's wheelie bins stand at a perfect right angle to his drive-way, lined up against the kerb like soldiers for inspection, handles facing outwards to make it easy for the refuse collectors. The plastic receptacles gleam like new beneath the street light. One of them is for everyday rubbish, the other is for recycling. I'm going to have a quick peek inside. Perhaps I'll find something incriminating.

The only problem is that once I step over to the bins, I'll be in full view of Martin's windows. I'll need to be quiet and I'll need to be quick. I glance all around me and creep over to his recycling bin first. Maybe I'll find packaging for nappies or milk formula. I should have brought my phone with me so I could photograph any evidence. But as soon as I spot something fishy, I'll have cause to call the police and then they can deal with him.

I ease up the lid and gently fold it back. The bin is only half full, not like ours, which is overflowing every week. I have to lean over to get a good look inside. The streetlight is on, but I could have seen the contents much better if I'd thought to bring a torch. So far, all I can make out are newspapers and flattened packs of ready-made custard. I gingerly delve a bit further, wrinkling my nose in distaste. Beneath the newspapers are empty tin cans lined up on their sides – tomato soup, apricot halves, prunes, condensed milk, chilli con carne—

'Hello, Kirstie.'

I go cold at the sound of Martin's voice.

CHAPTER TWENTY

I grip the side of the black plastic bin, a hot ball of panic in my chest. We're outside and we're alone. The smell of newspapers and rotting food wafts into my nostrils, making me gag. I clamp my lips together, hold my breath and turn around.

Martin is standing at the end of his driveway wearing a checked dressing gown and matching slippers, his hair sticking up at odd angles.

'What are you doing out here?' he asks, his expression stern, the light from the streetlamp casting a strange shadow across his face.

My mind races with possible excuses before settling on the most plausible. 'Hi, Martin. I was just… checking that everyone is recycling properly. Sorry, it's a bugbear of mine. I'll go.' I release my grip on Martin's recycling bin, and flip the lid closed with a loud clatter, wondering if I'm going to have to make a run for it. If I scream, will the neighbours hear? Will I be loud enough to wake Dom? Would he get down here in time to save me?

'Very commendable, Kirstie,' Martin says. 'But you won't find anything amiss in my bins. I'm extremely fastidious about recycling. Not like some other people I could mention. I would lay bets on young Melinda and the Cliffords not bothering to sort their general waste from their recyclable materials.'

'Okay, well, that's great. G'night.' I start backing away, almost tripping over in my haste to get home.

'You shouldn't come out here with bare feet,' Martin admonishes. 'There could be broken glass or bits of builder's rubble. You could hurt yourself. In fact, you shouldn't be out here alone. You might think this is a lovely little close, but it's not safe to be out at night. You're a young woman all alone. Anyone could be out here.'

'Thanks. I'm fine,' I mutter as I stumble away, wondering if that was some kind of veiled threat.

I hear soft footfalls behind me and give a startled yelp as his voice sounds almost in my ear. 'I'm impressed that you care about looking after the planet, Kirstie. We need more people like you in the world.'

I don't reply. Instead I break into a jog, keen to put as much distance as I can between me and my oddball neighbour, praying he doesn't come after me. He wouldn't dare – anyone could be looking out of their window. But as I finally arrive back at my front door, throwing a final panicked glance over my shoulder, I see that my pathway is empty. He hasn't followed me, as far as I can tell.

My skin still prickles with the sensation that someone is watching me. I glance up at the Parkfields' house and almost scream with fright as I see an ethereal figure at one of the upstairs windows. It's Lorna, her blonde hair loose around her shoulders. She's scowling as usual, but this time I can't blame her. I probably woke her up when I slammed the bin lid shut. I'm too shaken up to do anything about it tonight. I'll apologise when I next see her – make some excuse. All I want right now is to be at home, where Martin can't get at me.

Safely inside, I close the door with a soft click, pull the chain across with clumsy fingers, and sink down onto the hall floor almost sobbing in relief. What was I thinking? I have to stop going out there at night. Stop imagining that everything I see is a threat. Martin is undeniably odd, but does that make him dangerous? I didn't see anything strange in his recycling, but that doesn't mean it wasn't in there, stuffed beneath the newspapers and other innocuous things. And unless I go back for a second look, the evidence will be removed tomorrow, crunched up in the jaws of the bin lorry. But there's no way I can go back out there now – my nerves are shot, my legs like jelly. I doubt I'd make it back down the path without collapsing. Besides, Martin is awake and could be staring out of his window, waiting for me to return.

I brush the grit off the soles of my feet and attempt to stand, taking deep, steadying breaths. Before going back upstairs, I have to go through my usual lock-checking routine. Once I'm satisfied that everything is secure, I begin to tiptoe back up the staircase. My heart sinks as Dom appears on the landing in his boxer shorts.

'Kirst? That you?' His voice is gruff. 'What you doing?'

'Nothing,' I reply in an upbeat whisper. 'Go back to sleep.'

'I will, but what are you doing?'

I can't tell him I was getting a glass of water as my hands are empty and I can't think of an excuse, so I stupidly tell him the truth. 'Sorry if I woke you up. I was just checking Martin's rubbish bins in case he had anything dodgy in there.'

'You were *what*?'

It sounded even worse when I said it out loud. 'Don't worry about it. Just go back to sleep.'

But instead of shuffling off to bed, he switches on the hall light. I wince at the brightness, and at the realisation that we're about to have a row.

'Kirstie,' he says, 'do you know how crazy that is?'

'Shh, you'll wake Daisy.'

'Come into the bedroom,' he says, turning his back on me and striding away into our room.

I follow meekly, wondering how I can make my actions sound saner. Dom is sitting on the edge of the bed in the semi darkness, light from the landing casting a yellow glow up the wall and across a triangle of carpet.

I stand in front of him, hanging my head, understanding I've crossed a line in the what's-acceptable stakes.

'This has to stop, Kirstie,' he says, rubbing at his forehead.

'What has to stop?' I say, knowing full well what he's talking about.

'Don't think I can't hear you going downstairs at night, triple-checking the locks, laying out Daisy's toys as some kind of booby trap against imaginary burglars.'

My shoulders sag. He knows.

'I'm not stupid,' he says. 'I didn't say anything before, because I thought things would get better if I didn't make a fuss. But it's getting worse, isn't it?'

I don't respond. Humiliation coats my skin and furs the inside of my mouth.

'Kirstie, I'm not angry; I'm worried about you.' He pats the space next to him on the bed, but I can't move. So instead, he gets to his feet and takes my limp hands in his firm ones. 'What did you think you were going to find in Martin's bins?'

I clear my throat. 'Nothing.'

'Come on, Kirst. What were you hoping to find? I'm on your side here.'

I shrug. This isn't the first time I've felt like a naughty school-child this week. 'Something incriminating, I suppose.'

'Like what?'

'Baby formula tins, nappy bags, baby toy packaging.'

'You seriously think Moaning Myrtle could be a child abductor?'

'I don't know,' I snap. 'That's why I was looking in his bins. I wanted evidence before I came to you, or the police.' Unable to look at my husband's incredulous expression any longer, I get to my feet and walk over to the window. I peer behind the curtain and stare out across the silent close, the stillness out there a deep contrast to the turmoil inside my body. On the one hand, I can see why Dom is so worried about my behaviour, but on the other hand, I know I'm right to be anxious about this.

'Do you think…' he begins, but then trails off.

'Do I think what?'

'Do you think you might need to talk to someone?'

I turn around to face him. In the gloom, I see his eyes are full of concern.

'I'll be fine,' I say.

'But, Kirstie—'

'Honestly, I think if I just try to get a few nights' good sleep, I'll get back to my old self. That baby monitor thing last week freaked me out, but I'll be okay.'

'But if you went to your GP, she might be able to—'

'I don't need to see my GP. I just need to get some sleep.' I turn away from my husband again and go back to staring out of the window. This time I don't see what's outside, instead, my distorted reflection stares back at me. The truth is that I'm scared to put into words how I'm really feeling. I'm afraid that if I go to a doctor and unburden myself, they will say I'm having some kind of breakdown. They may even say I'm not fit to look after Daisy. And no one is taking my baby away from me. *No one.*

CHAPTER TWENTY-ONE

Dom is upstairs getting ready for bed while I'm curled up on the corner of the living-room sofa watching the end of a feel-good chick flick. The girl is getting the guy as the lights twinkle on the screen and the music soars, but I feel detached from the movie, not warm and fuzzy like the producers intended.

At least today felt like almost a normal day. Dom went to work, I stayed home with Daisy and we played inside. I also managed to read some of my book while she napped. I made a vegetable bake for dinner and only checked the locks three or four times all day. Dom now knowing about all my insecurities means that I don't feel quite so alone. I mean, he might not agree with me, he might think I need professional help, but he's not giving me a hard time about it. This morning he hugged me extra tight and told me he loved me. Tonight he was late home from work, but he brought flowers and said he would skip the training. He's being supportive and understanding. That helps.

I've been trying not to think about Martin. To blank him out. To blot out even his house from my mind. I've been attempting this thing where I imagine that the houses in our road end at number four – our house – and to our left are simply fields and empty spaces. If I picture his house gone, then my panic recedes. Every time Martin or the image of his basement pops into my head, I push them right out again. Maybe it's not the right thing to do, but it's got me through the day without having any type of meltdown.

As the credits roll on the movie, I pick up the remote and switch off the TV. I should go to bed. I'm still not secure enough to leave Daisy alone in her own room, but I'm not being too hard on myself about it. Baby steps.

I stretch my arms and give a noisy yawn, about to move, when my phone lights up and starts vibrating on the sofa cushion next to me. I glance at the screen and see it's an unknown number. Probably someone trying to sell me something. I ignore it and uncurl my legs, get to my feet and pick up my phone. It needs charging. I take it into the kitchen to plug it in when it buzzes again – an unknown number *again*. Must be the same person. Probably not a sales person if they're this insistent. I swipe to reply.

'Hello?' I say.

'*Kirstie.*' It's a gruff male-sounding voice.

'Yes?'

'*Stop poking your nose in where it's not wanted, or you'll regret it.*' The line goes dead.

I drop the phone onto the kitchen counter like it's a hot coal. *What the hell?*

With shaking hands, I scrabble for my phone again and flee the kitchen, thundering up the stairs to our bedroom, where Dom is drawing the curtains. He turns around, takes one look at my expression and his face blanches.

'Kirst? What is it? What's happened?'

'Someone called,' I stammer. 'A man. It was withheld… the number I mean. They knew my name. They threatened me.'

'Threatened you? What man?'

'They said I was poking my nose in. They said I'd regret it. Oh my God, Dom. Who could it have been? Do you think it was *Martin*?'

'Kirstie, slow down, you're not making any sense.'

I inhale deeply through my nose and out through my mouth, sit down heavily on the end of the bed and try to explain. 'My phone just rang.'

'Okay.' Dom's eyes are wide with concern.

'It was an unknown number, so I didn't answer it the first time. But then they rang again so I picked up.'

'What did they say?' Dom's eyes narrow.

'They said my name. Then they told me to stop poking my nose in where it's not wanted.'

'They said that?'

'Mmhm. Then they said, "or you'll regret it".' I exhale through my mouth. 'Who do you think it was? It must have been Martin, mustn't it? I was looking through his bins last night. Maybe I was onto something and he's done this to scare me off.'

'Come here.'

I step into my husband's arms and try to let myself be soothed, but the voice on the phone keeps going round and round in my head on a loop. It didn't sound like Martin's voice – it was deeper, gruffer. But he could have made it that way on purpose so I wouldn't recognise it.

'Let me see your phone,' Dom says.

I step out from the circle of his arms and pass him the phone. He looks at the screen, frowning.

'What is it?' I ask.

'Nothing. It's like you said, there's one missed call from an unknown number and another call that you answered. If they threatened you, we should probably call the police.'

I nod, clasping both hands together to stop them from shaking, wondering whether the police will believe me. This will be the third time I've rung them in the last few days.

'Shall I call them for you?' he asks.

'Okay. Yes please.'

★

We sit downstairs in the lounge while we wait for the police to arrive. Dom has made us both a cup of tea and I sip the scalding liquid, not caring that it's burning my tongue and stripping the top layer from the roof of my mouth.

'You okay?' Dom asks.

'Mmhm,' I reply, not meaning it. I feel numb.

Car headlights pan across the closed curtains like anti-aircraft searchlights. Dom jumps to his feet, goes to the front door and opens it. I stay on the sofa, picking at the skin around my nails, wondering if the police will be able to trace the call.

Two uniformed officers follow Dom into the lounge – a dark-haired man and a blonde woman, both young, their dark uniforms looming above me. Dom gestures to the other sofa where they both take a seat while Dom comes and sits back down next to me. I suddenly realise that if whoever called me lives in our road, they will see the police car outside. They will know that I have reported them. I hope it's made them nervous. I hope they're really worried about getting caught.

'Would you like to tell us what happened?' the female officer says to me with a professional smile.

I tell her about the phone call while the male officer takes notes in a pad.

'Did you recognise the voice?' she asks.

'No.' I shake my head. 'But it sounded really deep, like someone was trying to disguise their voice.'

'You're sure it was a male voice? Could it have been a woman trying to pretend to sound like a man?'

'I don't think so. No. It was too deep.'

'May we see your phone?' she asks.

Dom stands and takes it to her. They both lean over the screen while Dom points out the call history.

'Unknown number,' the officer says, clicking her teeth.

'Can't you trace it through the phone company?' Dom asks, taking back the phone and returning to my side.

'You can call your phone company to find out,' she says, 'but the caller may have used an unregistered phone. Unfortunately, anyone can buy a phone and a sim card without registering the number. Is your mobile number private? Do you have it listed anywhere online?'

'No,' I reply. 'Definitely not. Only friends and family have it.'

'Have you fallen out with anyone recently?' she asks. 'Two of our officers came out to see you last week. And we were also called to this address on Monday. Could this be related to either of those incidents?'

'I am a little suspicious of my neighbour,' I say to her without catching Dom's eye.

'Your neighbour?' she asks.

'Yes. Martin Lynham. He lives next door at number five. I thought I heard a baby crying over there the other night. And I noticed he has a basement and toy shop carrier bags.' As I rush to get the information out, I know how it sounds – like I'm a paranoid woman with nothing better to do than imagine sinister occurrences. Dom puts a hand on my forearm and squeezes slightly. The two officers glance at one another. I daren't tell them I was looking in Martin's recycling bin last night. Maybe that could even be construed as trespassing.

'I would suggest only answering the phone to recognised numbers,' she says. 'If you do answer the phone to an unknown number, don't confirm your name or address. If you receive any further threats, please give us another call.'

I shake Dom's hand off and get to my feet. 'Aren't you going to talk to my neighbour?'

'Was it definitely his voice you heard on the phone?' she asks.

I hesitate. 'It… It didn't sound like him, but like I said, I think the person was putting on a fake voice.'

She twists her mouth into a sympathetic expression. 'We haven't really got enough to go on. But if your neighbour does or says anything threatening towards you, please let us know.'

Both officers get to their feet, obviously satisfied that there's nothing to worry about here.

'What about the crying baby?' I ask.

'Like I said, a crying baby is not really enough to go on either.'

'Please, can't you just go round there? Look in his basement?' Dom's warning hand reappears on my arm, but I shake it off again.

'Tell you what,' the officer says. 'We'll knock on his door and ask him if he's seen anyone suspicious in the neighbourhood. That way, if he *did* have anything to do with the call, our presence might be enough to deter him from continuing with any anti-social behaviour.'

I don't reply, disappointed but reluctantly understanding that they have to follow the law. They can't go storming into someone's house on the say-so of someone else.

'Thank you,' Dom says, getting up to see them out.

I plop back down on the sofa, dejected. A visit from the police didn't deter Martin before. It won't deter him again.

CHAPTER TWENTY-TWO

I wake with a gasp and a start, the memory of last night's phone call lodged in my brain like a poisonous thorn. Daisy is fussing in her cot, so I sit up and open my tired eyes, the brightness of the room in direct contrast with my grey mood. I stretch out the kinks in my neck caused by lying on this godawful futon. My jaw is just as tense as my neck. My teeth must have been clamped together while I slept. I yawn and wince as my jaw gives a series of dull clicks.

A different memory assaults me. Last night's caller used the phrase 'stop poking your nose in'. That's the exact same phrase Martin used this weekend when he told me about Dom spending time over at the Cliffords. He said something like 'I don't want to poke my nose in'. That has to be more than a coincidence, surely. It's not *that* common a saying.

I get up and take two steps over to the cot to say good morning to my daughter, who gives a wide smile at the sight of my face. I pick her up and take her over to the changing table, trying to lie her down on the padded surface, but Daisy's not having any of it. She clings on tight like a koala. She wants a cuddle. I give up for the moment and bring her back to my chest, smiling as she looks up at me and grabs at my nose. My days should be spent revelling in the joy of my daughter, not worrying about evil people trying to snatch her. I've only got a couple more months until I have to return to work. How can I go back to work when Daisy's life may be in danger?

'Morning, Kirst.' Dom pokes his head around Daisy's bedroom door. 'Sleep okay?'

'On and off,' I reply. 'Mostly off.'

'How you feeling?' He comes in and plants a toothpaste kiss on my lips, and another on Daisy's head. Then he pings one of my curls to try and get me to lighten up.

'Still a bit weirded out,' I say. 'I'm not looking forward to turning my phone on this morning in case there's another missed call, or a message.'

'I'll check for you,' he says. 'Where is it?'

'Charging in the kitchen.'

'Usual pin code?'

'Yeah. Dom…'

'What?'

I tell him about Martin using the same phrase that was used by the caller last night. 'What do you think?' I ask. 'Should I tell the police about it?'

Dom frowns. 'To be honest, I don't think you should be making any more accusations without evidence.'

'But it's pretty coincidental, don't you think?'

'Yeah. But that's all it is, Kirst – a coincidence.'

'You don't believe me, do you?' Tears prick behind my eyes.

'When have I ever said I don't believe you?'

I take a breath. 'Sorry, just woken up. Bit grumpy and all over the place.'

'That's okay. Look, do you want me to stay home with you today?'

I would love nothing more than for Dominic to stay with me. I'm craving his company, the comfort of his words, his arms, his support. 'You need to be at work though, don't you? Show them that you're committed in case of redundancies.'

'One day shouldn't hurt.' But he looks nervous, like one day *will* hurt.

'How about if you knock off a bit early instead?' I suggest.

'Are you sure? I can stay home if you need me.'

'I'm sure.' But I go and ruin it all by allowing a tear to slide down my face.

Dom peels Daisy from my arms and places her back in her cot. 'You're not okay, are you?' he says. 'How much sleep did you actually get last night?'

'Not sure.' I sniff. 'Maybe an hour or two.'

'Two hours? That's nowhere near enough. No wonder you're tired and tearful. Go back to bed – *our* bed – and I'll bring you up some breakfast.'

'But what about work?'

'I've got time to make you breakfast. Then you can go back to sleep for a bit.'

'I'm not sure if I'll have the chance to sleep,' I say. 'I have to change and feed Daisy, and she won't be ready for another nap for ages. I'll have to play with her to tire her out.' More tears slip down my cheeks and I feel like a useless, soggy mess. I sink cross-legged to the floor and put my head in my hands.

'Kirstie?' Dom's voice sounds anxious. Probably because I don't normally cry about stuff. Even when I miscarried, I didn't really cry. I was quiet, sad, angry, but rarely tearful.

'I'll be okay in a minute,' I murmur, a sob catching in my throat.

'I'm calling the doctor. You're exhausted. Stressed.'

'I don't need a doctor.' I try to sniff back my tears. 'I'm just tired. I'll be fine.' But I'm not fine. I'm a shuddering wreck.

'Kirstie.' He crouches down in front of me. 'I'm going to make you a doctor's appointment, okay? If I call the surgery as soon as they open, I'll probably be able get you an appointment for today. You can tell them that you're not sleeping and that you're anxious.'

'Don't forget paranoid and deluded,' I add.

He tuts. 'I don't think that at all. Maybe she'll give you something to help you sleep, then you won't feel so bad during the day.'

'Do you really think I need to see a doctor?'

'I don't think it can hurt.'

'What if I don't want to go?' I get to my feet once more and glare out of the bedroom window, not seeing anything.

'Well, obviously you don't *have* to go.' Dom comes and stands by my side. 'But honestly, Kirst, I don't know how much more of this I can take.'

I whip around to face him. 'You don't know how much you can…' I trail off and shake my head.

'Sorry, that came out wrong,' he says, hunching his shoulders. 'I just meant we're both under a lot of strain with everything. And you have to admit, you haven't been acting like yourself these past few days.'

'That's because there's someone out there who's… Oh, forget it.'

'No,' he says. 'Someone out there who's *what*?'

'Trying to take Daisy,' I whisper.

'Do you really believe that, Kirstie?'

'Um, let's see: the baby monitor, the flower bed, the spilt paint, the person out in the fields at night, your car being keyed, Martin's basement, that threatening phone call… Isn't that enough to make any parent worried for their child?'

'I'll admit, the phone call was odd. But honestly the other things could just be kids mucking around, or coincidences. And the fact is, Kirst, no one has actually tried to take Daisy.'

'Fine,' I snap, fed up with trying to justify myself. 'Whatever. I'll go.'

'You'll go? To the doctor's? Today?' I hear the lift in his voice and it makes me want to scream.

'I just said I would, didn't I?'

He puts an arm around me and kisses the side of my head as I grit my teeth. It's all I can do not to push him away. I'm starting to feel like I don't know my husband any more.

★

'Hello, Mrs Rawlings,' Dr Sloane says. 'Please take a seat.'

I do as she asks and sit on the plastic chair opposite her own, a faint smell of disinfectant in the air. The room has been arranged so that there is no barrier between us. Instead, the cherry-wood veneer desk is pushed up against the wall beside her.

'How are you today?' she asks.

'I'm okay,' I say automatically, before correcting myself. 'Actually, no, I'm not okay, but I don't think it's anything you can help me with.' I bite my lip trying to stop myself from crying. *What the hell is wrong with me?*

'What's the problem?' she gives an encouraging smile, her tired brown eyes filled with compassion, something I didn't expect.

'I've been having trouble sleeping,' I say, my hands resting in my lap.

'Your daughter is six months old, right? Is she keeping you up at night?'

I glance across at Daisy, who is currently asleep in her pram by my side. 'No, she's good as gold – sleeps through till five thirty most nights. Then goes straight back down for another few hours.'

'That's good to hear. So what else is keeping you awake, do you think?'

I consider the question, trying to work out how to explain the turmoil in my brain. 'Recently, I always seem to be worrying about everything. My mind won't switch off at night or even during the day.'

'And what are you worried about?'

I tell her about the voices I heard in the monitor, about the flower bed and the spilt paint, and also about the threatening phone call. 'And ever since I heard those voices, I'm scared that whoever it was might come back and snatch Daisy.' I don't mention Martin and his basement – it sounds too 'out there'. I don't want to give her any reason to doubt my sanity. I just need help sleeping at night. 'So, you see, it's not really a medical issue. It's more that I'm worrying about the safety of my child.'

'I see.' Dr Sloane leans over to her desk and begins tapping at her computer keyboard. 'It sounds like you've had a few quite traumatic experiences.'

'And I seem to be on the verge of crying all the time. It's not like me,' I add.

'Anything else out of the ordinary?'

'I've lost my appetite.'

'Okay.' She carries on typing.

'I also… I also think I might have a bit of OCD,' I blurt out, surprising myself that I've actually admitted to my compulsive checking. I think deep down I knew what it was, but I hadn't said the word out loud until now.

'Obsessive compulsive disorder?' She stops typing for a moment and turns back to face me. 'What makes you think you have that?'

'I keep checking the locks on the doors and windows. To make sure no one can get in the house. But even after I've checked them, I worry that I've missed one, and so I have to start checking them all over again. I feel itchy and antsy if I can't check them again.' An image of Martin pops into my head and I suppress a shudder.

'I see. Kirstie – do you mind if I call you Kirstie?'

'Sure, that's fine.'

'Have you had any difficulty bonding with Daisy at all?' she asks.

I'm surprised by her question. 'No.' I shake my head. 'Not at all. Quite the opposite. I had three miscarriages before having Daisy, so when she came along I could hardly believe it. I love my daughter so much. I'm terrified of anything happening to her.' I glance over at the pram again. 'Maybe that's why I'm always checking the house is secure. Maybe it's not OCD. Maybe it's just me being over-protective.'

'You said you heard voices in the baby monitor,' Dr Sloane says. 'Was that an isolated incident, or have you heard any other voices?'

'I'm not crazy, if that's what you think.' I give a nervous laugh. 'I googled it and apparently it's pretty common for older monitors to pick up other signals.'

'I wasn't suggesting you were crazy,' Dr Sloane says with a smile. 'We just have to rule these things out. Hearing things can be indicative of certain conditions.'

Yeah, it can be indicative of being crazy.

A car pulls up outside the doctor's window and a nurse gets out. She calls to someone out of my view and waves to them, a beaming smile across her face. She looks so young and happy and carefree that I experience an unexpected pang of envy.

'What about friends and family?' Dr Sloane asks. 'Do you have support at home?'

'I've got my husband.' *Well, I've got him when he's actually at home and not flying out the door to go training every spare moment.* 'He was the one who suggested I come and see you today. But he does work long hours. He's training for this triathlon at the moment so he's out most weekends…'

She purses her lips. 'Do you have any other supportive family close by? Parents? Siblings?'

'Yeah. My mum and dad live in Wimborne – they're always happy to help out.' *Unless they've got their friends round for lunch.* But I know that's not fair. They'd be round like a shot if they were free. I don't call on them as much as I should. And I've barely spoken to them since all this baby-monitor business started.

'It sounds to me like you're an overtired mum who's had a lot on her plate recently,' she says.

I breathe a sigh of relief. 'That's exactly what I told my husband.'

'Don't worry,' she says with a reassuring smile. 'Fatigue and anxiousness is all part and parcel of being a new mum. And there's a lot you can do to help combat it. Do you exercise at all?'

'Um, not really.'

'Well, as a minimum, I recommend going out for a brisk walk every day. Running would be better – something to release those endorphins. The exercise and fresh air will also help you sleep. Meditation is also good, along with a healthy diet and no alcohol, especially if you're breastfeeding. It will take time, but if you follow my advice, things should gradually improve, you'll see. Book in an appointment to see me again in a few weeks' time. And there are some leaflets on the side about mother and baby groups, you might find going to one of those gives you some routine to your day.' She gets to her feet to signal that our consultation is over. 'So, remember: exercise, meditation, healthy eating and no alcohol. Make another appointment to see me in one month, and we'll see how you're getting on.'

*

At 5 p.m. I'm standing behind the sofa staring through the lounge window, waiting for Dom to get home. He said he would leave work at four thirty today, so surely he should be home by now. Daisy is upstairs napping. She's likely to wake up any minute so I have an ear out, listening for her cry.

I went to the doctor's like Dom asked, but I don't feel any different at all. I'm still exhausted and worried, and I still have to keep checking the doors and windows. I keep in mind Dr Sloane's advice, but I already feel as though my insides are cracking, like I can't quite keep myself intact. I wonder if I should have asked her for some medication for my nerves.

My heart gives a little leap as I see Dom's car pull into our road. I'm looking forward to telling him about my trip to the doctor. Telling him that there's actually nothing wrong with me other than overtiredness. But instead of driving straight ahead towards our house, Dom veers away. Where is he off to? I turn away from the window and think about sneaking outside to see. Instead, I jog upstairs to look out of our bedroom window. I can get a good view of most of the cul-de-sac from up there. I have the uneasy feeling I might know where he's going.

CHAPTER TWENTY-THREE

I peer out past the Parkfields' house to the Cliffords' place. Sure enough, Dom's car is parked right outside their house. Has he gone over there to hang out with Jimmy? Dom is getting out of his car, walking down their driveway and up to the front door. I watch as he rings the bell. The door is answered seconds later and I catch a glimpse of Rosa's long, dark hair and her tanned legs. My husband follows her inside.

My heart beats erratically as all kinds of thoughts flash through my mind. Thoughts I would rather not be having. Jimmy's California isn't parked in their drive – only Rosa's cream Beetle. He's in there alone with Rosa. Should I go over there? Confront them? But what if it really is something completely innocent, and I end up making a total idiot of myself? I'll wait a while, see how long he spends in her house. Am I a fool for waiting, or a fool for worrying about it?

While I stare at the Cliffords' place, wishing I could see through walls, a movement from next door catches my eye. A boy. He stumbles out of the Parkfields' front door, trips and falls to the ground. Not a boy, it's Callum Carson. Behind him, Stephen Parkfield strides out of the house, shoulders back, chest puffed out, his face scarlet with rage. He's yelling something, but I can't make out the words through the double glazing. I turn the key in the window lock and edge it open slightly. A warm breeze floods my nostrils, heavy with the scent of burnt grass and honeysuckle.

'I told you before,' Parkfield's nasal tones fly upwards, now clear as a bell, 'come round here again and you'll be sorry.' He's standing above Callum and I wonder if he's about to hit him. Just then, another figure comes striding up their driveway – a man, but I can't make out who it is. He bends down and helps Callum to his feet. Callum scowls and shakes the man off. The man looks up and I step back, but not before he catches my eye. It's the builder, Rob Carson, Callum's father. I feel embarrassed that he's caught me spying, but it wasn't done on purpose – I was trying to spy on my husband, not on my neighbours.

I peer back around the curtains to see Carson squaring up to Parkfield, whose body still quivers with anger.

'Tell your son to stay off my property and away from my daughter,' Parkfield cries.

'Did you push him?' Rob growls at Parkfield. He tries to put an arm around his son, but Callum shrugs him off again. 'Did he push you, Cal?'

'No. Leave it, Dad.' Callum strides away up the path and heads back towards the building site.

Carson jabs Parkfield in the chest with his forefinger, but I don't hear what he says. I just see Parkfield's face turn white. He takes a step backwards, then turns and heads back into his house, slamming the door behind him. Carson shakes his head and stares at the ground for a moment. He looks up and catches my eye once more, giving me a long, cool look. I squirm, but I don't duck out of sight this time, as that would be even more embarrassing. Finally, Carson turns away and leaves.

The incident must be to do with the crush Callum has on Hannah Slater. I wonder what she's been doing while all this has been going on. Maybe she's upstairs watching out of a bedroom window too. She's always been a troublemaker, but I do feel a little sorry for her. It must be hard if your parents don't approve of your friends. I was lucky – my parents always loved Dom. But then they've known him since he was young. Parkfield is such a snob, probably judging Callum because he's left school.

My eyes stray once again to the Cliffords' house. Still no sign of Dom, his car still parked outside their house. Surely, if my husband was up to no good, he wouldn't leave his car in plain sight for everyone to see. As I lock the window, a short cry comes from the room next door. My daughter is awake.

I bring Daisy downstairs into the lounge, trying to decide how long I should leave it before marching over to number two and demanding to know just what it is my husband is doing over there. But, just as I'm gathering up my courage, I hear a key in the lock and the sound of the front door opening.

'Hey! I'm home!'

'In here,' I call out, my nerves jangling.

Dom pushes open the lounge door and gives Daisy a huge grin. 'Missed you today. How are my two favourite girls?' He loosens his tie and opens the top button of his shirt as he comes over to give us a kiss. He's obviously being overly nice because he made me go to the doctor's.

'We're okay.' I decide not to question him straight away. I'll give him the opportunity to volunteer the information himself. 'How was work?'

'Work was fine. Have you seen my white sunglasses? The ones I use for cycling? They're not in the car or on the hall table.'

I think for a couple of seconds. 'Sorry, no.'

'Sure you haven't tidied them away somewhere?'

'I'll have a look in a bit.'

'Thanks. How did you get on at the doctor's?' He takes Daisy from me and she giggles as he pulls a funny face for her.

'It was okay.' I sit on the sofa and pull a cushion onto my lap. 'She said it's nothing more than overtiredness.'

Dom stops gurning at Daisy and stares at me. 'Overtiredness? Is that all?'

'She said it's quite normal after having a baby.'

'Did you tell her everything?' He comes and sits by me with Daisy on his lap. 'About the not sleeping and the anxiety? Did you tell about checking the locks and—'

'Yes, I told her all that,' I snap.

'So what did she say? Did she give you any advice?'

I give a shrug. 'Apparently I've got to exercise and meditate.'

'Right.' He doesn't sound too happy.

'I've got to go back next month.'

'Well that's good,' he says, trying to keep Daisy from flinging herself off his lap. 'At least they can check your progress.'

'Progress? It was a waste of time, Dom. My sleeplessness and anxiety are not about my health, they're to do with the baby-monitor thing and the awful phone call I got. And Martin.'

'I know it's hard, but you should try and put all that stuff behind you. Concentrate on looking after yourself now. Do what the doctor said and get some exercise, find a meditation class.'

I give a murmur of assent, but when will I get time to do any of that with a baby to look after? And I honestly don't think I'll feel better until I know exactly what it is that Martin is hiding in his basement. A few half-formed ideas flit through my brain, but I'll think about them later. Right now, I want Dom to tell me what he was doing at Rosa's place.

'Anything interesting happen today?' I ask.

'Nothing out of the ordinary.' Dom places Daisy on the floor in her play ring then comes back to sit by me. 'She's such a little wriggler.'

'I know, she'll be on the move soon.'

'Yeah, then you won't have time to think about anything.'

'Thanks for coming home early,' I say, trying to steer the conversation back to what he was doing earlier. 'How was the traffic?'

'Fine.'

'You were a bit later than you said you'd be, so I thought it must have been busy.'

'No, traffic was fine. It just took longer than usual to finish up in the office.'

This is hopeless, he's obviously not going to tell me, and I'm not going to torture myself for the rest of the evening wondering. 'Was that you coming out of Jimmy and Rosa's place earlier?' I ask, trying to keep my voice light.

I'm pretty sure he frowns for an instant. 'Oh, yeah. Jimmy just asked if I could help him move a piece of furniture.'

'How is he? Jimmy?'

'Yeah, he's good. Looking forward to the barbie next week.'

'So he was there today, was he?'

'Yeah, I just said, I helped him move some furniture.'

I want to ask Dom what piece of furniture he was moving, and why Jimmy's van wasn't parked outside their house. I want to know when Jimmy asked for Dom's help, because I saw Dom drive straight over to the Cliffords' house, so he couldn't have just asked him – it must have been arranged beforehand. But I can't think of a way to ask my husband without it sounding like I don't believe him. And right at this moment, I don't.

'Hey,' Dom says, 'did something happen out the front earlier? I could've sworn I heard shouting while I was round at Jimmy's place.'

I'd almost forgotten what I saw out of the window. 'It was Parkfield throwing Callum out of their house.'

'Really? Who's Callum?' Dom asks, picking invisible lint off his trousers.

'Callum Carson. The builder's son.'

'Oh, yeah, I know him. What was *he* doing round there?'

'According to Lorna, Callum's got a crush on their eldest, Hannah.'

'I bet Parkfield isn't happy about that.'

'Understatement. It looked like Parkfield physically threw him out of their house. How do you know Callum, anyway?' I ask.

'I don't really know him, but I caught him leaning against my car a while back so I asked him to move. He flipped me the finger. Right little charmer. Moaning Myrtle came out of his house and told me his name.'

'That doesn't sound like Callum. He was always so well-behaved in class.'

'Yeah, well, he's obviously turned into a little shit. Wouldn't be surprised it if was him who keyed my car.'

'That's a bit harsh.'

Dom shakes his head and scowls.

'So anyway,' I continue, 'Callum's dad came marching round and started jabbing Parkfield in the chest.'

'Bloody hell.'

'I know. I thought there was going to be a proper fight, but Parkfield backed down and went back into his house.'

'Where were you while all this was going on?'

'In the bedroom. Saw it out of the window. Which is when I saw your car over at the Cliffords.'

Dom's cheeks flush once more, and I definitely didn't imagine it this time.

'Want a cup of tea?' he asks.

'I'll make it,' I offer.

As I go to stand up, Dominic stops me, putting his hand on my arm. 'Everything okay, Kirst? You seem a bit…'

'A bit what?'

'I dunno. A bit annoyed. Is it because I wanted you to go to the doctor's? Because it's only because I care about you. You know that, right?'

I shrug.

'Or have I done something else to upset you?'

'I don't know, have you?' I say it with a smile on my face, but my heart is aching a little at the thought of him over at Rosa Clifford's.

'That would be telling,' he replies with a wink. 'Seriously, though, are you all right?'

'Apart from being a basket case, you mean?'

'Oh, Kirst.' He pulls me into his arms and I let myself be hugged, but I can't help feeling like my husband is lying to me. That he's holding something back.

CHAPTER TWENTY-FOUR

Dom is at work, and Daisy is propped up in her inflatable ring with an assortment of toys ranged around the edge for her to grab at and explore. I'm sitting at the kitchen island with the laptop open in front of me, sipping iced water. I woke earlier, aching and uncomfortable on the futon, and I thought, *Why am I sleeping in here, away from my husband?* Why am I afraid to be more than a few steps away from my daughter when we're already locked up tight inside our house? I don't want to cower like a fox in a hole any more. I'm going to be proactive. Do something.

Dr Sloane said it would take a while to start feeling more myself, but I'm already feeling a lot better; my head is clearer, my outlook more hopeful, more determined. Maybe it's psychosomatic – maybe the fact I'm feeling better in myself is because the doctor didn't seem overly worried about me. I'm still convinced that being a new mother isn't the sole cause of my anxiety. The main reason is my suspicion of Martin. So if I can find out more about his basement, then that will bring me a step closer to feeling safe in my own home once again.

Besides, it will take my mind off the unsettling thoughts I'm having about my husband. There's no reason for me to think that anything illicit is going on between him and Rosa Clifford. Yes, Dom has cheated on me in the past, but we were younger then, and he was genuinely devastated at what he'd done. He swore he would never ever betray me again. And I believed him. I still believe him. We have to trust one another. Otherwise, what kind of relationship have we got?

Dom has been as kind and loving as ever. But he was definitely acting shifty when I asked him why he went round to the Cliffords. If I see him going over to their house again, I won't hide behind the curtains and watch, I'll go and knock on the door.

I tap Martin's address into Google, and it doesn't take me long to find out what I've been looking for; the local planning website shows applications going as far back as 1946. At some point in the recent past, an admin assistant must have spent a meticulous few months transferring all the old paper records to digital. The record I'm interested in is from almost ten years ago.

The page opens and I skim the application, which confirms that the house next door did not originally have a basement. Chills slide down my back. Martin Lynham applied for planning permission to build a basement in his house on 2 March 2008. That's two years after his wife died. The application was refused twice, went to appeal, and was finally approved in 2009.

Why did he wait until after his wife died to build it? He's one man living alone in a three-bedroom house. What would he need the extra space for? What if something sinister is going on in the basement? What if there really is a child locked away down there?

*

I decide to spend the rest of the day heeding Dr Sloane's advice – going for a brisk walk with Daisy in her pram and clearing my mind of negative thoughts at the same time. We walk to a park that's fifteen minutes away, a woodchip-covered rectangle filled with brightly coloured play equipment, set at the edge of a large playing field. It's busy enough that I don't feel vulnerable, yet empty enough that I won't feel hemmed in and panicky. The fields at the back of our house where I always used to go are now out of the question for me; I'd feel too vulnerable since I saw someone lurking out there.

I end up doing brisk laps of the park. Daisy faces me and I chat and sing to her as she coos and smiles back. Dr Sloane was right – this is good for me. Getting away from the house is therapeutic. Away from Magnolia Close. From the proximity of my neighbour. The sun on my face and fresh air in my lungs. By the sparkle in her eyes, Daisy seems to appreciate it too.

But my attempts to tune out my worries aren't completely successful. After a couple of laps of the field, images of the long-limbed Rosa talking to my husband flash into my mind, along with creeping thoughts of dark basements and Martin's yellow-toothed smile, blighting the sunny afternoon. He built that basement almost a decade ago. What's down there? Why can't I stop thinking about it?

The sun has been getting hotter all afternoon, like a laser boring into the top of my head, and makes me close my eyes momentarily against the silver glare. Why didn't I bring sunglasses and a hat? At least Daisy has a stick-on parasol on her pram, keeping her nice and protected. A thought pops into my head that I could wait until Martin goes out and snoop around the side of his house – check again to see if there are any vents or windows in his basement. I could check the online plans first. I would have to make doubly sure he was out though, as the thought of him catching me on his property isn't appealing at all. I shudder.

A strange feeling sweeps over me – nausea and a wave of dizziness. I should stop thinking about Martin, and try to focus on happier thoughts like the doctor said – clear my mind, meditate. But, I can't seem to focus. Black spots appear at the edge of my vision and I stop walking for a moment, taking a moment to rest beneath a leafy oak on the edge of the field as a respite from the heat. I pull a bottle of water out from the basket beneath Daisy's pram, unscrew the cap and chug down the cool liquid. I should have stayed in the shade. But I know the heat isn't what has caused my breath to shorten and my vision to blur. I'm having a panic attack.

I angle Daisy's pram out of the sun and sit on the dry grass next to her, slowing my breathing and stretching out my fingers to try to get rid of the pins and needles. *Don't cry*, I tell myself, feeling the tears behind my eyes. *You'll be fine in a minute. Nothing is going to happen. No one is here. It's just you and Daisy.* I can't allow myself to pass out. The play park is right at the other side of the field. No one can see me here beneath the trees, no one will come to my aid. Daisy will be alone. I sit cross-legged and put my head between my knees, my hands splayed out on the grass.

The pins and needles spread along my arms and up my legs. Just breathe.

*

'Are you okay?' A male voice floats through my brain, like in a dream. Where am I? The scent of grass, the distant sound of children playing – I'm at the park.

'Is she alive, do you think?' A female voice this time.

'Think so,' he replies. 'I should probably check her pulse.'

I flutter into consciousness once more. 'I'm all right,' I croak.

'We saw you from across the field,' he says. 'And then, when you didn't move for ages, we came to check if you were okay.'

I crack open my eyes and squint. A man's face peers over me, blurry and pale. I vaguely recognise him. The woman behind him looks familiar too, but I can't place either of them. My mind is still silted up with darkness.

'Can you move?' he asks, his voice soft and concerned, almost crooning.

I'm lying at an awkward angle on my side, my neck twisted and aching. *Daisy!* I force my eyes to focus, but I can't see her anywhere. 'My daughter, where is she?' I try to sit up, but everything swims so I'm forced to lie back down, heart racing, palms clammy.

'She's fine,' he says.

'But where is she? Just tell me where my daughter is!' I cry, my breathing getting heavier.

'She's freaking out,' the woman says to him.

Too bloody right I'm freaking out. Who are these people?

'Here.' The woman pushes Daisy's pram into my line of sight, but I still can't actually see my daughter. Everything looks indistinct and wavy, like it could all disappear in the blink of an eye. Like I'm in a nightmare.

CHAPTER TWENTY-FIVE

'Miss?' he asks. 'Are you okay, miss?'

I turn my head slightly to look at him again, willing my eyes to focus, and for the fog in my brain to clear. He's calling me 'miss'. Must be one of my students. And then it comes to me where I've seen him before. This man isn't a man, he's still a boy really. It's *Callum*. Callum Carson. I take a breath and sit up, ignoring the sensation that my brain has come detached and is floating freely inside my skull.

I also realise that the woman standing by Daisy's pram is actually a teenage girl – it's Hannah Slater. These two wouldn't harm my baby, would they? I haul myself up onto my knees and reach up to grasp the handle of Daisy's pram, sighing with relief as I see my daughter, sound asleep.

'We'll call an ambulance,' Callum says.

'No, please,' I say. 'Don't want any fuss. I'll be fine in a sec. How long was I out for? Do you know?'

Callum looks at Hannah, who shrugs. 'Only a few minutes, I think,' he replies.

'Was she okay when you got here? My baby?'

'She seemed okay,' Hannah says.

'But was she upset?' I ask, suddenly terrified at what could have happened if Callum and Hannah hadn't been around. Someone could easily have taken her.

'No, she's been fine,' Callum says. 'Hasn't cried once. Been sound asleep.'

'Thank goodness,' I reply, my heart rate finally slowing. How could I have thought these kids could have meant us any harm? 'And thank you. Thank you for coming over and making sure we were okay. I'm grateful.'

'It's no problem, miss,' he says, blowing a dark curl out of one eye. 'We'll walk you home if you like.'

My water bottle is at my feet. With an unsteady hand, I pick it up and drain the last few drops. The liquid revives me a little. 'Thanks, but I think I'll be okay now.' I put the empty bottle to my forehead to try and cool myself down, but the plastic is disappointingly warm.

'What if you pass out again on the way home?' Callum says.

I don't want to rely on Callum and Hannah to look after me like I'm some kind of invalid, but actually, I don't think there's any way I can walk home alone in this state. I really do feel wobbly.

'You already know Hannah, don't you?' Callum says. 'Seeing as you live next door.'

'Yes.' I smile up at my beautiful young neighbour and she gives a grudging smile back. I never really warmed to this girl, either as a neighbour or as one of my pupils, but here she is, helping me, so I have to be friendly.

'Don't tell my mum and stepdad, will you?' she says, tucking a strand of pale blonde hair behind her ear. 'About me being here with Cal, I mean. They'd go mad, even though we're just friends.' She rolls her china-blue eyes.

'Sure,' I say. 'It's none of my business.'

'Thanks.' This time her smile is more genuine, and so is mine.

Lorna won't be happy if she finds out they're seeing each other, even if it is just as friends. She made her feelings about Callum pretty clear. But I won't be the one to snitch on Hannah. Anyway, it'll be hard for the two of them to carry on their friendship once the Parkfields move away from the area.

Callum holds out his hand to help me up, and I accept, struggling from my knees to my feet like an old person. 'Thank you,' I say, panting a little. 'I feel like a bit of an idiot, fainting like that.'

'You couldn't help it, could you, miss? Probably got dehydrated or something.'

'Yes. Stupid of me to be out in this hot sun without a hat.' I begin to walk unsteadily alongside the two of them while Hannah pushes Daisy in her pram.

'I can take her,' I say.

'I don't mind,' Hannah replies, 'if you still feel ill.'

'Honestly, it's fine,' I say, itching to get to my daughter. 'I can use the handle to lean on.'

Hannah stops pushing and I take back my daughter's pram. We all seem to have run out of conversation and the journey is becoming slightly awkward.

'Do you know,' I say, 'I'm actually feeling loads better. I think I'm okay to go on by myself.'

'Are you sure?' Callum says. 'You still look really pale, miss.'

'Honestly,' I reply. 'I'm fine.'

'But—'

'She said she's fine, Cal.' Hannah nudges him in the ribs and he flicks her cheek with his finger. They have a mini play fight, laughing, eyes flashing, and I think that even if they aren't romantically involved now, they soon will be. I wonder if Dom and I were ever like that – unable to tear our eyes off one another.

'So, thanks again,' I say. 'Take care.' I walk away before Callum has the chance to protest further. By my calculation, it will take me at least twenty minutes to get home. I'm not even sure how I'm managing to stay upright at the moment, but I don't want to intrude on Callum and Hannah's afternoon. I'm relieved that they took the time to check on me but I just want to get home now.

I continue walking, leaning heavily on the pram handle to keep my balance. As long as I don't pass out, everything will be fine.

*

By the time I eventually get to my house, the sun has dipped in the sky. I go straight through to the kitchen and have a long, cold glass of water and two paracetamol. Daisy is still asleep so I check the locks before taking a cool shower. Feeling a shade better, I bring Daisy into my room and lie on the bed in my cotton dressing gown while she nurses. As she feeds, I stare out of the window at the distant tree tops and the azure sky, my mind pulsing with everything that's happened today, softening at the memory of Callum and Hannah's concern over my wellbeing.

The click of the front door brings me back to the present.

'Hey, it's me!' Dom's home.

'Up here!' I call back, my voice weak. I wonder if he heard me, but then I hear his footsteps on the stairs.

'Hi.' He comes into the bedroom bringing a welcome dose of normality with him. I instantly feel less strange and woozy.

'Hi. Good day?' I ask.

'Not bad. You?'

I tell him about my funny turn at the park, and also about my two unlikely rescuers.

'Hannah and Callum? What was she doing there with that waste of space? You sure he wasn't helping you so he could get a reward?' Dom asks, his expression darkening.

I frown. 'You really don't like him, do you? I know he was rude to you, but he's just a young lad, that's all.'

Dom sighs. 'He's not my favourite person, but I'm glad he was there to help you.'

'Me too. It was pretty surreal, passing out like that.'

'Must have been scary.' He sits on the edge of the bed and kisses my cheek. 'Maybe you should go back to the doctor's. Are you still feeling dizzy?'

'To be honest, I think it was a just mild case of sunstroke. Stupid really. I shouldn't have gone out for so long in that heat.'

'Well, as long as you're okay now. Can I get you anything?'

'Thanks, but no, I'm fine. Daisy's almost finished, we'll come downstairs with you.'

'Okay, great.' He stands and starts unbuttoning his shirt. 'I'll get changed. Going to go training in a bit if that's okay? But I'll make you a cup of tea first.'

Five minutes later, I'm sitting on the sofa in the back room, while Dom paces around the kitchen with Daisy propped over his shoulder, rubbing her back in the hope that she will give a nice, big, satisfying burp.

'I found out something interesting today.' I dunk half a digestive biscuit into my tea, and wonder how Dom will take my news.

'Oh yeah?'

'I had a look online and saw that Martin *did* build that basement. It wasn't built with the house. He applied for planning permission in 2008.'

'Kirst, you went online to look for that? You really think Martin is some dodgy sex fiend?'

'Ugh, no. I don't know. But it's a strange thing to build, don't you think?'

'Maybe. Maybe not. It could be a wine cellar. To be honest, I really don't care what he gets up to, as long as it doesn't affect us.'

'But what if it does affect us? What if he's after Daisy? Don't forget, I saw those Toy Shack bags at the top of the cellar stairs.'

'I thought you were over all this, Kirstie?' Dom stops walking around and gives me a long stare. 'Moaning Myrtle is not after Daisy. That's just… ridiculous.'

'How do you know?' I feel my blood pressure rising at Dom's dismissal of my fears. 'You're not the one home alone all day with our daughter. I feel… I feel like he's always watching us.'

'Watching you?' Dom's expression darkens. 'Have you seen him out there? Looking at the house.'

'No,' I say. 'It's just a feeling I get.'

'Have you thought that maybe it's just that you're overtired, like the doctor said?'

I roll my eyes.

'What?' Dom says. 'It could be, couldn't it? The anxiety and lack of sleep.'

'Is this going to be like the thing where men blame everything on our periods?'

'No! Course not. I just wondered if, maybe…'

'Maybe what?'

'Maybe you might be a little paranoid – but don't take that the wrong way. I'm just trying to reassure you about Martin.'

'Well, telling me I'm paranoid is not reassuring.'

'I don't mean paranoid, I mean…'

'… paranoid.' I finish his sentence for him.

'Kirstie.'

'What?' I snap.

'I don't want to argue about Moaning bloody Myrtle. Can't we just have an evening without talking about the neighbours?'

'I wish we could,' I say, getting to my feet, 'but I can't help it if I'm worried for our daughter's safety.'

'So what do you want me to do?' Now it's his turn to snap.

'I don't know… maybe just take me seriously for a moment, instead of making me feel like a crackpot!' My voice has risen to a cry, but I know that last comment was unfair. It's more likely that I'm doubting my own sanity. My head pounds, whether a hangover from the sunstroke or in reaction to our argument I'm not sure. Either way, I feel like shit.

'Look, Kirst, if you really are worried about Martin and his basement, how about I go over there right now and ask to see what's down there?'

I let out a long, slow breath and try to absorb what he's just said. 'You can't do that,' I finally say. 'He'll know we've been snooping.'

Dom clears his throat theatrically. 'He'll know *you've* been snooping. But seriously, I'll go over there now if it will get you to relax.'

My heart misses a beat as I consider the possibility for a second. 'It could be risky to go asking him questions. If there's something strange going on, he might try to hurt you. To shut you up. I've already had a threatening phone call, remember?'

'You've been watching too many of your Scandi crime thrillers,' Dom says. 'It's Moaning Myrtle; I'm pretty sure I could take him if it came to it. Look, do you want me to go over there or not? If yes, I can go now before my bike ride.'

'No,' I say, panicking at the thought. 'Don't go over there. Promise me you won't.'

'I won't go if you don't want me to. Just thought it might help put your mind at rest.'

I'd never forgive myself if Dom got hurt. I know he thinks this threat is all in my head, but I can't take the chance that it's real. I'll have to get proof of what's going on next door without tipping Martin off. Which means going round there while he's out. And I can't tell Dom about what I'm planning. He's already starting to worry about my mental health, this would just confirm things. No, I'll sort this out on my own. It's the safest way.

CHAPTER TWENTY-SIX

I'm making up batches of pre-prepared meals for Daisy, blending them into a smooth mush and freezing them for when weaning starts in earnest. At the moment we're still on the banana and avocado stage – introducing different foods slowly. I spoon the gloopy mixture into the multicoloured ice-cube trays. I've also done some baking. The act of following a recipe always has a calming effect, and I need things to calm me after the events of last week.

I've been keeping myself locked up in the house with Daisy for the past couple of days. Dom was training most of the weekend and now he's on a two-day course in Bristol, so he won't be back until tomorrow.

The oven timer beeps, signalling that the cakes are ready, although I already knew that by the warm vanilla aroma wafting through the kitchen. Daisy is strapped into her high chair sucking on a rice cake and watching my every move. I stick my tongue out at her and she gurgles at me as I don the oven gloves and lift out the tray of cupcakes. I'm going to ice them and take them over to Mel as a peace offering.

She tried calling round here a couple of times over the weekend, but I wasn't up to seeing anyone, so I either ignored the doorbell or asked Dom to tell her I was asleep. I heard them whispering together downstairs. I hate the thought of them talking about me, discussing how over-protective I've become and how paranoid and forgetful. I wouldn't be surprised if Dom has told her about my trip to the doctor and they're feeling sorry for poor nutty-as-a-fruitcake Kirstie. I know that's uncharitable – they'll have my best interests at heart, but it still makes me feel crappy. I don't want to be the subject of people's gossip and sympathy, even if it is my husband and my best friend. *Especially* if it's my husband and my best friend.

So, I'll go over there and clear the air. Make sure there's no bad feeling between us about money, or about Tamsin. Make a joke about myself if I have to. Mel always responds well to humour. We'll have a laugh about my crazy baby-brain, and all will be forgotten.

Once the cakes are cooled and iced, I change Daisy into a pretty blue and white polka-dot dress and walk across the road. Mel's car is in the drive, so I'm assuming she's home.

'Hey.' I give a sheepish smile as she opens the door.

She looks at me for a second, before pulling me and Daisy into a squishy hug. 'I've been worried about you, Kirst. Come in.'

I follow her through to the kitchen and hand her the Tupperware container of cupcakes. 'A peace offering for ignoring you over the weekend.'

'You didn't need to do that,' she says. 'But I'm bloody glad you did. Tea and cakes, yum.' Mel sets the cakes on the counter, puts the kettle on and takes Daisy from my arms.

'I'm so glad I came over. Definitely need a bit of normality.' I plonk myself on a stool and peel the lid off the cake tub.

'I'm touched you think I'm normal.' Mel raises an eyebrow and pulls a face, making me laugh.

The kettle boils, but Mel is still holding Daisy so I offer to make the tea.

'Go on then,' Mel replies, making baby noises at a giggling Daisy. 'Oh, Kirstie, you know last week when Tamsin came over? I think you were right.'

'Hmm?'

'Yeah, she was really over-friendly, asking me round to her place, saying to bring the kids over for a playdate. And when I suggested inviting *you* along, she made an excuse that Daisy was younger than our kids and that it would be annoying having a baby crying and fussing. Can you believe it?'

'Charming!' The woman's unbelievable.

'I know, right. Think she realised she'd gone too far. She backtracked and said she just meant we wouldn't be able to relax and talk. Not sure how relaxing she thinks it would be with four young children running around anyway.'

'I'm not surprised, though,' I say, taking a couple of mugs out of the cupboard. 'She hates my guts.'

'I think she's just resentful,' Mel replies. 'Because Dom realised he made a mistake with her. That's why she pretended to be pregnant. To try and get him to stay with her.'

I nod. 'But that was years ago. Why would she hold on to such ancient history… unless she still has feelings for Dom?'

'No,' Mel says. 'I'm sure she doesn't.'

'She's divorced though.'

'So am I; doesn't mean I'm going to ravage your husband.' Mel raises an eyebrow at me.

'Sorry, I just meant—'

'I'm just messing with you.' Mel gives a throaty laugh. 'Now can we stop talking about Tamsin, and start talking about how fabulous my new haircut is? You haven't even mentioned it yet. So rude!'

I laugh, feeling so pleased that I decided to come over here. Whenever things get tough, I know Mel will always be there for me, cheering me up with her silly banter, and vice versa. In fact, we're more like sisters than friends. We share everything. As I reach up to get the sugar bowl out of the cupboard – Mel takes three sugars – I notice a pair of white wraparound sunglasses in her fruit bowl.

'Are these Dom's?' I ask, picking them up.

Mel follows my eye line and I see her expression falter for a moment, her mouth falling open. She stutters, 'Nope, don't think so. Must be Chris's.'

I know she's lying. Her ex isn't sporty and there's no way he would wear a pair of non-branded glasses like these. 'Yes, they are. They're Dom's. He wears them for cycling. He's been looking all over the place for these. What are they doing here?'

'Uh, no idea.' She turns away and reaches up to get a couple of flowery plates from her duck-egg-blue Welsh dresser. When she turns back around, her face is more composed. 'Maybe he dropped them out the front, and one of the kids picked them up, brought them home. They're like a couple of magpies, those two. Always bringing back random crap – stones, leaves, ring-pulls. Syringes – joke.' She rolls her eyes – an attempt at nonchalance.

But I'm not buying it. I'm not laughing either. Dom's been round here, and it wasn't at the weekend, because he lost his sunglasses last week. 'Don't lie, Mel. Just tell me, are these Dom's glasses?'

She drops the act and nods.

'So why did you lie? Was Dom round here last week?' All my earlier good humour is disappearing fast.

'I'm sorry, Kirstie, I can't tell you.'

For a second, I think she's joking, until I realise she isn't. My pulse quickens. 'What do you mean you can't tell me? Of course you can. You just open your mouth and the words come out.'

'It's… It's not my place to say,' she says, her face reddening. 'You'll have to ask Dom. I'm sorry.'

'You're *sorry*?' Heat floods my face. Why is she refusing to say any more? 'Just tell me what the big secret is.'

Mel shakes her head. 'I can't.'

My throat tightens as I remember how Mel and Dom were whispering in the hallway over the weekend, and also how Dom defended Mel when I told him about her borrowing money. 'Are you having an affair with my husband?' the question pops out before I can stop it. Silence hangs between us for a moment. Daisy babbles happily in Mel's arms, unaware that her mummy's heart is being twisted.

'No!' Mel cries, a look of outrage on her face. But of course she would deny it. 'Speak to Dom,' she repeats.

I grip the counter top as my head begins to swim. Not this again. I can't faint. Not here, not now.

'Are you okay?' Mel asks.

I'm far from okay, but I shake her off, unable to even look at her. I take a steadying breath, stride over and retrieve Daisy from her arms. 'I thought you were supposed to be my best friend! I'll let myself out.'

'Kirstie! Please. It's not what you think. Just stay and have some tea.'

'You're joking, aren't you?' I stomp down her hallway and out of the front door, slamming it behind me, hoping the vibrations rattle her bones. I let out a growl of frustration.

Why wouldn't Mel tell me why Dom's sunglasses are in her kitchen? What reason would he have to be at her house? Yes, they're friends, but Dom's never gone over there on his own to hang out and chat. I mean, I don't suppose I would mind if he did, but why would they keep it secret? That's the part I can't understand. There's no explanation I can think of other than the obvious one – Dom and Mel must be having an affair. But he wouldn't do that to me, would he? Not after last time. Not now we've got a daughter together. Would he? Would she? If they have, I'll kill them both. I'll… Truth is, I don't know what I'd do.

Tears of hurt and anger burn behind my eyes as I march back towards to my house, Daisy wriggling in my arms. So much for going over to Mel's and clearing the air – it's more toxic now than it's ever been. I want to call Dom this minute and demand answers, but I also want to see the expression on his face when I ask him if he's sleeping with my best friend. That's the only way I'll know if he's telling the truth and I can't do that over the phone. Why does he have to be away on a bloody course today of all days? How am I going to wait until tomorrow? I stand in the hallway of our house, panting, a space opening up inside me like a vast black hole.

CHAPTER TWENTY-SEVEN

A night and a day of waiting and stewing and pacing and biting my nails and jumping out of my skin at every creak of the house and cry from Daisy. A night and a day of ignoring my husband's text messages and phone calls. A night and a day of not eating, of rolling tears and black thoughts.

And now, finally, the wait is almost over. It's Tuesday night and Dom will be driving back from his course.

Daisy is asleep upstairs while I sit downstairs, curled up on the lounge sofa like a cat who appears relaxed but could spring up at any moment. Could fight or flee with a wail and a screech. But for now, I wait in the dark with TV on and the sound turned off. I wait, anticipating the conversation to come, but also dreading it. Dreading it so much it makes me feel physically sick.

My body tenses as I hear Dom's car pull into the driveway.

My stomach turns in time with my husband's key in the lock. Click.

The hall light comes on and I take a breath. Try to work out what I'm going to say. Try to anticipate what his response will be. Is my marriage over? Will I be a single mum? Maybe it really is nothing. Maybe Dom and Mel aren't involved and it's my brain making unwanted connections. But if it's nothing bad, then why wouldn't Mel tell me what was going on? Why did she tell me to speak to Dom? Why didn't she come over to see how I was doing?

'Hey, Kirst!' The lounge door swings open and I see him standing there, illuminated in the doorway. He already looks different, already distant. Not the Dom I've known for most of my life. My husband, the stranger.

'Hi,' I reply, the word almost jams in my throat.

'Why are you sitting in here with the light off?' he asks. 'I missed you guys. How've you been?' He puts his keys on the hall table and steps into the lounge. 'Is there something wrong with your phone? I've been texting and calling.' He switches on the light.

I squint and look down at my fingers twisting in my lap.

'Kirstie?' he says, a note of irritation creeping into his voice.

'How was the course?' I ask, sure that Dom will notice my voice is too high, too bright.

He gives me a quizzical look before answering. 'Yeah, it was okay. Learnt a couple of new sales techniques, but nothing earth shattering. You know, the usual. They could probably have condensed it into two hours. Dying for a beer. Want one?'

'I can't,' I say. 'Breastfeeding, remember?' I get up and let myself be kissed, follow him into the kitchen.

'You haven't said how you and Daisy have been?' he says, opening the fridge and pulling out a bottle of Peroni.

'Fine.'

'Feeling any better... you know, since going to the doctor's?'

'Yeah, I'm okay.' I shrug.

'Oh. Good. Well, how's our little girl?'

'She's fine.' Dom can't fail to notice that my voice is becoming sharper.

He takes a bottle opener from the drawer, pops the cap and takes a long slug from the bottle. 'Look, Kirst, I wanted to say I'm really sorry. About... you know, the whole taking Daisy out shopping while you were asleep thing. I should've made sure you heard me explain. I knew you were half asleep when I was talking to you. I really am sorry that I worried you like that. But it was a genuine mistake.'

I nod, my lips tight. He thinks I'm angry about *that*. But he's wrong.

'So, am I forgiven?' Dom stares at me, with a hesitant smile, clearly thinking he's won me over.

'I found your sunglasses,' I say, stony faced, watching for his reaction.

'My sunglasses?' He breaks into a proper smile. 'Oh, amazing. I'd thought I'd lost them for good. It's not that they were expensive or anything, but they're my favourites. Where did you find them, anyway?'

'They're at Melinda's house,' I say. 'I went over there to clear the air and saw your sunglasses in her fruit bowl, of all places.'

'What are they doing over th—' He stops for a moment and clears his throat. 'What are they doing over there?'

'You tell me,' I say, folding my arms across my chest.

'What does that mean?' he says, eying me over his bottle of beer. 'You're looking at me like I've done something wrong.'

'I asked Mel why your glasses were at her house, and she told me it wasn't her place to say. She told me to ask *you*. So, I'm asking you.'

'Shit. Bloody Mel. I told her not to say anything.'

Tears sting the back of my eyes and I can't hold back the question burning in my throat. 'Are you two seeing each other?'

'Seeing each other?' Dom's eyes widen. 'No! Did you think…? Have you been thinking that she and I were…? Oh, Kirstie, no. Come here.' He puts his bottle on the counter and tries to hug me, but I push him away.

'Well, what am I supposed to think?' I cry. 'Mel was all tight-lipped and telling me to talk to you about it. What would *you* think if you were me?'

He nods. 'I know. I'm an idiot. But she really shouldn't have said… Oh, never mind.'

'So? Why were you over there? What's the big secret?' I suddenly have the awful thought that it might not be Mel who's having an affair with Dom – what if it's Tamsin? What if she's been seeing Dom again, and Mel knows about it? That she's keeping it a secret and that's why Mel said it wasn't her place to tell me. Please, please, don't let it be that.

'You're not going to be happy,' Dom says.

I'm already not happy. 'Just tell me, Dom.' All I want is for him to spit out the truth.

He sighs and takes another sip of beer. 'Mel sent me a text last week, asking me to go round there. She said she had a favour to ask. She wouldn't tell me on the phone, so I nipped over to her place last week after training.' He looks at me, waiting for a response.

I don't speak. I'm waiting for him to go on.

'It was the usual thing, Kirst – she's skint. She's maxed her credit cards and her overdraft is up to the limit. So she asked if I could lend her three hundred quid to tide her over until Chris sends through her next maintenance payment.'

I wasn't expecting that. But I immediately wonder if this is simply a convenient story they've concocted to keep me in the dark. 'How do I know you're telling the truth?'

'Jesus, Kirstie. Why would I lie? I'm your husband.'

'If you're having a thing with Mel, or anyone else—'

'I am not having a thing! Mel's not even my type.'

'She's everyone's type,' I snap.

'She's too high-maintenance, too in-your-face. I love her to bits, but not like that. She's our friend, and that's *all* she is. I'm married to you! If you don't believe me, then I can show you my bank statement – I took out three hundred in cash last week to give to her.'

'So she really was asking you to lend her money?' I sit down heavily on one of the kitchen chairs, letting his explanation sink in.

Dom nods, his face flushed.

'And you lent it to her.'

'What was I supposed to do? She's our friend, she's in a jam. She said she'd pay me back next month.'

I exhale.

'I knew you'd go mad,' he continues, 'so I told her not to tell you about it. I'm so sorry. I'm such an idiot.'

'It's not the money, Dom. It's the lying. It's the fact that I've been at home stressing for two days, thinking you and Mel were sleeping together. You've made me look like a fool in front of my friend. And you've made me doubt our marriage. I mean, forgive me for suspecting you of an affair, but it's not like you haven't done it before!'

'Kirst!' He gives me a wounded look.

Maybe I shouldn't have brought up his one-night stand with Tamsin – it's ancient history that he spent months apologising for early on in our relationship, and I chose to forgive him. But his lies have made me doubt him again. And right now, I'm too keyed up to feel anything but pissed off.

'No, Dom. It's like you're deliberately trying to ruin our relationship at the moment.'

'I am so sorry, Kirstie. I know I'm screwing everything up. What can I do? How can I make it up to you?'

'Maybe you could start by not having secrets from me and not lending money we don't have to my best friend.'

Dom nods, his body hunched, his expression one of remorse. But then he drops his shoulders and tilts his head. 'Um,' he says.

'Um, what?'

'Well,' he says, 'it's just, you're telling me not to go behind your back and lend Mel money, but isn't that exactly what you were doing before?'

'Yes,' I reply, 'but I came to you and told you what was going on, and we agreed together that we wouldn't lend her any more.

Now you've gone behind my back and made me look bad. You've basically driven a wedge between me and Mel.'

'You and Mel will be fine.'

'You don't know that. At the moment I'm pissed off with the pair of you. You lent her money after I called her out on not paying me back. You've made me look like the bad guy.'

Dom chews his lip.

A wave of exhaustion hits me. I should be happy that Dom isn't having an affair, but my body is itching with irritability and disappointment. Of course I'm relieved my husband and Mel – or even worse, Tamsin – aren't seeing one another behind my back, but there are still so many other issues we need to work out. I thought Dom and I were a team, a tight unit. But we seem to be drifting further and further apart, and I don't know how to fix it.

CHAPTER TWENTY-EIGHT

I stand before the bathroom mirror, carefully applying my makeup. I desperately need it to cover up the suitcases beneath my eyes. After our bust up earlier in the week, Dom and I have reached an uneasy truce. It's Saturday, the day of Jimmy and Rosa's barbecue. To be honest, I'd much rather go for a family picnic on the beach, or a walk in the countryside, or maybe stick some rusty pins in my eyes, but Dom thinks this will be good for us. And if I don't go, it will be another reason for us to argue. So now here I am trying to make myself look presentable for the neighbours, who all know about the humiliating episode where I thought Daisy had been snatched.

The music from number two has already been cranked up, and I recognise a muffled version of some chart tune I can't remember the name of. The thump of the bassline has the added effect of quadrupling the number of butterflies in my stomach. But as long as I show my face over there, I won't have to stay long. An hour tops, then I can say I have to get back to feed Daisy, or make some other excuse. It'll be fine.

'You nearly ready, Kirst?' Dom calls from the landing, giving a short rap on the bathroom door.

'Two minutes!' I reply.

'I'll wait downstairs!' The excitement in his voice irritates me. Why does going to some twenty-something's barbecue make him so happy? Are we growing apart, is that it? Am I becoming boring and staid, while he still has an abundance of partying years left in him? As I apply bronzer to my cheeks, I try to think about this objectively. Before we had Daisy, I probably would have been excited to go to a party too. Now, it feels like nothing makes me excited. And everything makes me either anxious, angry or miserable. I hold my breath for a moment to stop the flow of threatening tears. Why the hell am I always crying?

That doctor was probably right – I'm overtired and I should probably book myself onto one of those meditation courses like she suggested. But to admit that I haven't been coping feels like a weakness, like I'm a failure as a mother. I wanted a baby for years, and now I finally have Daisy, but I can't enjoy her because I'm too busy crying or whining or locking myself away from the world. I need to stop my mind from going down this rabbit hole. I'm supposed to be going to a party, not analysing how crap my life is. I'm going to go to this barbecue and I'm going to try and squeeze some enjoyment out of it – if only to prove to myself that I'm still the same person I used to be. That I haven't lost myself.

'Kirstie! You coming?' Dom's voice flies up the stairs, more urgent now.

I smear on some lipstick, blot my lips together and take another steadying breath. I can fake it for an hour, surely. 'Yep, coming!' I yell back, smoothing my red dress down over my hips and teasing out my dark curls.

*

Jimmy and Rosa's garden is like something out of a magazine, with slate paving, a hot tub, dark wicker furniture, emerald-green grass (Martin would freak at such blatant disregard for the hosepipe ban), a white brick-built outdoor oven, and a cedar-clad summer house complete with a bar. Dotted amongst this glamour, like tropical birds, beautiful people sip their drinks, vape and generally appear at one with the universe.

Daisy sits on my hip, her eyes wide, taking everything in. Dom is trying to spot anyone we might recognise. I'm trying to remain anonymous. I breathe in the aroma of barbecue smoke and perfume, cocktails and sun cream. Even the sunlight feels different at the Cliffords' – brighter and somehow more exotic, like we're a couple of pasty-faced tourists who have just arrived at a tropical holiday destination.

'You made it!' Rosa appears through a crowd of guests and sashays over to us, wearing an insanely short broderie anglaise playsuit and cork wedge heels. I smile up at her and hand over a chilled bottle of prosecco. 'Lovely,' she says. 'Thank you, Kirstie. Hi, Dom. Jimmy's around here somewhere – probably inside messing about with the music.'

We air kiss and she offers us drinks.

'I'm not drinking,' I say, pointing to Daisy with a smile, 'but we've brought some non-alcoholic beer, so I'll have one of those.'

Rosa opens the bottle for me and hands Dom a beer. 'Oh, here's Jimmy,' she says with a smile.

'Hey, hey, Kirstie. Dom, my man.' Jimmy and Dom clink bottles and immediately start talking about racing-bike specifications.

Rosa and I make small talk, but my mouth goes dry as I catch sight of a familiar figure further down the garden peering into the brick oven. I grab hold of Dom's arm and squeeze.

'Ow!' He turns to me. 'Kirstie, what are you doing?'

I can sense Jimmy and Rosa staring at me, but I can't take my eyes off the person by the oven. 'Martin's here,' I hiss.

Dom, Rosa and Jimmy turn to stare at our neighbour.

'What's the matter?' Rosa asks. 'Is he a bit of a weirdo? He's all right, isn't he?'

'Kirstie thinks he's got sex slaves in his basement,' Dom says with a dead-pan face.

Jimmy and Rosa stare at Dom, wide eyed, before bursting into hysterical laughter. I don't find it funny. Dom puts his arm around me by way of an apology, but I don't appreciate him getting cheap laughs at my expense. He knows that man makes me nervous.

'Oh my God. Has he really got a basement?' Rosa asks. 'Or are you winding us up?'

'Kirst found his planning application online,' Dom says. 'He built the thing ten years ago.'

Rosa pulls a face. 'That's so creepy.'

'Hey!' Jimmy shouts down the garden. 'Martin!'

I cringe with embarrassment. What is Jimmy going to say to him? Surely they're not going to ask him about it.

Martin looks over, shading his eyes, a bemused expression on his face. His gaze rests on me and Daisy and he gives a brief wave. I look away quickly, my heart in my throat, my head starting to swim. I tell myself it's fine. We're in a public place. My husband is here. Nothing is going to happen. But the sight of that man now turns my insides to water. I set my bottle down on the table behind me, and grip Daisy a little tighter, turning back to the others.

'Hello, Kirstie, Daisy.'

I look up to find Martin has come over and is now standing uncomfortably close. I take a step back so that I'm pressed up against the table. My throat seems to have closed up, so I simply nod at him and take a sip of my drink.

'Dominic, how are you?' he asks.

'Fine thanks, Martin. You?'

'Not too bad at all.' He turns to the Cliffords. 'It was nice of you to invite me to your gathering.'

'Glad you could make it,' Jimmy says, while Rosa looks as though she's trying not to laugh.

'I wanted to ask,' Martin says to our hosts, 'did you pre-cook the meat in a regular oven, or will you be cooking it from scratch in that outdoor oven. Because, in case you were unaware, there are very high instances of food poisoning arising from improperly cooked food at barbecues. Now, I'm not casting any aspersions, I'm just hoping to avoid any food-related sickness.'

'Don't worry about it, mate,' Jimmy says, clapping Martin on the shoulder and almost knocking him over. 'Rosa's brother Gino is a chef and he's in charge of the barbie, okay?'

'That is reassuring,' Martin replies, sipping his orange juice.

Rosa giggles, and ordinarily I'd find Martin's mannerisms amusing, too. But I can't stop viewing him as a possible predator. I don't want to be anywhere near the man. I'm hot and my throat is dry. I reach behind me for my drink and down the rest of it. Rosa hands me another of my beers and I take a sip.

'Now, Martin,' Jimmy says. 'Is it true you have a basement in your house?'

The noise from the party recedes as all my attention turns to Martin. To study his reactions and listen to his response.

Martin's face turns a deep shade of crimson. He thrusts his jaw out and balls his fist. He looks as though he might punch Jimmy, or maybe even cry. 'It really is no one's business,' Martin says. 'What I do in my own house is private, and I'll thank you to remember that.'

Jimmy raises his hands in apologetic surrender. 'Sorry, mate. Didn't mean to offend.'

'Yes, well,' Martin continues, 'do I ask you what you get up to, with people coming and going from your house at all times of the day and night? No, I do not. And I expect the same courtesy from you.'

'Wow, sorry,' Jimmy says. 'Forget I asked.'

Despite the music and the laughter from the party, an awkward silence descends on our little group.

'I think I need to go and change Daisy,' I say. 'I'll just pop back home for a minute.'

'No need to go home,' Rosa says. 'Take her upstairs. The spare room is just to the left of the bathroom.'

'You sure?'

'Course.' She raises her eyebrows at me over Martin's head.

I smile back, relieved to be getting away from our next-door neighbour. He didn't deny having the basement, but he also didn't explain why he built it. He was defensive, angry. His response has made me more certain that something is going on next door.

I can't put it off any longer. I'm going to have to find out what's down there.

CHAPTER TWENTY-NINE

As I make my way inside the Cliffords' house with Daisy in my arms and my heart still pounding from the encounter with Martin, I bump into Mel. I'm really not in the mood to speak to her, but it would be more awkward not to, so I force out a limp smile.

'Hi Kirst,' she says guardedly.

'Hi.' We stand there for a moment, unsure how to proceed.

'I don't suppose… Did you speak to Dom?' Mel asks.

I nod. 'He explained about lending you the money.'

'I'm sorry,' she says. 'I really wanted to tell you about it the other day, but Dom thought it would be easier to keep it secret. So when you found his glasses, I wasn't sure if it would be better to tell you about it myself or let Dom tell you. I was completely out of order to go to Dom behind your back. I've got no excuse other than I was desperate. Don't blame him for my mistakes. If there's any way I can make it up to you…'

'Forget about it,' I say, meaning it. Suddenly, I'm exhausted with all the arguing and mistrust. I know I can't erase the events of the past fortnight, but I just want everything to go back to normal. I want Dom and me to be close once more, and I want my best friend back. We'll talk about the money she owes some other time. I just don't have the strength to think about it at the moment. 'Let's just put it behind us, Mel. Be friends again.'

'Really?' she says. 'Are you sure you're not mad at me?'

'I'm sure.'

'Pinky swear?'

I roll my eyes. 'Cross my heart and hope to die.'

She leans in and kisses Daisy's cheek before giving me a hug. 'I'm so glad. I've been miserable all week. And I promise to manage my money better.'

'Let's not talk about it any more, okay?'

'Fine by me,' she says.

'Where are your two?' I ask.

'They're with Chris's mum today. She's taking them to the theatre. Good luck with that, I told her. Those two can't sit still for two minutes, let alone two hours.' She takes a sip of her drink. 'Uh oh, look who it is.'

I tense up, thinking she's talking about Martin. But when I turn to look, I see it's actually Lorna and Stephen Parkfield deep in conversation, heading our way. To be honest, I didn't think they'd even be here. I wouldn't have thought a barbecue at the Cliffords' was their thing – but then again, it's not *my* thing either. They haven't spotted us yet, so maybe I can make a break for it. I could do without another awkward conversation.

Too late.

Lorna looks up with a scowl which stays on her face when she catches sight of us. 'Kirstie,' she says. 'Melinda.'

'Hi, Lorna,' Mel says breezily. 'Hi, Steve.'

I laugh inwardly, knowing how much Parkfield hates to be called Steve. But Mel has no qualms about pissing him off.

'Afternoon,' Parkfield says in that pompous tone of his.

I take a swig of beer to settle my nerves, and then I remember that it's alcohol free.

'When's the big move?' Mel asks.

'Hopefully sometime next month,' Lorna says.

'Moving far?' Mel probes.

'Yes,' Parkfield says without elaborating.

'Okaay,' Mel says.

'I've just got to change Daisy,' I say, making my excuses, my head beginning to pound. This barbecue is turning into some kind of twisted obstacle course, where the object of the game is not to get snarled up in uncomfortable conversations with your neighbours.

'Want a hand?' Mel asks, begging me with her eyes.

'I'll be fine,' I say, feeling bad that I'm abandoning her, but I desperately need a minute alone. 'Back in a second, okay?' I make my escape into the hall and up the stairs. I push open the door at the top of the landing, behind which lies a stunning grey and white designer bathroom. The room to the left is a smart single bedroom, which I enter, closing the door behind me. Daisy doesn't need a clean nappy, it was simply an excuse to get away from Martin and the Parkfields. I'm grateful for a few moments to get myself together.

I sip my drink and gaze out of the window to see if I can get a glimpse of Martin again despite being repulsed by him. Maybe I could go to his house while he's occupied over here. He might have left a window open. I could climb in and check the basement. This really would be the perfect time. I can't quite believe I'm considering breaking and entering, but if it's to discover what's going on next door, then surely the end justifies the means.

Scanning the guests below to see if I can spot him, I catch sight of Lorna's two youngest girls sitting cross-legged on the grass, chatting. The music is more muffled up here, but the relentless beat is exacerbating my headache; the dull throbbing inside my skull has become a sharp pounding. My forehead suddenly feels clammy and my head is starting to whirl. I actually don't feel good at all.

I sit on the edge of the bed for a second, sliding Daisy into my lap, taking slow breaths to try to stop my head spinning. Is this a panic attack? I don't think so. I'm not short of breath. It feels more like I'm drunk. But that can't be right. I examine the beer bottle and see that it contains zero per cent alcohol. So definitely not drunk. The bottle falls out of my hand onto the floor, amber liquid pooling on the cream carpet, but I don't have the strength to lean down and retrieve it. How can this feeling have come on so quickly? Maybe I'm coming down with flu or something. I exhale. I'm not going to be able to check out Martin's basement, not feeling like this. I think I need to go home. Now.

Making sure I've got a firm hold of Daisy, I rise to my feet. The room suddenly swirls, reams of walls scrolling past my eyes. I shuffle towards to the door as a wave of nausea sweeps over me. This is not good.

I put my hands out to steady myself against the wall, bite back another wave of sickness and pull open the door. The noise from the party below hits me. I need to find Dom. Give Daisy to him to look after while I get myself home and lie down. After everything he's done to persuade me to come to the party today, he'll think I'm making this up to get out of being here. He won't believe I genuinely feel ill. Why is this happening to me? I swallow down my panic. I just need to keep it together until I can get home.

The staircase in front of me looks like a precipice. It's too risky to walk down it while I'm carrying my daughter, so I sit on my bottom and shuffle down, one step at a time, hoping no one sees me. But my hopes are dashed as two giggling women appear at the bottom of the stairs, a blurry mass of shiny hair and bright clothing.

I sense both sets of eyes on me, but I'm too busy concentrating on not falling over or throwing up to worry about what they think.

'You okay?' one of them asks while the other splutters with laughter – at me, no doubt.

'I'm okay.' The words come out heavy and slow.

'Oh my God, I know her,' one hisses to the other.

'Who is she? What about her poor kid?'

'Her name's Kirstie. Looks like she's pissed out of her head.'

Through another wave of dizziness and nausea, I recognise that voice. I stop my downward shuffle for a moment and look up to see Tamsin Price staring at me with an ill-concealed grin on her face. What's she doing here? How does she know the Cliffords?

'Not drunk,' I slur. 'Feel ill.'

'It's probably better to stay off the booze when you're supposed to be looking after your baby,' Tamsin says.

'You know her?' the other woman asks Tamsin in a horrified whisper.

'She never used to behave like this,' Tamsin says. 'She was always such a little square at school. Must be having a mid-life crisis.'

'Why are you here?' I ask, slurring my words.

'Dom invited me,' she says with a smirk. Or at least I think that's what she said. But that can't be right, can it? Dom would never do that.

The women step apart as I reach the bottom of the staircase. I don't have the energy to respond to Tamsin's lies. I'm too concerned with keeping myself upright and not dropping Daisy. In any case, they allow me to pass, their horrified stares and whispers following me.

Need to find Dom. I somehow make it through the hall and into the kitchen where a sea of faces turn to stare as I stagger and push my way past as though in slow motion, everyone's expressions a fuzzy mass of wide eyes and open mouths.

My husband is outside somewhere. *Need to get out. Need to give Daisy to him.* He won't be happy about that. He won't be able to enjoy himself properly, not if he has to look after her. As I head outside, I misjudge the step and my right heel catches on the door threshold. My knee gives way and I topple sideways with a scream, throwing myself as far onto my back as I can to keep Daisy from tumbling onto the hard slate patio.

I fall so slowly, like I could right myself at any time. But then, like a switch being flicked, everything speeds up. I desperately try to keep hold of my daughter, terrified I'm squeezing her too tightly, or not tightly enough. But as I hit the ground, landing on my side with a thud, Daisy jolts out of my arms, sliding across the patio onto the grass. Shocked cries and screams are followed by silence, apart from the music, which thumps away, oblivious.

Then Daisy lets out a piercing wail.

'Oh my God!'

'Is the baby okay?'

'Are you okay?'

'She fell over.'

'Is she drunk?'

'Is she high?'

'Her name's Kirstie.'

'She dropped her baby.'

The voices swirl around me, but I'm more worried about my daughter than about the party guests. 'Daisy all right?' I ask, reaching out for her, but she's scooped up by a stranger. 'Is she 'kay?' I wipe my brow and my mouth with the back of my hand. 'She 'kay? I… not… I.' What the hell is wrong with me? I definitely sound drunk. My body is numb, unhurt, even though I know I landed heavily on hard slate.

'She's off her face!'

'Who is she?'

'Think she's one of their neighbours.'

'Kirstie! Are you okay?'

It's Dom. I crawl up onto my knees. 'Fell over,' I manage to say before vomiting across the pristine slate patio.

'Ew!' a woman cries.

'That's gross.'

'What the fuck. She's puked on my shoes!'

Dom's aftershave cuts through my senses. I feel his arm around me. My head lolls into his chest. His voice in my ear, angry, hissing, 'Are you drunk, Kirstie? *You are.* You're totally shitfaced. How could you? You could have seriously hurt Daisy. Killed her even!'

'She 'kay?' I persist. 'Daisy? She okay?'

'She's fine, no thanks to you.'

'Not drunk. Feel ill.' I throw up a little bit more, this time all down Dom's immaculate shirt.

'For fuck's sake,' he cries. 'I'm taking you home.'

'Bring Daisy,' I say, my head tipping backwards and then forwards again.

'No. You're in no fit state to look after her. I can't believe this. I can't fucking believe it. You're a mess, Kirstie. There's no way you should have been drinking. You're breast feeding, for Christ's sake. This is so irresponsible.'

'Daisy,' I persist. Even though my mind is woozy, I'm paranoid that this could be the perfect opportunity for Martin to snatch her.

'Daisy's fine,' Dom snaps. 'She's with Mel.'

I try to tell Dom that I'm not drunk. That I only had two bottles of non-alcoholic beer. That something else has happened to me. Maybe an allergic reaction or something. But the words won't come out. My mouth is thick, my brain sluggish. As though I'm not here. Disembodied. It's no good. I need to close my eyes. I need to sleep.

I blink heavily. Once. Twice. Three times. I catch sight of Rosa's shocked expression, of Mel with Daisy in her arms, Tamsin, the Parkfields. All of them staring at me like I'm insane.

My eyes close and their faces fade…

CHAPTER THIRTY

I wake with a fuzzy head and realise I'm lying on the sofa in the lounge, still wearing yesterday's red dress, infused with the faint smell of vomit. I try to sit up and the whole of my right side screams in pain while the events of the barbecue tumble into my brain: Martin, the dizziness, the fall. And worst of all – I dropped Daisy! I actually dropped my baby!

'Dom!' I try to yell, but it comes out like a croak. My throat is raspy, my stomach hurts, I feel nauseous and my body is in absolute agony. 'Dom!' I try again, but it's no good – I have no strength in my voice whatsoever.

I gingerly rise to my feet. Once I'm upright, I hitch up my dress to examine my body. My right leg is a mass of red and black bruises. My hip is swollen and tender to the touch. My arm is in the same knocked-about shape. I really took a tumble. But I can't even think about that now. I need to find out if Daisy is okay.

Flashbacks of yesterday evening assault me like a stop-motion video. Dom telling me I was drunk, and bruised down one side, but not seriously hurt. I remember trying to explain that I wasn't drunk, that I hadn't even been drinking, but my words were slurred. I felt and sounded drunk to myself, so why would anyone else believe me?

I make my way into the kitchen to try to find my husband. To apologise and tell him that I wasn't myself. That something else is going on here. Something I can't explain. Every step sends a volley of sharp knives into my side, and every movement feels as though my brain is becoming dislodged, like it's sloshing about in my head. Dom is not in the kitchen. The time on the cooker clock says 8.05 a.m. Early for a Sunday, but he's an early riser. Perhaps he overslept. I rinse out an empty glass from the draining board and fill it with water. Take a few sips to ease my throat.

Everyone thinks I got drunk yesterday. But I didn't knowingly have one single sip of alcohol. Could somebody have spiked my drink? I think back to the party. All I drank were a couple of bottles of alcohol-free beer that Rosa opened in front of me. I left one on the table behind me for a while. How long was it there? Could someone have slipped something into it? I don't know. Could it have been an allergic reaction to something? I drain the glass of water and set it back on the counter.

Through the kitchen window I see that it's another glorious day out there, a day for picnics and families and fun and relaxing. I can't see my day turning out anything like that. I make my way up the stairs and enter Daisy's room. My pulse quickens when I see she's not in her cot. It's okay, she's probably in with Dom. I go to our bedroom next, but there's no sign of either of them. He must have taken her out. I tell myself not to panic.

As long as Daisy is okay. But what if she's not? What if that's why Dom isn't here? What if he's had to take her to the hospital? She could have hit her head yesterday and had a delayed reaction. She could be in intensive care.

Stumbling out of the bedroom, I head back downstairs. I need my phone. I need to call Dom to make sure Daisy's okay. But I can't see my bag anywhere. I frantically search for it, hoping I didn't leave it at the Cliffords' place. There's no way I'm going back over there to retrieve it. I don't know how I'll ever be able to show my face in the street again. I pick up the landline handset and call my mobile. *There!* It's ringing! I follow the sound of the ringtone into the lounge where, thankfully, I find my bag wedged under a sofa cushion.

I call Dom and he answers almost straight away.

'Is Daisy okay?' I pant.

'*She's fine,*' he says tersely.

Relief floods my body and I sit on the sofa getting my breath back. 'Where are you?'

'*Mel's.*'

'Mel's?' A sudden chill coats my spine. 'What are you doing over there?'

'*She messaged me this morning to see how you were. You were still asleep so I decided to come over here for a coffee.*'

'With Daisy?'

'*Yes, with Daisy. You were asleep. And anyway you were pissed out of your head last night. I didn't think it would be appropriate to have you breathing your alcoholic fumes all over our daughter first thing this morning.*'

'You didn't think it would be *appropriate*?' My chest is thumping with anger, with outrage. 'I wasn't pissed, Dom. *You* probably drank more than I did.'

'*You were off your face, Kirstie. I saw you.* Everyone *saw you.*'

'It was non-alcoholic beer. You know that.'

'*It obviously wasn't. And anyway, you were inside for ages. I wasn't exactly keeping tabs on you. But whatever it was you did or didn't drink, you were totally out of order. You could have done some serious damage to Daisy, dropping her like that.*'

'Someone spiked my drink!'

'*Who would do that at a neighbour's barbecue, Kirst?*'

'I'm coming over there,' I say, rising to my feet, my whole body trembling with rage.

'*Don't bother. I'm coming home now.*'

'Bring Daisy.' I end the call with a stab of my finger, throw my phone onto the sofa and pace the living room, trying to calm down, trying to work out how I can convince my husband that he's got it all wrong. I know it must have looked really bad with me falling over, and slurring my words and vomiting all over him, but surely he knows me better than that? He knows how careful I am around our daughter. How I would never endanger her in such a reckless way.

I stand at the window, staring at Mel's place, all yesterday's warm feelings of friendship hardening into a frozen lump of hatred. How could she take Dom's side in this? She didn't even come over to see if I was all right. She just assumes that I'm guilty. Same as Dom. Like she's so perfect. Like either of them are.

Finally, Mel's front door opens and Dom steps out onto the pathway, like a toy figure. I reach out my hand as though to hold him in my fingers. Mel stands in the doorway wearing a short dressing gown, talking to him with my baby in her arms. How bloody dare she think she can keep hold of Daisy without my permission? I drop my hand back down by my side. She closes the door and Dom heads over this way *without* our daughter. My emotions bubble over.

I march outside, the morning air tinged with the scent of burnt charcoal. Dom is walking down the drive, and I stride up the path to meet him. 'I thought you were bringing Daisy,' I cry.

'She's with Mel.'

'I know she's with Mel, but she should be with me!'

'We need to talk about this, Kirst. Let's go inside.' He takes hold of my good arm but I shake him off.

'I'm not going inside. I'm not going anywhere until I've got my daughter back.' I try to push past him, but he bars my way with his body. How did it come to this? To me and Dom arguing in the street like this. Like people you see on TV soaps. We're not those kinds of people.

'Kirstie, please,' he says, trying to sound reasonable, like I'm the one who's out of line. 'You haven't been yourself. I know you're anxious about things, but you can't put our daughter's safety at risk like that.'

His words come like slaps. '*Me* put my daughter's safety at risk?' I spit. 'I've thought of nothing but Daisy's safety for weeks!' I'm trying to keep from screaming. Trying to stay calm, but it's almost impossible; the volume rises of its own accord. 'You didn't seem bothered when I heard those baby snatchers in the monitor, or when I got that threatening phone call, or when I told you about Martin's creepy basement. And even now, when I'm telling you that someone did something to my drink yesterday, you're still not listening. You prefer to blame me than believe me.'

'Look at it from my point of view, Kirstie.' Dom inhales and releases a breath out slowly through his mouth. 'You've been paranoid, anxious, moody… and yesterday you were out of control at that party.'

'You don't believe me,' I say. 'You actually don't believe me.'

'I want to believe you, Kirst. There's nothing more I'd like than to believe you, but I don't think that going along with your… delusions, is going to do us any favours.'

'Delusions? Fucking hell, Dom. I don't believe this.' I sit on the path cross-legged, letting my head fall into my hands. My husband thinks I'm deluded. He thinks I'm crazy.

'I'm sorry, Kirstie.' Dom crouches down in front of me. 'I hate seeing you like this. Honestly, it kills me. I sat up all night with you last night, making sure you were still breathing, making sure you didn't choke on your own vomit. But I can't tread on eggshells any more. I think you should go back to the doctor's. Maybe… Maybe it's not your fault. Maybe you're depressed or something.' His voice cracks.

My husband is a good man. He loves me, I know he does. Which is why I'm so gutted that he isn't taking my word for what happened yesterday. He's clearly upset, but I don't know how to convince him that something else is going on here. That someone has it in for me. I just need to work out who.

'Why did you invite Tamsin Price to the barbecue?' I ask.

'What?' He frowns. 'I would never invite her to anything. I saw her there, but it was nothing to do with me. And I didn't even speak to the woman. Why would I?'

'She told me you invited her.'

'Is that what all this is about? Is that why you got so drunk?'

'How many times do I have to tell you, Dom, I didn't touch any alcohol.'

'Look, Kirst,' Dom says gently, 'I haven't spoken to Tamsin in years, and I was as surprised to see her there as you were. I think it's best if you take some time to get yourself straight. Go and see your doctor tomorrow. Rest, sleep. In the meantime, I'll go and stay with my mum and dad for a few days.' He pauses, 'And, Kirst, I'm going to take Daisy with me.'

'No.' I snap my head up. 'You're not taking our daughter.'

'This isn't up for negotiation.'

'She needs me. She needs my milk.' Talking of which, I'm going to have to express all my milk and throw it away – God knows what substance was added to my drink yesterday.

'There's enough breast milk in the freezer for a week at least,' Dom says, 'and anyway, she's eating more solids now so she'll be fine. I can top her milk up with formula if I need to.'

'You're not taking her,' I say. 'I won't let you.'

'Sorry, Kirstie.' He stands and heads into the house.

I scrabble to my feet and follow him. 'What are you doing?' I shout.

'Getting some of Daisy's things together,' he replies calmly. 'It won't be for long. Don't worry. I'm doing this for you as well as for Daisy. You need a break.'

He breezes through the house packing up her things as I shadow him, pleading, begging, threatening, yelling. Trying to sabotage his attempts at packing by childishly pulling things out of his hands. But he's ignoring me now, grim-faced. I know I must appear deranged, but I'm so desperate that I can't help myself. And I know the more I yell, the worse I sound, and the more likely he is to stick to what he believes.

I hoist up the bag he's just packed – the one which contains all Daisy's things.

'What are you doing with that?' Dom asks.

I don't reply. I don't tell him that I've decided to go to Mel's and get my daughter back. He wants to take Daisy to his parents, well maybe I can take her to *my* mum and dad's instead.

'Kirstie.' He follows me out of Daisy's room and down the stairs. 'What are you doing? Where are you going?'

'You're not taking her,' I say, snatching up my car keys from the hall table.

'You're not driving,' Dom says. 'You'll be way over the limit.'

I pause. Could he be right? No. I feel perfectly sober. Maybe a bit fuzzy headed, but certainly not drunk.

'Kirstie, don't get into your car.'

'I'm getting my daughter.'

'No. If you get Daisy, I'm going to have to call the police… and social services.'

'You wouldn't!' I cry, turning back to face him.

'They won't let you take her,' he says. 'Not after what happened yesterday in front of all the neighbours.'

'You bastard.' I want so much to make him understand, to see that I'm not a danger to our daughter.

'No,' he says, continuing down the staircase towards me. 'I'm not doing this to be a bastard. I'm doing it to protect Daisy and to give you a chance to get better. That's all.'

I can't allow him to call the police, and especially not social services. Dom knows he's got me. There's nothing I can do. I drop my car keys back onto the table, and let Daisy's bag slide out of my hand onto the hall floor. Everything is slipping through my fingers, falling away. Maybe Dom's right. Maybe my mind has come loose and I need help. I catch sight of my reflection in the hall mirror, and I'm shocked by the dishevelled, hollow-eyed woman staring back at me.

CHAPTER THIRTY-ONE

The water cascades over my body in a gentle stream, an attempt to wash away the disaster that my life has become. I stare at the gathering droplets on the shower screen wishing I could become one of them – a single, innocuous bead of water. I focus my gaze on one, then smear it away with my fingertip. Gone. Disappeared. It's thoughts like these which have driven away my husband. My fingers curl into loose fists. I flex them, wincing at the painful pull of scratched, bruised skin on the back of my hand.

Dom has gone to his parents' house. He's taken our daughter with him, and I'm here alone in this house that has become more like a self-made fortress, a prison. Turning my face up to the shower head, I close my eyes and stand, unmoving, letting the water flow. For how long, I don't know. Eventually, my mind clears a little and the dark thoughts recede to be replaced by a small flutter of determination.

The shower dial creaks as I switch it off. I push open the steamed-up cubicle and step out onto the mat. A damp towel hangs on the back of the door. I use it to dry myself, carefully patting the livid bruises, and then I go into the bedroom and pull on a cotton sundress – one that's loose enough not to irritate my tender skin.

Downstairs, I drink more water, determined to flush any toxins out of my body. I've already poured two boobs' worth of milk down the sink, but I don't know how much more I'll need to ditch until it's safe for Daisy to drink again. Just thinking about her gives me a physical ache in my chest. I bend forward with my hands on my hips, sucking in breaths to ease the hurt. Will she be crying for me? Surely she'll be missing her mummy? I dread to think what Dom has told Geoff and Audrey. They've always spoiled Dom, so they'll take his side, no questions asked. I get on with his parents, I love them, of course I do, but when it comes down to it, he's their son and they will happily believe the worst of me. Of that I'm quite sure.

I pour myself another glass of water and drift into the lounge, but I'm too restless to sit. Instead, I stand and stare out of the window, at the stillness of the cul-de-sac. It's Sunday, so the builders aren't around. Nobody's around. I glower across at Mel's house, unsure if our friendship will ever recover from this. Why did she text Dom rather than me? I think she must still bear a grudge about the money. I sigh. Perhaps I was too judgemental, too harsh. Maybe I should have given her the money gracefully without any demands. After all, she's like family. But I can't think about that now. I have more important things to worry about, like the state of my marriage, and when Dom is going to bring Daisy home.

It's funny, but without Daisy here, I don't even feel an urge to check the locks. What's the point? Maybe it's a good thing she's at Dom's parents. She's safer away from home because, although Geoff and Audrey's house is only a few minutes' drive away, at least Martin doesn't know where they live.

I notice that my neighbour's car is missing from his driveway. My heart thumps uncomfortably as I realise what this means… Martin is out. But when did he leave and when is he coming back? I don't know the answers to those questions, which means he could be back any minute. Do I dare to do what I know needs to be done? Couldn't this be the perfect opportunity, while Daisy is out of the house? I still don't feel as though I'm quite in my right mind. My thoughts are scattered and shaky. But what

I do know is that I won't be able to relax until I see who or what is down in Martin's basement. I need to prove to myself that I'm not losing my mind, that something really is going on next door. And, if I'm honest, I have a strong urge to prove Dom wrong. To say *I told you so*.

I scoop up my shoulder bag from the sofa and slide my phone inside. I decide to go out the back way in case any neighbours are looking out of their windows. I ease the back doors open and step outside, scanning the garden and the fields beyond. No movement. Nothing but patchy grass, trees and sky. Gripping the heavy wooden patio table with both hands, I heave it off the flagstones and onto the grass. From there, I drag it over to Martin's fence, churning up the dry grass and leaving two parallel gouges across the lawn.

Nervously, I glance around once more, but I'm still too close to the house for the Parkfields to spot me from their windows, unless they decided to lean out for some reason. My side is throbbing with pain again, but I ignore it. What I'm doing now is more important than any physical discomfort I might feel. I clamber up onto the table. Kneeling, I hold my breath and peer over Martin's fence. His garden appears to be empty. All the while I have one ear cocked for the sound of an engine or car door slamming, but so far, all is quiet.

Okay, this is the point of no return. I'm about to break the law.

Gingerly, I grip the top of the fence and wiggle it, testing its strength. Our side of the fence is grey and faded, but Martin's side has been coated with wood-preservative and it feels strong enough. With shaky limbs, I swing one leg over, then the next, and drop down into his garden. My whole body jars, and it's all I can do to stop myself from crying out as the pain in my right side flares. With watering eyes, I stand for a moment and wait for the feeling to subside a little. But time is not on my side – Martin could be back at any moment.

I scan the back of his house for an open window, but there are none, so I scoot around the side where there are two frosted-glass windows, both shut. The only options open to me are to either go back home and forget this, or to break into Martin's house.

I've come this far, I can't back down now.

All of Martin's windows are double glazed, impossible for me to break, but his back door is half-glazed with what looks like a single pane of opaque glass. A large stone would do the trick, and then I could reach in and hope that the key is in the lock. I glance around the garden, searching for anything suitable to use. By my feet, I see a metal trowel in an empty plant pot. I pick it up. The handle is solid metal. A hard jab on the door pane should be enough to break it. I realise I'm biting my bottom lip so hard that I can taste blood.

Creeping over to the back door, I test the handle, just in case. To my utter amazement, the door opens. I almost drop the trowel in shock. Could Martin actually have gone out without locking his back door? It doesn't seem very likely. Does that mean he's at home despite his car not being here? My heart twangs. What should I do? *What should I do?*

'Hello?' I murmur through the open door, tensing up. If Martin is in, I can simply say I saw someone snooping around, and came over to check. Then, I'll make my excuses and get the hell out of here. 'Hello?' louder this time. I walk into the kitchen, my whole body on alert. 'Martin!'

Nothing. Not a creak or a sigh.

Okay, well, I'm in here now. I set the trowel down on the kitchen counter and step into the hall, the stench of air freshener assaulting my nose, throat and lungs. I walk past the basement door, heading towards the bottom of the stairs. I stare up, convinced Martin will be standing at the top, a look of outrage on his face. But the landing is empty, a dark space. I force myself to call up one more time. 'Hello?' I wait, frozen…

Nothing.

Before I go down to the basement, I peer into the lounge and out through the net curtains. His car is still not back. *Good. Okay.* I return to the basement door, take a breath, and pull it open. What am I going to find down here?

There's a light switch on the wall which I press, illuminating a newish-looking wooden staircase. At the bottom lies another door with key sticking out of the lock. What is behind that door, and why does it need a lock? I give a shiver. My fingers are shaking. I check that I still have my bag over my shoulder with my phone inside, in case I need to call the police. *Yes.*

I can't put it off any longer. I have to go down there. The blood whooshes in my ears as I put one foot on the first step, then my other on the next. Soon I'm halfway down and I throw a panicked glance up over my shoulder, listening out for footsteps above me. All I hear is my own breathing, amplified in the narrow space.

I take the final few steps to the bottom and stand in the small uncarpeted area before an innocuous, veneered wooden door. Despite the air being cooler down here, I feel sticky and short of breath, like the walls are closing in. I grasp the key and try to turn it while throwing glances behind me up the staircase. Down here, I'm vulnerable. I wonder if I would even. be able to get a phone signal if I needed to. The key doesn't turn, but I realise that's because the door is already unlocked. So I press down on the handle and push open the door.

'Kirstie? Is that you?'

I whimper, frozen in place.

He's standing there behind the door, a puzzled expression on his face. 'What are you doing down here?' Martin asks, his frown turning into a half-smile.

CHAPTER THIRTY-TWO

I'm in shock. Martin's face is so close to mine that I can smell his rank eggy breath. But I'm too terrified to turn away. My instinct is to run as fast as I can back up the stairs and out of his house. But the door to the basement is open. I have to see what's back there. If I don't find out now, I'll never know.

'I saw someone hanging around your house,' I say, bluffing, my voice unnaturally high.

His eyes narrow. 'Where? And what are you doing down here? You know you shouldn't have come down here.'

I can't help shuddering. He reminds me of an anaemic spider, gangly and creepy.

'Anyone there?' I cry out, trying to look over his shoulder into the space beyond.

He presses a switch and the room behind him goes dark. 'What are you doing, Kirstie? Why are you shouting? No one else is down here.'

'Hello!' I yell, ignoring him. 'Is anyone in there?' I try to edge past him, pushing at his torso through his thin shirt, feeling an unpleasant combination of protruding bones and loose flesh.

'Kirstie,' Martin says. 'Are you quite all right? I witnessed your behaviour yesterday at the party, and I have to say it seemed quite out of character. I never pictured you as the drinking type. Are you intoxicated again?'

Finally, I manage to move past him into the breathless dark of the room. I slam the heel of my hand into the wall, trying to locate the light switch. Martin is behind me, agitated, still talking. I know I'm in a vulnerable position now. He could easily lock me in here. I realise too late that I should have taken the key out of the door. I can't seem to find the light switch, so instead I turn around and stare into the gloom, shards of light from the stairwell helping me to see. But I still can't quite understand what it is that I'm looking at.

The room is large. It must be around thirty foot long and twenty wide. A massive table takes up the majority of the space, on top of which sit strange shadowy shapes. I also notice a pile of bulging Toy Shack carrier bags stacked up in the corner of the room. My heart thumps uncomfortably. I want to get out of here, but my feet are glued to the ground. I can't seem to move.

'What *is* that?' I whisper, turning back to look at Martin, who has followed me into the room.

'I don't appreciate you barging in like this, Kirstie…'

Then I spot something else. Something that makes my skin go cold. To my left, pushed up against the wall, stands a child's cot. With a cry, I stumble towards it.

'What do you think you're doing?' Martin shouts.

Suddenly the room is bathed in artificial light and I blink and squint against the brightness. My eyes gradually take in the struts of a white painted cot, pink blankets inside and the hard, plastic, unmoving face of a doll. The doll from the photograph in Martin's lounge upstairs.

'Get away from her!' Martin shouts, making me jump.

I ignore him, pulling aside the blankets, my hands scrabbling around inside the cot, searching beneath the covers for a baby. But there is no baby inside this cot; not a real one at any rate. 'It's a doll,' I say, letting out a sigh.

I turn back to face Martin, his mouth a hard, thin line, his eyes narrowed, blazing, his body trembling. 'Priddy keeps me company while I'm working down here,' he says, folding his arms across his chest.

'*Keeps you company? Working down here?*' I step away from the cot, my heart beating wildly. Martin has kept his late wife's doll to keep him company, to give him comfort. I don't know whether to feel sorry for him or completely creeped out.

Martin glares at me. 'I was trying to keep my project a secret until it was finished. I was going to have a grand unveiling. But you've spoiled the surprise.' His voice is petulant, like a child who didn't get their own way.

'Unveiling?' I echo stupidly, slowly realising that I may have got things completely wrong.

He holds his hand out, gesturing to the space behind me.

I turn around, still disorientated by the brightness. The table I saw earlier is now thrown into sharp relief beneath two buzzing, fluorescent strip lights. On top of the table are hundreds of multicoloured blocks – Lego blocks. Most of which have been made into buildings. 'Lego?' I say, exhaling. 'I thought you were… Actually, what *is* this?'

'Well,' he says, 'like I said, I was hoping to keep this a secret until I had my grand unveiling… But if you must know, I'm actually creating a replica of our cul-de-sac. It's Magnolia Close in Lego form.' His features become more animated. 'It's a scale model and will be an exact copy of our close and of each house and its occupants.'

'I… I don't know what to say.' I'm aware my mouth is hanging open and that I'm trembling with shock. I'm also aware that I may have made a monumental error in judgement. I don't know whether to laugh with relief, or to cry with the realisation that all my paranoia regarding Martin was totally unfounded. 'But why did you need to build a basement for this?' I ask. 'Wouldn't it have been easier to put it all in the loft?'

'No, Kirstie, I couldn't do that. My train set's in the loft.'

Of course it is. Of course his train set is in the loft. Here's me thinking my odd neighbour is some kind of pervert, when in reality he's a harmless man who I've managed to malign with my paranoid thoughts. I've been so obsessed with Martin and his basement that I didn't even consider the possibility that I might have been mistaken. My instincts were way off. I think about what Dom will say when I tell him about this. He'll probably laugh his head off. I miss Dom already. I miss our easy relationship. Where did it go? How did I let it deteriorate? I've screwed this up so badly.

'I would show you my train set-up,' Martin says apologetically, 'but it's undergoing track repairs at the moment, so maybe another time.'

I stare at my geeky neighbour, still wondering how I managed to get things so wrong.

'Now, Kirstie,' he continues, 'I'm disappointed in your quite frankly antisocial behaviour today. You shoved me out of the way a minute ago and you quite frightened poor Priddy. But, more importantly, my model is nowhere near finished yet. I've only completed my house and yours, so you must promise me you won't breathe a word of this to the neighbours. Like I said, I'm going to have an unveiling ceremony once it's complete. I think the local paper might be interested, too.' His eyes bore into mine and I realise he's waiting for me to agree.

'No, I mean, yes. Of course, I promise I won't say a thing.'

'Would you like to see your house?' Martin's eyes glitter.

'Um...'

He walks over to the opposite end of the table and I reluctantly follow.

'Now this,' he begins, 'is number four, your house. You can see, I've faithfully copied the interior as well as the exterior. Here's Dominic in the lounge...'

I look through the front window and spy a tiny Lego figure that looks uncannily like Dom sitting on the sofa. The layout of the room is spot on, down to the positioning of the coffee table and footstool. I wonder how he managed to make everything so accurate. 'How did you…'

'… and this is you upstairs with Daisy in her room,' he continues, pointing through an upstairs window.

Pinpricks of unease dot my back as I peer through the miniature window to see a Lego version of me sitting on the futon in what appears to be an exact replica of Daisy's room. In my Lego arms, I'm holding a Lego version of Daisy. How does Martin know what Daisy's room looks like? I should ask him, but I'm scared to hear the answer.

'Wait a minute,' he says, his eyes narrowing, 'didn't you say you saw an intruder? We must go upstairs and check.'

I can't admit my reasons for breaking in here. I can hardly tell him I suspected him of being a child-snatcher. 'Yes,' I lie, 'I thought I saw someone go around the back of your house. But, well, I haven't been feeling myself lately so I suppose I could have been mistaken. I just thought I'd better come and investigate. I know you would have done the same for me if you'd seen someone hanging around my house. All part of the Neighbourhood Watch service, right?'

'Yes, absolutely. We must all look out for one another. After all, that's why I set up the Neighbourhood Watch in the first place. Look, Kirstie, why don't you go back home and I'll have a check around, make sure it's all clear?'

'Are you sure?'

'Yes, yes. You don't look well at all. You've gone quite green around the gills. Go back home, I insist. Thank you for coming to investigate, dear. Thank you.'

'Okay.' I let my shoulders slump. Suddenly I feel quite weak, as though the slightest gust of wind could blow me over.

'Well,' he says, his face brightening, 'there is a silver lining to all this, of course.'

'There is?'

'*Yes.* I now have someone to discuss my model with! It's been a terrible strain trying to keep it all a secret.'

That's all I need – hours spent listening to Martin bombard me with details about his creepy model. But in light of what I thought him capable of, I guess listening to him talk about Lego is the least I can do. Something else occurs to me. 'Where's your car, if you don't mind me asking?'

'Ah, yes, my car. I was in a traffic collision last week – not my fault, I hasten to add.'

'That's awful, are you okay?' I ask, trying and failing to forget that Martin is creating tiny models of all the neighbours.

'Mild whiplash. Would you believe the insurers wrote off my car? Apparently it's cheaper to get a new vehicle than to fix the old one. Terrible state of affairs, very wasteful. Nevertheless, I'm waiting for the cheque to come through from them before I can purchase a new one.'

'Sorry to hear that.'

'Yes, well. Nothing I can do about it. Luckily, I have my Lego model to take my mind off the stress of it all. You know, this project is the reason I've been so concerned with the building works next door – the vibrations from their drilling have resulted in some of my buildings destabilising. It's extremely frustrating.'

I nod and give a sympathetic murmur as I turn to leave the basement, running my eyes one last time over the table with the Lego, and the strange doll lying in the cot. It's then that I notice a large mirror at the end of the room, and next to the mirror, set into the wall, is another door, painted white to match the walls, its silver handle glinting.

'What's through there?' I ask, pointing at the door, a strange ringing starting up in my ears.

'Boiler room,' Martin says, his face going blank. At that moment, the room plunges back into darkness as he switches off the light.

I gasp and head for the exit, at the same time wishing I had the courage to go and try that boiler-room door to see if Martin is telling the truth. But my nerves won't take it. I need to get out of here, back into the fresh air, before I pass out.

I rush past Martin out of the Lego room, trying to quell the resurging panic in my chest, telling myself that Martin is probably telling the truth. He's building a Lego model, nothing more sinister than that. That other door is probably nothing but a boiler room, like he said. I need to stop imagining things where there is nothing. I need to keep my runaway thoughts in check.

As I race up the stairs, away from my neighbour, a million things fly through my head. I must go home and try to put my thoughts in some kind of order. Because something else is also occurring to me – if it wasn't Martin's voice in the baby monitor, and if *he* wasn't responsible for that threatening phone call, then who was?

*

At last, I'm back in my own quiet garden, slightly shell-shocked and somewhat chastened, with nothing but the sound of birdsong in my ears and the sigh of a warm breeze on my skin. It feels like hours since I was last here, but it can't have been more than twenty minutes ago. My legs are trembling and my dress is sticking to my back and to my legs. I need to go inside and sit down where it's cool and quiet. To process everything. I can't be sure if Martin was telling me the truth when he said the other door leads to the boiler room. He could be lying. The Lego room could be a cover for something more sinister. But, no, I should stop this. I'm doing it again – making wild assumptions without any proof.

I realise I left my back door open – not a smart move. I must really be out of sorts. Now I've discovered that Martin may not be responsible for whatever's going on, I need to be even more on my guard. It could be someone else out there who threatened me on the phone. Someone else who attempted to snatch a baby. After all, didn't I hear two voices in the monitor that night?

I quickly head inside and turn to close the doors, but as I do so, I feel a prickling sensation snake its way down my back.

I'm not alone. Someone else is in my house.

CHAPTER THIRTY-THREE

'Don't freak out.'

A male voice. He sounds almost as scared as I feel.

I remain where I am, facing the bifold doors, afraid to turn around. 'What do you want?' I ask, a tremor in my voice.

'It's okay, it's only me, miss.'

'Callum?' I turn around and let out a huge sigh of relief when I see the boy standing by the kitchen table, his hands raised as though in surrender, his puppy-dog eyes brimming with worry. 'You scared the life out of me,' I snap. 'What are you doing in here? You shouldn't be inside my house.' I know how ironic that sounds considering my recent actions, but Callum doesn't know that.

'Sorry,' he says, lowering his hands. 'Didn't mean to scare you.'

'So?' I ask. 'Have you got an explanation for what you're doing here? And don't tell me you're looking for your football.'

'No. I was in the fields out the back, trying to get hold of Hannah – she hasn't replied to my texts – and I saw your back door was open…'

'So you thought you'd wander in?' I need Callum to leave. My mind is still churning from my encounter with Martin.

'No,' he replies. 'I rang your doorbell first. But you didn't answer, so I came round the back again to see if you were okay.'

'And what made you think you could just come inside?' I ask in my most serious teacher voice.

He shifts from one foot to the other. 'I was worried, miss.'

'Worried?'

'I heard what happened at the barbecue yesterday.'

My face heats up at the thought of it. A breath of wind blows in from the garden, ruffling my dress, my hair. I smooth my dress and push the curls off my face.

'I know your husband took your daughter away this morning.'

My heart begins to beat faster. 'Are you spying on me, Callum?'

Now it's his turn to flush. 'No. I just heard about it. You know what it's like, people talk. I wanted to say I'm sorry about what went on.'

'You didn't just break in here to say you're sorry.' A myriad of possible reasons why he could be here race across my mind, but none of them make any sense.

'I didn't break in!' He thrusts out his jaw. 'When you didn't answer the door, I was worried. I knew your husband had gone and I thought you might have…' He tails off.

'You thought I might have *what*? Hurt myself? Come on, Callum, you'll have to do better than that.'

'It's *true*, miss. I was really worried. You were my favourite teacher at school. I knew you wouldn't have got shitfaced at the party and dropped your baby like they said you did. Thing is… I know something.'

'What! What do you know?' The look on his face is scaring me. He seems uncomfortable, like he knows something bad. Something I won't want to hear. The trees and bushes are rustling outside. A dog barks in the distance.

'For starters, your husband shouldn't have taken your little 'un away,' Callum says with a scowl. 'You should get her back off him.'

'It's not what you think,' I say, wondering why I'm discussing my personal life with an eighteen-year-old boy. 'I haven't been myself recently,' I continue. 'Dom's taken Daisy to his parents to give me a break. Now, if you don't mind, I'd like you to leave. I appreciate your concern, though,' I add.

'Don't you wanna hear what I've got to say?' he asks.

I'm not sure I do. But he obviously has something he wants to get off his chest. 'Go on then, Callum. But make it quick. I'm not feeling too great.' The events of the party are catching up with me. I really think I need to go and lie down.

Callum tilts his head. 'I know something about your husband.'

A chill settles on my shoulders. I walk over to the kitchen table, pull out a chair and take a seat, crossing my legs and then my arms. 'What? What do you know about him?' I'm telling myself to stay calm. This boy can't possibly know anything about my family. He's just a kid who believes whatever ridiculous gossip he's heard.

'Well, for starters, he's getting juice from Jimmy Clifford.' Callum grips the back of a chair and tips it towards him.

'*Juice?* What are you talking about?' I don't like the sound of this.

'Steroids, miss.'

'What?' As shocking as this sounds, I'm almost relieved. I don't know what I was expecting, but it was something far worse than steroids. 'You think Dom's taking steroids? Who told you that? You can't come round here and start accusing...' But suddenly it all starts to make sense – Dom's brief visits to the Cliffords after work, his obsession with training.

'Everyone knows about Jimmy,' Callum says. 'I've scored there myself from time to time.'

I raise my eyebrows.

'Nothing heavy, miss. Just dope.'

'So? You buy dope. So what. What makes you think Dom's taking steroids? Jimmy's a friend, that's all. He goes round there for the occasional beer sometimes.'

Callum pulls the chair out and sits down, starts drumming his fingertips on the table. 'I saw Dom there once with the gear in his hand. Told him his secret was safe with me, but he hates me now. Thinks I'm going to tell someone.'

'Well, Callum. You have told someone. You've just told me.'

'Yeah, but that's different. You're his wife. You deserve better than that scumbag.'

'Excuse me!'

'Sorry, miss, but Dom's a tosser.'

I rise to my feet and take a step towards the open back door. 'Okay, Callum, I'd like you to leave now.' I grit my teeth, tiring of this conversation, of this boy and his talk of drugs and steroids. I've got more important things to worry about, like who's threatening me and my baby and how I'm going to get Dom and Daisy to come back home.

'Sorry,' Callum says, sounding anything but, 'I know he's your husband and you probably love him and everything, but you shouldn't. I haven't told you the rest.' His drumming fingertips are getting faster, louder.

'Do you think you could stop that?' I ask, nodding at his hands.

Callum splays his fingers flat on the table, then looks back up at me, his dark eyes full of something – pity? I can't tell. 'It's a bit awkward,' he says. 'This thing I've got to tell you.'

I shake my head, impatient. 'Go on. Spit it out.' I notice a damp patch up on the corner of the ceiling, right below the bathroom. We must have a leak somewhere. I'll have to get Dom to check it out when he comes home… *If* he comes home.

'You know you called the cops about that baby-monitor thing?' Callum says, jolting me back to the present.

'How do you know about that?' I ask, tensing.

'That doesn't matter, miss. The thing I need to tell you is that there *is* another baby in your road.'

'What?' I take another step back. This boy is in my house. Only he's not a boy, he's a man. And he's just admitted that he knows about another baby. Maybe he's not the sweet person I thought he was.

'It's not what you think,' he says quickly, his eyes wide, realising he's frightening me.

'You better tell me what the hell's going on, Callum.'

'It's Hannah's baby.'

'Hannah? But she's only fifteen!' I realise that was a naive thing to say. Hannah has been flirting with boys at school since she was twelve.

'She's sixteen now,' Callum replies. 'Anyway, her family's trying to keep it quiet. Trying to stop it turning into a scandal. Parky'll probably lose his job if the school finds out his daughter got pregnant when she was fifteen – got to keep a squeaky-clean reputation and all that crap. That's why they're moving house. Parky's got a new job up north. Hannah's pissed off – she said her parents are going to pretend the baby's theirs.'

'Is it *your* baby?' I ask. 'Is that why you've been hanging around next door? I thought you said you two were just friends.' Something else occurs to me – I bet it was Parkfield behind that anonymous call, trying to warn me off. Trying to stop any gossip from flying around school. My blood heats up as the realisation begins to dawn. All that stress and fear caused by a pompous man trying to save his reputation.

'No,' Callum says, 'the baby's not mine, even though her parents think I'm the dad. That's why they hate me. Me and Han, we're just friends. We've never slept together. Never even kissed. She was a virgin until…' Callum's hands curl into fists and his face turns red.

'Callum?' I prompt.

'I'm sorry, miss. I didn't want to tell you this.'

'Tell me what?' The room begins to close in as I wait for him to go on. My heart drums in my ears and pulses in my fingertips. I don't want him to finish his sentence. I don't want to hear what he has to say. The air stills as if holding its breath.

'Hannah was a virgin,' Callum says, 'until she slept with your husband.'

CHAPTER THIRTY-FOUR

The air leaves my lungs and it feels like an eternity until I take my next breath. He can't possibly be telling the truth. 'Why would you even say something like that?'

'Because it's true. I'm sorry, miss, but it is.'

'Dom was right about you,' I cry. 'You're a troublemaker.'

'Yeah, well he would say that, wouldn't he? He knows I'm on to him.'

'Get out!' I cry. 'Go on, just get out!' I cross the room and pull at the shoulder of his T-shirt, attempting to haul him to his feet. 'Maybe you're right about the steroids, Callum. Maybe. But what you're accusing Dom of – cheating on me, sleeping with an underage girl – no, I don't believe it. We've been together for years. I know him, and he wouldn't do that. He just wouldn't.'

'I know it must be a crap thing to hear,' he says, getting to his feet, cringing against my rough treatment of him, despite the fact he's bigger than me, 'but I'm not lying, miss. I promise. Hannah told me herself. I thought you deserved to know the truth, especially after he's gone off with your little 'un. It's not right. He shouldn't have her. Your baby should be with you, not that paedo.'

'Don't call him that!' I propel him in the direction of the back door, trying to get him out of my house. 'And I don't suppose you've considered that it's Hannah who's lying?' *That must be it*, I think, relieved. *She's always been a little madam. She's lying through her teeth. She has to be.*

'Hannah's not like that,' he says, shaking his head vigorously. 'She wouldn't lie to me. We're friends. She tells me everything. Look, miss, before I go, there's something else—'

'Something else? What else can there possibly be?'

'It was *my* voice you heard in the monitor that night. I'm sorry I scared you.'

'*Your* voice?' I take my hand off him and take a step back. What exactly is he telling me here?

'Yeah. I was in Hannah's room that night when the cops came round asking if there was another baby in Magnolia Close.'

'You were in Hannah's room?' I frown. 'I find it hard to believe that Lorna would let you into her daughter's bedroom.'

'Yeah, well, course she didn't know I was up there. Me and Han heard the cops tell her mum and stepdad that you reported an attempted baby abduction. They said you heard voices in your baby monitor.'

'I did hear voices. And now you're saying it was *you*?'

Callum gazes down at his trainers for a moment. 'I was telling Han she didn't have to put up with her parents taking the baby. I said we should just take him ourselves and go off, run away somewhere. She knows I'd do anything for her. I'd help raise Leo. We could do it together. Her parents couldn't stop us.'

'Oh my God, that really was you!' I stagger backwards and sit back down on the kitchen chair, letting my head fall into my hands, letting his words sink in.

'Yeah,' Callum continues. 'We didn't know that Leo's monitor was being picked up by yours. Then, when the police came round to ask about a baby, well, me and Hannah nearly died. Couldn't believe it. Parky went mental. He hadn't realised I was upstairs. When he found me up there, he threatened to kill me. And Hannah's mum was just as bad. We all had a right barney. I'm not allowed back there, so me and Han have to meet up in secret now.'

I'm trying to get my breathing back under control. 'So, you're telling me that it was really you in the monitor? That all this time, I thought… Do you realise what you've put me through?' My voice rises to a screech as the implications of this sink in.

Callum's eyes widen. 'Calm down, miss. I didn't exactly know you were listening—'

'Calm down?' I bang the palms of my hands down on the table, ignoring the shards of pain shooting up my bruised arm and shoulder. 'Your little whispered conversation put me through hell! I thought there was someone out there trying to snatch my baby! I've been a paranoid mess for weeks!'

'That's not my fault,' he says, glowering at me. 'I mean, I'm sorry you were a mess and everything, but I thought I was having a private conversation with Hannah.'

I know what he's saying is right, but I can't help the wave of rage sweeping over me. These teenage kids have basically screwed up my sanity and may have cost me my marriage. No one is trying to take Daisy. It was Callum all along. He was simply trying to persuade Hannah to take her own baby. How did I manage to get things so wrong? All this time I've been thinking there's someone out there who's trying to steal *my* child.

But even if that part is true, can I really believe that Dom slept with a fifteen-year-old girl? That her child is… is Daisy's half-brother. It can't be true. It just can't. But then why would Hannah lie about it? Why would Callum lie? What possible reason could they have? Money? Extortion? I look up at the boy.

'Does my husband know?' I snap. 'About the baby?'

Callum shakes his head. 'I don't think so. Hannah never told him. I think the only person she's told is me. And, like I said before, her parents think I'm the dad, too.'

'Okay, so if it's true that Dom's the father, then why didn't she tell him about the baby?' I ask.

'Han said she doesn't want him getting in trouble with the police, or with her parents.'

'Nice of her to be so considerate,' I mutter. 'But I still don't believe that Dom would do that.' He wouldn't, would he? He loves me and Daisy. Hannah's just a child – Dom wouldn't be so stupid, surely.

'I didn't want to show you this, miss,' Callum says, pulling his phone out of his jeans' pocket.

'Show me what?'

Callum is tapping and swiping at his phone, muttering to himself, his dark hair falling forward over his eyes. 'Here,' he says, holding out his phone screen.

Sunshine reflects off the screen so I stand and take the phone from him, moving further into the room where it's darker. I'm looking at a photo on WhatsApp. A selfie of Dom and Hannah, heads bent together as they smile at the camera. The caption below reads: *Now do you believe me?*

The date is last November, when I was six months pregnant with Daisy.

Hannah looks beautiful, way older than fifteen, about twenty maybe. But still way too young for Dom. How could he? *How could he?* I pace up and down the kitchen, staring at the image until it blurs in front of my eyes. Callum is telling the truth. This picture proves it. My husband and this… this… *child*.

'Miss.'

I want to smash the phone, but I don't. Instead, I grip it so tightly that it feels like I could crush the metal and glass beneath my fingers.

'Miss? Are you okay?'

'What?' I look up at Callum, who's standing over by the open doors.

'Can I have my phone back?' he asks, a worried expression on his face.

'If I give you my number, can you send me a copy of that photo?' I ask.

'Uh, yeah, I think so.'

I finally wrench my gaze away from the damning photo and give Callum his phone back. 'Can you send it to me now?' I give him my mobile number and he punches the digits into his phone. In a shocked daze, I take my phone out of my bag and wait for him to send the image through. 'So, Hannah and… are they still… seeing each other?' Bile rises up in my throat, but I swallow it back down.

'Dunno,' Callum says with a scowl. 'She won't talk to me about that.'

'I thought you said she tells you everything.'

'She does, mostly. It's just, I think she's trying to protect him or something. She knows I hate his guts. She knows I want to be with her. But for some reason she still likes him. He's old enough to be her dad. I think it's gross. He should be in prison.'

I realise that that's exactly where Dom will end up if this gets out. And maybe it's what he deserves. My phone pings and I open Callum's text. My heart twists as the photo pops onto my screen.

'Can you leave now?' I ask, unable to hear any more. I need to be on my own and process this. I need to work out what I'm feeling, because at this precise moment I'm starting to become numb, to shut down.

Callum stares down at his feet. 'There's one more thing, miss.'

I don't know if I can cope with 'one more thing'. But I let him continue.

'I'm sorry,' he says softly, 'but it was me who scratched your husband's car. I don't normally do stuff like that. I'm not a vandal or nothing. But, well, to be honest, I wish I'd torched the fucker.'

At this point I couldn't care less about Dom's car. But something else is bugging me. 'Was it you who trampled my flowers? And tipped that paint over my step?'

Callum hangs his head and then nods.

I don't know what to say to his silent admission. Those things all seem so trivial now, after what I've just learnt about Dom.

'I'm sorry, miss. I did it to get back at your husband, not you. I was so angry.'

'Just go, Callum.'

'Okay. I'm sorry,' he repeats.

As he steps out of the back door, I remember something else. 'Wait!' I stand and turn to face him.

He stops and turns, his dark eyebrows raised.

'Was it you who rang me that time?' I ask.

'Rang you?'

'That anonymous call telling me to back off.' I trawl my brain to remember the exact words… '"Stop poking your nose in." That's what they said. Was that you as well?'

'I dunno what you're talking about. I didn't even know your number before just now so how could I have called you?'

'Do you promise?'

'Look, I just came round here to tell you some pretty serious stuff. Why would I lie about a phone call?'

'I don't know. I don't suppose you would.'

'And why would anyone say that to you?' Callum asks. 'Maybe it was a wrong number.'

'They used my first name.'

'So what did they say exactly?'

'What I just said. "Stop poking your nose in or you'll regret it."'

'Shit. So it was like a threat or something.'

I nod. If it wasn't Callum who called me, then it doesn't make sense. Who could it have been? Unless… *No.* Dom wouldn't do that to me, would he? I don't know. My husband is not the person I thought he was. 'I really need you to leave now, Callum.'

'Sorry, miss. For… you know. Everything.'

I don't reply. I just sit where I am, wishing I could blot everything out.

After Callum has gone, a deep silence overtakes the room.

My husband and Hannah Slater. I picture them together, more intimately, his hands on her body, and I rush over to the sink, vomiting up all the water I drank this morning. I wipe my mouth with the back of my hand. Is Dom still seeing her? Are they in love? It can't be possible, can it? But then again… it might be.

I grip the edge of the sink and take a breath as my mind unlocks and starts racing ahead. What if Dom hasn't been working late these past few weeks, and instead he's been meeting up in secret with Hannah Slater? What if he wants to be with her permanently? I squirt washing-up liquid into the basin and run the hot water tap to clean out the sink. Something else occurs to me – maybe my own husband has been setting me up to look crazy, making me appear neglectful. Could he have spiked my drink at the party? He could have. But he wouldn't have, would he? Or maybe… was Hannah there yesterday? Did *she* do it?

Once the sink is clean, I pour myself a glass of water, rinse out my mouth and spit. Then I square my shoulders. I'm not going to sit around here all day speculating. I've done enough of that over the past couple of weeks.

I'm going next door right now to find out the truth.

CHAPTER THIRTY-FIVE

I lock up the back door with sweating, trembling fingers. Then I grab my bag and keys, leave the house and march next door to the Parkfields'. As the soles of my sandals slap against the pavement, I remember it's Sunday morning, so the whole family will probably be home. Fine. Who cares? Let them all hear. If Hannah really is sleeping with my husband then her parents need to know exactly what's been going on.

I stride up the front path and hammer on their door, ignoring the sharp pains shooting up my bruised arm. No one answers straight away so I put my finger on the doorbell and hold it down.

Eventually, I see a dark shape approaching through the frosted glass. I remove my finger from the bell and stand there, arms folded across my chest, preparing myself for a confrontation.

Lorna opens the door with a scowl of annoyance, wrapping her arms around her body. 'Kirstie? What are you doing hammering on our door? Have you gone mad?'

'I don't know, Lorna. Maybe I have. Is Hannah home?'

'Hannah?'

'Yes, you know, Hannah, your eldest daughter. Can I speak to her please?'

'Are you drunk again?' Lorna asks, with a faint sneer.

I give a short laugh. 'You'd like that, wouldn't you? You know, Mel was right – you are a snobby cow. I always stuck up for you, but I don't know why I bothered. Now, are you going to get that daughter of yours out here, or do I have to come in and drag her out?'

Lorna's mouth drops open before she snaps it shut with a glare. 'Okay Kirstie, you better leave right now, or I'm going to call the police.'

'Do it,' I say. 'Call the police and then I'll call the school governors and let them know that the headmaster's daughter got pregnant when she was fifteen years old.'

'What?' Her face blanches. 'I don't know what you're—'

'Save it, Lorna. I know you're a grandma.'

'What are you doing here, Kirstie?' she says. 'My daughter has got nothing to do with you. What my family does is none of your business.'

'Look, I need to speak to Hannah.'

'Why?'

'Just give me ten minutes with her, and then I'll leave.'

'What the hell is wrong with you, Kirstie? First, your behaviour at the barbecue yesterday, and then today, coming over here like this… I don't think you're right in the head.'

'Ten minutes with Hannah, or I'm on the phone to the school governors. Your choice.'

'Lorna! Who is it?' Parkfield calls from a distant room.

Lorna sighs. 'Wait here.' She closes the front door and I see her dark shape recede through the opaque glass.

As I wait for her to return, I try to rein in my emotions. If Callum is to be believed I'm about to confront the teenage girl my husband is sleeping with. I need to hear Hannah admit it. To tell me to my face that my husband is the father of her child. Of all the things I expected to have to deal with today, this was not one of them. I don't think it's even sunk in yet.

A few minutes later, the front door opens again and I'm staring into the faces of both Lorna and Hannah.

'You better come in,' Lorna says. 'Stephen's working in his study. I've told him you're here to pick up some of the girls' old clothes for Daisy. I don't want him to be disturbed by any of this. We'll go into the living room.'

I step inside and follow them into the front lounge. We stand facing one another, the air between us crackling with tension and hostility.

'Well?' Lorna says, 'Say what you've got to say and then leave.'

'I need to speak to Hannah alone.'

'No way,' Lorna says. 'You can say whatever you've got to say in front of me.'

'I told you what the deal was, Lorna.' I have a feeling Hannah won't be quite as truthful if her mum's in the room. 'I'm not bluffing about calling the governors of our school *and* the new school.'

We remain deadlocked for a few moments, neither of us backing down until Lorna finally caves, 'Fine,' she says. 'Five minutes.'

'Mum!' Hannah cries. 'Where are you going? Don't leave me with her.'

'Don't make this more difficult than it is, young lady,' Lorna says to her daughter. 'Your stepfather could lose his job because of your behaviour. He doesn't need any more aggravation.' She turns to me. 'And you,' she points at me, 'remember she's still a child. Whatever it is you've got to say to her, say it nicely.'

Finally, Lorna leaves the room, and I close the door behind her.

'Why are you here?' Hannah asks. 'What do you want?'

No point beating about the bush. 'Are you sleeping with my husband?'

'What? No!'

My pulse skips a beat. Hopefully Callum has got the wrong end of the stick. 'Really?' I ask, 'because Callum seems to think you are.'

'Fucking Callum,' she mutters.

'He also said that my husband is the father of your child.'

To my horror, Hannah starts to cry. She sniffs and wipes her eyes with the back of her hand.

'Why are you crying?' I ask. 'Is it true? Is that why you're upset? Because you're scared to tell me?'

'No!' she says.

'Because if it is true, I need to know. You were a minor when it happened, so I won't be mad at you. I just need to know the truth, that's all. This is my husband you're accusing, so tell me. Please.'

'Just go away,' she snarls.

At that moment the lounge door opens and Stephen Parkfield walks in, his eyes blazing.

'I just need a couple more minutes,' I say. 'I'm talking to Hannah.'

'No you're not,' he replies. 'Hannah, go to your room.'

Hannah scuttles away. I call after her. 'Please, just tell me the truth!' But she's gone already and I can't exactly chase her through the Parkfields' house.

'Get out,' Parkfield says to me. 'Now.'

'You don't even know why I'm here,' I say.

'I don't care,' he says. 'You're a drunk and a troublemaker and you need to leave.'

A million and one retorts come to my mind, but they all remain unspoken, lying thick and heavy on my tongue. Tears prick behind my eyes. Why can't I just get the answers I need? Why is it so hard to find the truth about what's going on? I take a couple of steps towards the lounge door, where Lorna is lurking. She gives me an evil stare and something inside me snaps.

'Fine, I'll go, but you both need to keep your daughter away from my husband.'

Lorna's face drops. 'What's that supposed to mean?'

'Exactly what it sounds like.'

'You're delusional, Kirstie,' she says.

That's not the first time today someone's called me delusional, but I really don't think I am. 'Ask her who the father of her baby is.' I turn to Parkfield. 'You can kick me out of your house, but it doesn't change the fact that your daughter's sleeping with my husband.'

'Nonsense!' Parkfield says. 'We already know who the father is.'

'Callum, right? You think it's Callum,' I reply. 'But maybe that's just what Hannah wants you to believe because the truth... the truth is...' My voice cracks, but I force myself to keep going. 'According to Callum, your daughter has been sleeping with my husband, and he's the father of her child.'

Lorna blanches.

'My wife is right,' Parkfield says, 'you're delusional.'

'I wish I were,' I say. 'I bloody wish I were.'

*

As I let myself back into my house, I get the feeling that I've just made everything a whole lot worse. I should never have gone next door shouting my mouth off. If Dom is found guilty of sleeping with a minor, then he'll go to prison. When she's older, Daisy will discover that her father is a sex offender. There will be a huge scandal and all the kids at school will find out about it. My colleagues, family and friends will be shocked. Our world will implode.

But what the hell else was I supposed to do? Ignore it? Hope it goes away? If Dom really did do this thing, then he deserves to be punished, but it's Daisy and I who will have to live with the fallout. I find myself back in my kitchen, standing at the sink once more, looking out of the window into the back garden. It all looks so peaceful and idyllic out there. So calm. The complete opposite of the frantic whirlwind inside my head.

Although, if I know anything about Parkfield it's that he loves his precious career above anything else. He won't report Dom to the police because he'll want to avoid the scandal. No, it suits him to believe that Callum is the father.

I don't know why I'm standing around here. I know what I need to do. I need to confront my husband. But I'm putting it off. If Dom admits to this, then I'll have to accept that my marriage is over. I'll have no choice but to leave him and bring Daisy up on my own. I don't want it to be true. *Please don't let it be.* My throat tightens and my eyes sting. But I can't fall apart. Not yet.

CHAPTER THIRTY-SIX

I park my car at an untidy angle on my in-laws' gravel driveway, next to Dom's Audi, his scratched paintwork a stark reminder of everything that's happened. *As though I need reminding.* I get out of the car and run my fingertip along the scarred surface of the scratch, the roughness scraping my flesh. I imagine how Callum's anger at Dom must have turned to temporary satisfaction as he dug his key into the side of the gleaming vehicle. If Dom tells me that it's true – that he's having an affair with our neighbours' daughter – perhaps I'll give him a matching pair, and balance out the other side of his car. Or perhaps I'll do what Callum wishes he'd done and 'torch the fucker'.

I take a breath and pull my fingers through my curls. This won't be easy. Before I get to speak to Dom, I'll have to navigate his parents. I can already picture the disapproving looks, overlaid with distant politeness. But I can't let their judgement distract me or make me feel guilty for something I haven't done. I crunch over the gravel and ring the doorbell.

I hear laughter from inside. Footsteps approaching. More laughter. The door opens. It's Audrey in full make-up, wearing an Emma Bridgwater apron over a knee-length, floral-print dress, her open smile turning to mild shock when she sees me. 'Ah, Kirstie. We weren't, uh, expecti— Never mind, come in, dear, come in.'

I step inside their expansive hallway, the smell of roasting meat wafting under my nose, making me fight the urge to retch. It's thirty degrees out, but heaven forbid Geoff and Dominic don't get their roast lamb with all the trimmings for Sunday lunch.

'I've come to speak to Dom,' I say. Male laughter floats out from the back of the house. Nice to hear my husband's having such a jolly time.

Audrey purses her lips and lowers her voice. 'I think you should give Dominic some space, dear. It's all been a bit of a shock – your breakdown, and yesterday's unfortunate incident. Maybe give him a day or two.'

I bite back my sarcasm. If she knew what her precious son had been up to, she might be a bit less judgemental. 'I won't stay long,' I say. 'I just need to have a word with him about a few things.'

'Well, the boys are in the den watching the athletics. Why don't you come into the kitchen and give me a hand with lunch? Speak to him after.'

'Where's Daisy?' I ask, my whole body yearning to hold her.

'Ah, the little darling is up in her room having a nap,' Audrey says.

Her room. Since when does Daisy have her own room here? 'Which room have you put her in?' I ask. 'Dom's old room?'

'No, dear. The small front bedroom. It's perfect for her as it's cooler than the others – north facing. It's not good for babies to be too hot.'

I ignore the passive-aggressive advice. 'Okay, I'll just nip up and see if she's all right.' I make a move towards the sweeping staircase behind us.

'Like I said…' Audrey puts a bony hand on my bruised arm, making me wince at the sudden pain. 'Daisy's having a nap.'

I would be quite within my rights to kick up a fuss and insist on seeing my daughter, but I don't want to cause a scene before I've even spoken to Dom. It takes all of my willpower to accede. But I do it, letting my shoulders slump as I turn away from the stairs. Right now, more than anything, I need to have this conversation with my husband. 'Okay, well in that case, I need to speak to Dom. I'm afraid he'll have to watch *the athletics* later.'

'Fine,' Audrey says, removing her hand from my arm, her eyes widening as she notices the livid bruises and scratches on my skin. She looks like she's about to say something, but then she clamps her mouth shut before opening it again. 'Go into the sitting room, dear. I'll fetch Dominic.'

I step into the vast lounge, an eighties time warp with its dark wooden drinks cabinets, Laura Ashley wallpaper and chintzy sofas. I wish I didn't have to have this conversation in this house, on his territory, but it's too late now.

'Kirstie, what are you doing here?' Dom comes into the lounge, a puzzled look on his face. Audrey follows him in. 'We won't be long, Mum,' he says. 'Give us a few minutes?'

'Of course. Can I get either of you a drink?'

'We're fine,' Dom replies, answering for the two of us.

She leaves the room, closing the door behind her.

Dom glances out of the window. 'You *drove* here, Kirst. I told you not to drive. You're probably still over the limit.'

'I'm fine. This is the most sober I've ever been in my life. How's Daisy?'

'Asleep.' He turns to face me.

'I know that,' I say. 'But how is she? Has she been okay?'

'A bit grizzly. But yeah, fine.'

She's probably grizzly because she's missing her mummy, I think angrily.

'You look tired,' he says.

I bring a hand up to my face self-consciously. 'Yeah, well, it's been a stressful morning. A stressful week. A stressful bloody month.' I exhale. 'I need to ask you something, Dom. And I need you to be completely honest with me.'

'I'm always honest with you, Kirst.'

I drove over here angry, ready to demand answers. But now I'm here, faced with my husband, I can't think what to say.

'Well? What's this thing you need to ask?' he prompts.

I stare into my husband's eyes, terrified to ask the question. 'Kirstie?'

'I heard something today,' I begin. 'An accusation.'

'What have you done now?'

'This is about *you*, Dom.'

'Me?'

I swallow and lick my lips. I can't put this off any longer. 'Are you sleeping with Hannah Slater?'

'*Who?*' He gives a disbelieving snort and shakes his head. 'This is a joke, right?'

'No joke,' I reply. 'I wish it was.'

'First you think I'm sleeping with Mel, then Tamsin, and now someone called Hannah. This is getting ridiculous, Kirstie.'

'Don't pretend you don't know who she is. I'm talking about Lorna's daughter Hannah, who lives next door.'

'Oh, right. And you actually think I'm sleeping with her?'

'I found Callum Carson in our house today and he had some interesting things to say about you and Hannah.'

'That little shit. What do you mean you found him in our house?' Dom's face clouds over. 'Did he break in? Don't tell me you believed a word that came out of his mouth. I already told you he's a liar.'

The lounge door opens and Audrey pops her head in. 'Everything all right in here? I heard raised voices.'

'We're fine, Mum,' Dom snaps, then immediately softens. 'Can you give us a minute?'

Audrey's face flushes. 'Of course.' She glances from Dom to me and then backs out of the room, closing the door once more.

'You still haven't answered me, Dom.'

'Of course I haven't answered you,' he cries. 'Because it's a ludicrous question. Am I sleeping with Hannah Parkfield? I mean what am I supposed to—'

'Slater,' I correct him. 'She's Parkfield's stepdaughter.'

'Well, the very fact that I don't even know her surname should tell you that *of course* I'm not sleeping with her. I'm not sleeping with anyone – least of all you!'

I nod, flushing. 'Well, that's not all my fault,' I say.

'Sorry,' he says, running a hand over his hair. 'That was uncalled for. But Kirstie, how could you take the word of a teenage boy over your own husband?'

'I'm not taking his word for it,' I reply, 'I'm asking you, aren't I?'

'Well I'm telling you, I am not and never have slept with that girl. How old is she anyway?'

'Just turned sixteen.'

'Christ, he's accusing me of sleeping with a child. I'll bloody kill him.'

'There's more,' I say. 'You know that "phantom" baby I heard crying?' I add air quotes to the word phantom.

'What about it?' Dom asks.

'It's real. It's Hannah's baby and she's saying it's yours.'

Dom's face turns white. He staggers two paces and sits heavily in one of the flowery armchairs. I almost feel sorry for him. Or I would if I could truly believe he was innocent. But after the last few weeks, I'm just not sure I do.

CHAPTER THIRTY-SEVEN

'Kirstie, listen to me,' Dom says, twisting his hands in his lap, his voice almost a whisper. 'I know I haven't been whiter than white in the past. But I swear to you that I never slept with that girl. I've barely even spoken to her.'

'Then how do you explain this?' I show him the selfie of him and Hannah on my phone.

His eyes narrow and his cheeks flush. 'What the hell?'

'So? Are you still going to deny it?'

'She said it was for some school project about the neighbours. She said she was taking pictures of *all* of us. I have no idea why she's pretending to be in a relationship with me! It makes no sense and it's total bullshit!'

He looks like he's telling the truth, but then again, he could just be an extremely good liar.

'For some reason that Carson kid hates me, and now he's roped Hannah into this – this sick prank,' Dom continues.

'Or maybe he hates you because you've been sleeping with the girl he likes.'

'No! Kirstie, what do I have to do to convince you?'

'That's the problem,' I say. 'I don't think there's anything you can do to convince me. I honestly don't know who to believe.'

'But I'm your husband!'

'Yes, and you took my child away and ran off to your mum and dad's when I needed you most. You're asking me to believe you, but you didn't believe me when I told you I didn't drink any alcohol yesterday, when I told you that someone must have spiked my beer. Trust goes both ways, Dom. Maybe if you'd listened to me then, I might be more inclined to listen to you now.'

'I'm sorry, Kirstie. You're right. It's just, you have to admit, you've been acting pretty strange over the past few weeks.'

'Yeah, for a *reason*. I've been worried because I thought someone wanted to snatch Daisy. You know that. And it wasn't me going mad either – I found out who that voice in the monitor was.'

'Who?'

'It was Callum.'

'Callum?'

'He was telling Hannah they should take her baby and leave. It sounded sinister, but it wasn't. That was the conversation I overheard that night.'

'Are you serious? So those voices you heard were real?'

'I *knew* you thought I was hearing things!'

'Well, look at it from my point of view, Kirst. It did sound a bit far-fetched.'

'Dom, you don't trust me and I don't trust you. Not a great situation for a married couple.'

'Look,' Dom says, getting to his feet, 'why don't I get Daisy and we'll go home now together. Sort this out. Talk things through properly.'

So now he's interested in coming home. Now that his reputation is on the line. 'No,' I reply. 'I think you should stay here for now.'

'What? Why?'

'Because I need some time. I need to think about all this.'

'But you do believe me though, Kirst? About the Slater girl?'

'Honestly? I don't know.'

'But—'

'No.' I cut him off. 'Can you go and keep your mum occupied while I get Daisy?'

'Daisy? You're not taking her—'

'Yes, I'm taking my daughter back home.' I move towards the lounge door, suddenly keen to be gone.

'But—'

'Don't try to stop me, Dom. I'll give you a call when I've had time to think about things.'

'Kirst, don't do this. Don't let a teenage boy dictate what happens to our marriage. I barely know that girl and I would never lie to you.'

'What about the steroids?' I ask. 'Or is he making that up, too?'

'Steroids?'

'Don't bother denying it.'

Dom drops his shoulders. 'Okay. Okay, that's true. I've been taking a little something to boost my performance. I'm not proud of it, but everyone else does it. It's not actually that big a deal.'

'If it's not that big a deal, why did you keep it from me?' I shake my head. 'You know what? It doesn't matter. I don't even care about the drugs right now. What bothers me is that I don't think I can trust you. What other skeletons in the closet have you got lined up for me?'

'I don't have anything in any closet. The performance enhancements are the only thing I kept from you, I swear.'

'I hope that's the truth. But I'm going home with Daisy now. I'll call you when I've had a chance to think.'

As I leave the lounge, Audrey materialises from the kitchen. 'You two had your talk? I hope you've managed to work things out. Will you stay for lunch, Kirstie?'

'Thanks, Audrey, but I'm off now. Dom!' I call out, as I head towards the staircase 'Explain what's happening to your mum, will you.'

I can't wait to fetch my daughter and go home.

*

It's 8 a.m., Monday, and Daisy is awake and smiling, babbling away to me in her inflatable ring while I kneel on the lounge carpet, passing her different toys to play with. For the first time in ages, I've stopped feeling anxious that there might be someone out there who's going to break in and snatch my child. Instead, I have a sick feeling in the pit of my stomach. A feeling that my marriage might be over. Whether or not Dom is telling the truth about Hannah Slater, the fact that I don't trust him says a lot about our relationship.

Since I saw him yesterday lunchtime, I've done nothing but think about Dom and whether or not he's been cheating on me. A few days ago, I thought he was having an affair with Mel. Now it's Hannah who's in the frame. I even think I suspected him of having a fling with Rosa Clifford at one point. So either he's guilty or I'm paranoid and suspicious. Or maybe it's simply circumstances conspiring against us. The truth is, I don't know what to think any more.

I jerk my head up at a tap on the side window. The knot in my belly tightens. Peering through the glass is Hannah Slater. What does she want? Is she here to admit that she and Dom are having an affair? Is she bringing evidence to show me? Or is she here to deny it once more? Why is she sneaking down the side of my house? Why didn't she ring the doorbell?

I stand and gesture towards the front door, but she shakes her head. I open the window. 'What are you doing here?'

'Is your husband in?' she asks nervously.

'Dom? No.'

'Can you let me in round the back?' she asks, glancing behind her.

'Okay. Wait there, I'll open the side gate.'

I scoop up my daughter, walk out into the garden and down the side of the house, easing back the rusted bolt on the wooden gate. Hannah is standing there, shifting from foot to foot, her hair tied up in a ponytail, her eyes red and swollen. It makes her look her age, or younger, and my guts roll at the thought of her and my husband together.

'Do you want to come in?' I ask.

She bites her lower lip and nods.

'Come on then.' I walk back through the garden and into the kitchen with Hannah following behind like a little puppy. 'Can I get you a drink?'

Hannah shakes her head.

'Sit down if you like.' I gesture to the chair that Callum sat in yesterday.

She sits, her hands in her lap, her eyes constantly darting to the window.

I strap Daisy into her high chair. 'Why are you here, Hannah?' She doesn't reply.

'Look, why don't you just tell me the truth. I told you before, I'm not angry with you, I'm angry with my husband.'

'You sure he's not here?' she says.

'I promise. He's at work. And anyway, he's staying at his mum and dad's place at the moment, in case you didn't know.' I take a seat opposite the girl.

'Did he leave because of me?' Hannah asks. 'Because of what Callum said?' She brings a hand up to her mouth and starts chewing her thumbnail. I notice all her nails are bitten down to the quick, the skin surrounding them chapped and flaking.

'No,' I say. 'But you need to tell me the truth about what happened between you and my husband.'

'I can't,' she says in a small voice.

'I told you, I won't be cross. But I really need to know, Hannah. If you don't tell me, I'll have no choice. I'll have to go to the police and report my husband's actions. If he slept with you when you were underage, there'll have to be an investigation, a paternity test.'

Her lower lip trembles and a tear rolls down her cheek. I also notice her hands have begun to shake violently. She sits on them, presumably to stop the shaking. 'Please don't tell the police. My dad will go mad.'

'You mean your stepdad or your biological dad?'

'Stephen. He'll kill me.'

'No he won't. But if he gets angry, it's only because he cares about you. Same with your mum. They don't want you getting into to trouble, that's all.'

'Bit late for that,' she says with a bitter laugh.

'So, it's true then?' I ask, my heart twisting. 'You and Dom…'

More tears slide down her face. She give a loud sniff and turns her face to wipe it on her shoulder.

The earlier anger I felt towards her has dissipated. Despite what she may or may not have done, Hannah is still only a child. She looks so young and vulnerable. I get up and grab a tissue from the box on the kitchen counter, pass it to her.

She blows her nose and gets to her feet. 'I shouldn't have come,' she croaks. 'I better go before Mum notices I'm missing. If Leo wakes up before I get back…'

'Leo,' I murmur, wondering if his surname will be Rawlings. Maybe she'll stick with Slater to keep things simple. 'Don't go yet,' I say.

'I have to,' she wails.

'Look,' I say sternly. 'Just tell me the truth. You'll feel much better if you get it off your chest. Then we can deal with it.'

'I don't know how to tell you.' She's sobbing now, gasping and shuddering.

I can't bring myself to comfort her, to hold her close and tell her it will all be okay. Not when she could be responsible for wrecking my marriage. 'Hannah?'

'I'm sorry,' she cries. 'Your husband isn't the father. I made it up. I'm really sorry.'

My whole body sags, followed by a sharp surge of anger. 'Why?' I cry. 'Why the hell would you make something like that up? You must have known something like that could ruin my marriage. Or didn't you care?'

'I know,' she cries. 'I know. But I had to tell Cal something. He wouldn't leave it alone – kept asking me who the father was. On and on and on, he wouldn't shut up about it. I don't even really know Dom, and I definitely never slept with him. His name just came into my head. I suppose because he's always friendly and funny. And he's probably the only person, apart from Cal, that I would want to be Leo's dad – he's so sweet with Daisy.'

'What about that selfie you took of the two of you?' I ask. 'Callum showed it to me.'

She flushes. 'I told your husband I was doing a school project on my neighbours. Asked if I could take a selfie with him. I needed a photo to show Callum, so he'd believe me and stop asking questions.'

'Oh my God,' I murmur, realising that Dom might actually have been telling the truth. It takes all my willpower not to take a step forward and slap this silly girl around the face. She and Callum have caused me and Dom weeks of misery and torment. Unless…

'Dom could have rung you yesterday or today, to warn you. He could have told you about the school project excuse. Maybe he came up with it on the spur of the moment.'

'What? No. I promise you. I made it all up. Dom is nothing to do with Leo, or with me. I swear.'

'If that's the truth, have you any idea what damage you've done to my life? Why didn't you just tell Callum who the real father is? Better than lying and causing everyone else pain!'

She nods, still sobbing. 'I couldn't tell Callum, because if I did, the real father, he said… he said he would hurt me.'

'Hurt you?' My skin goes cold. 'Who's the father, Hannah?'

'It's my stepdad. It's Stephen. He's Leo's father.'

CHAPTER THIRTY-EIGHT

'That's why I lied about your husband. I couldn't tell Callum the truth,' Hannah says through gasping sobs. 'I couldn't tell anyone. I should never have told you. Stephen's going to kill me. What am I gonna do?'

'No one's going to kill you, Hannah.' I can barely even process the fact that my husband is innocent. The horror of what this girl has told me overshadows everything. I put my arms around her, pull her close and stroke her hair as she cries into my shoulder. 'It's going to be okay. I'll make sure that man doesn't lay a finger on you ever again.'

She pulls away, her eyes suddenly wild. 'No! I shouldn't have said anything.' She presses her shaking fingers to her lips. 'Don't tell anyone, please. And please don't tell my mum.'

'Hannah, it will be okay.'

'No, it won't. You don't know what he's like. You don't know.'

No, but I'm getting a pretty good idea. She's obviously terrified of the man. 'You've done the hard part – telling someone else what he's been doing. It can't have been easy to tell me. But now that I know what's going on, I can help you. We can stop him.'

'But you don't understand…'

'Understand what?'

Hannah sobs. 'He said… He said as long as I keep quiet and don't put up a fuss, he'll leave Jess and Lydia alone.'

I'm shaking my head, at a loss to understand how anyone could do this. Especially someone in his position – a teacher, a caregiver, a man in charge of hundreds of children. I'm horrified. I feel physically sick that this man has been using this girl's younger sisters to blackmail her. 'He actually said that to you?'

'When I told him I didn't want to do it any more, he said, "That's fine, I'll pay Jess a visit instead." So I don't have a choice, do I? I can't let him do it to my sisters too.'

'How long has this been going on?' I ask.

She hangs her head. 'About a year and a half.'

I shake my head as I hear Hannah's painful confession. She would have been about fourteen years old when this started. Tears of my own begin to prick behind my eyes, but I have to stay strong for this girl. She can't see me fall apart. She's been through enough. 'Does your mum know about this?'

'Mum hasn't got a clue. She thinks Callum is Leo's dad. And Stephen is going along with it, *of course*. He wants us all to move away so we can pretend Leo is his and Mum's baby.'

'Couldn't you have told your mum the truth? She would have reported him, I'm sure.'

'I couldn't risk it. He's hit Mum before.'

Poor Lorna.

'I was too scared to tell Mum in case she confronted him and he hurt her again. And now I've ruined *your* life too.' Hannah stares at me with tear-filled eyes before looking down at her feet. 'I'm so sorry.'

'Hannah, listen to me.' I put my hands on her shoulders and look her in the eye. 'You have absolutely nothing to be sorry about. This isn't your fault, it's *his* fault. And his alone. You are brave and strong and selfless. And that man...' I can barely speak I'm so upset and angry. 'That man will pay for what he's done. I promise you.'

'How? How can I get away from him without him getting to my mum and sisters?'

'You just need to be brave for a little longer,' I say, thinking about what needs to be done. 'But he will never touch any of you ever again. I'm here for you, okay? And I'll be here for you for as long as you need me.'

She doesn't reply.

Why didn't I spot what was going on? I'm her teacher, her neighbour. I should have picked up that something wasn't right. Instead, I've been living next door to this monster for years while he… I can't bear to think about it. Well, today it stops.

'I'm sorry I was such a bitch to you at school,' Hannah says.

'You weren't a bitch,' I lie. At least I know the reason behind it now. This child has been scared and angry for a long time.

'He made me put something in your drink, you know.'

I'm not sure I heard her correctly. 'You put something in my drink?'

'At the barbecue. Stephen… he made me. He said you were getting too close to the truth. He said that if you found out about Leo, you'd report me, and then social services would take Leo away. So he made me drop something in your beer bottle.'

I swallow. 'What did you put in there?'

She shakes her head. 'I don't know. Some kind of clear liquid. Stephen said it would make you look drunk. He said it would mean that no one would take you seriously. They'd think you were lying if you ever found out about Leo and started talking. He made out he was protecting us.'

I thought finding out who spiked my drink would make me angry, but I also feel a strange sense of relief. I *knew* I hadn't been drinking, but I didn't know how to convince Dom. Now at least I know what really happened, that I'm not losing my mind. However, my relief is short lived. A tidal wave of fury floods my body. I will make Parkfield pay for what he's done to me and to this poor girl.

'I'm really sorry about making you sick at the barbecue,' Hannah says. 'Soon as I heard what happened I regretted it. Jess told me about you falling over and dropping Daisy, I feel so bad. I should never have done it.'

'I didn't even know you were there. I never saw you.'

Hannah sniffs. 'That's because I snuck in and out. I was at home looking after Leo because no one's supposed to know I've got a baby. But you won't let social services take him, will you?'

'You love him then?' I ask. 'Your baby?'

'More than anything. I know that probably sounds weird, because of who his father is. But it's not Leo's fault, is it?'

'No. It's not his fault.' But all the same, I wonder what she will think of her child as he grows older. If he starts to look like his father, will she begin to resent him? I hope not. Something else occurs to me. 'Was it Stephen who rang me that time?'

'Rang you?'

'Yes,' I say. 'I got a threatening anonymous phone call telling me to stop poking my nose in or else.'

'I don't know,' she says, frowning. 'But I bet it *was* him. Sounds like something he'd do. He's been paranoid ever since we brought Leo home. Really angry all the time, making sure Leo doesn't cry, and that all the windows are closed so no one can hear him.'

'Where did you give birth? Was it in the hospital? I know you've been away this summer…'

'We were in a cottage in Cornwall,' she says, her face clouding. 'Mum's cousin is a midwife down there. She helped me deliver Leo in the cottage. But then… well, she registered Mum and Stephen as his parents. Mum and Leo had all their health checks down there and they've managed to get away with everything so far. But Stephen's freaking out about getting found out and he's in a really crap mood all the time. Thinks it's only a matter of time before social services get suspicious. He's even blaming me for getting them into this mess, can you believe it?'

'But why are you all moving away if they're registered as Leo's parents?' I ask. 'Surely Stephen's covered himself by doing that? It's not a scandal for them to have a baby, is it?'

Hannah shakes her head. 'Yeah, but Mum didn't go through a pregnancy. People might talk. Stephen thinks that if we move to a different health authority, it will be easier to hide the fact that Leo's really mine. And anyway, Stephen doesn't trust Cal. Thinks he'll spill the beans. Turns out he was right about that.'

'Callum only spoke out because he's worried about you.' I glance at the clock. It's almost eight thirty. 'Has Stephen left for school yet?'

Hannah nods. 'I pretended I was ill today so I didn't have to go in. I couldn't face it. Then I waited till he'd left before coming over here.'

'Okay. Listen, if it's all right with you, I'm going to go and tell your mum what's been going on. Do you want to come with me? Or would you rather wait here?'

'No, you can't! Please. Please don't say anything.'

'We have to, Hannah. Otherwise it will carry on. You've got me on your side now.'

'What if she doesn't believe you?' She runs a hand over the top of her head and pulls at the ends of her hair.

'Why wouldn't she? Of course she'll believe you.'

'What if she confronts Stephen and he hurts her? Or hurts my sisters?' Hannah turns and paces to the far end of the kitchen then turns around and paces back.

'He won't hurt her,' I say, trying to catch her eye, trying to get her trust me, 'because we're going to put a stop to this, all right? We're going to put a stop to him. Today.'

But Hannah continues pacing and starts chewing her nails again.

'I know it's scary to be doing this,' I continue, 'but if we want him to stop, then we have to tell your mum. You've already been incredibly brave by coming over here and telling me. I just need you to be strong for a little bit longer while we sort this out.'

'What about *him*? Stephen?' She stops in the middle of the kitchen and turns to look at me. 'What will happen to him?'

'Hopefully they'll put him in prison and throw away the key,' I say, thinking he deserves far worse.

'Can I stay here while you tell my mum?' Hannah asks. 'It's just… I don't think I can do it. I can't tell her.'

'Of course,' I say. 'Of course you can.'

Hannah nods several times and stares off into the distance. I can't imagine what she must be going through.

With Daisy in my arms, I make my way next door. But I realise that this isn't going to be easy. I'm about to shatter all Lorna's illusions. I'm not even sure how I'm going to break the news to her.

She answers the door with her usual scowl. But behind the anger, I see pain and tiredness. I realise she could probably have done with a friend these past few years.

'Hi, Lorna. Mind if I have a word?'

'Haven't you caused enough drama this week, Kirstie? Hannah's ill in bed today, and I blame you for that. What were you thinking, coming over here and accusing her of such an awful thing? She assures me she hasn't so much as looked at Dom, and I believe her. I pity your husband.'

'You're right, Lorna,' I say. 'I was wrong about Hannah and Dom. It was Callum who told me about it, but he got hold of the wrong end of the stick.'

She sighs. 'Between you and Callum, you're going to send me to an early grave. If you've come here to apologise, that's fine, apology accepted. I'd also appreciate it if you didn't tell anyone about Leo. We're trying to protect Stephen's reputation and stop the school gossip-machine swinging into action.'

It's a bit late for that. I murmur something non-committal.

'Now if you'll excuse me…' she says, pushing the door.

With Daisy still clinging to me, I put a hand out to stop the door shutting in my face. 'Wait! There's something else…'

'Give me strength,' Lorna mutters under her breath.

'Can I come in? It's not really something I can say on your doorstep.' I tilt my head so I can see through the crack in the door.

'Fine, come in,' she says, pulling open the door once more. 'It's not like I've got fifty packing cases to fill or anything.'

I follow Lorna in to the lounge where she gestures for me to sit down on the sofa. As I do so, plopping Daisy on my knee, she raises an eyebrow, waiting for me to explain myself.

'I'm sorry, Lorna. What I'm about to say isn't easy. Maybe it's better if you sit down too.'

She huffs and perches on the arm of the other sofa, pushing her fringe out of her eyes. Her left leg is jiggling up and down – a nervous tick perhaps.

'Hannah came round to see me this morning,' I begin.

'Hannah? No, she can't have. She's upstairs. Like I said, she's ill.'

'She's not ill,' I explain. 'She just said that so she could stay home today.'

'Wait there a minute.' Lorna leaves the room and I hear her footsteps pound the stairs. Seconds later she's back down, a look of angry confusion on her face.

'Where is she?'

'She's at mine, Lorna, and she's upset. She wants you to know something but she's scared to tell you, so I said I'd come and speak to you on her behalf.'

Lorna sinks down onto the sofa, a weary look of resignation on her face. 'What's she done now?'

'She hasn't done anything. It's what's been done to her that's the problem.'

Her face drains of colour. 'Kirstie, you're scaring me. Just spit it out please.'

'Lorna,' I try to speak as calmly and clearly as possible. 'Stephen has been abusing Hannah. Leo is his child.'

Lorna grips the arm of the sofa, her knuckles whitening. 'You're lying.' Her eyes flash. 'Like I said when you came round before, you're a delusional bitch.'

'I know it's hard to hear, but I'm telling you the truth.'

'Where is she? Where's my daughter? What have you done with her?' she yells, rising to her feet, eyes wild.

At that moment there's a sound from above. A baby's angry cry.

'Fuck's sake,' Lorna mutters. A tear drips down her face and she swipes at it with her fingers. 'Where's Hannah? At yours?'

I nod.

'I need to see her.'

'Don't shout at her, Lorna. She's pretty fragile at the moment.'

'Don't tell me how to speak to my daughter! Of course I won't shout at her. What kind of mother do you think I am?'

I don't answer.

CHAPTER THIRTY-NINE

Back from the police station, we exit the car and walk up the driveway, emotionally battered, like we've all just fought in a war. I fumble for my keys and open the front door, Daisy in my arms. Lorna and Hannah tentatively follow me out of the sunshine and into the shade of the hallway; Hannah carrying a sleeping Leo It feels like days, not hours, since I was last here.

We spent all afternoon in the police station, going over everything with DS Callaghan and her colleagues. They wanted to know every gory detail from each of us. Precise dates, explicit descriptions, everything. I was debriefed separately from Hannah and Lorna, explaining all of it, from the baby-monitor incident, right up to the events with my spiked drink and then Hannah's awful revelation.

Hannah had a social worker sitting in on her interview. She and Lorna were in the station far longer than me, but I waited in my car for them. I didn't want them to have to get a taxi home alone. At the end of their interview, the detective asked Lorna where they could find her husband. Lorna told her he would be finishing work soon and heading back home. Callaghan said they would come to the house to bring Parkfield in to the station.

Lorna and Hannah have been assigned a family liaison officer – a woman who will keep them informed of what's happening with their case, and who they can go to if they need any further help or information. They will also be receiving a visit from social services to check on Leo and the other girls. It's all pretty overwhelming for them.

Neither Lorna nor her daughter want to be home when Stephen returns from work – which I completely understand – so I said they could come to mine and stay for as long as they needed to. Lorna has already arranged for her other daughters to spend the night at friends' houses.

Both Hannah and Lorna are jittery as rabbits as we head into the lounge. I settle Daisy upstairs in her cot for a nap and we decide to put Leo in her room too, where it's quiet. I offer tea, but no one wants it. Hannah keeps drifting over to the lounge window, staring into the peaceful afternoon sunshine, waiting for Parkfield to get home.

'What if he knows?' she asks, turning to look at me and Lorna, her eyes wide, face sallow. 'What if he's found out that I told you? That I've told the police?'

'He doesn't know,' I reply, shaking my head. 'How could he? He's been at school all day.'

'I know. I know, you're right.' She chews her nails. 'But he might,' she adds. 'And if he found out, then he won't come home right away. He might hurt Jess or Lydia. He might do something… drastic.'

'Jess and Lydia are safe at their friends',' Lorna says. 'He won't know where to find them. He won't do anything. Like Kirstie said, he doesn't even know. How could he?' But her voice is shaky, like she's trying to convince herself as well as her daughter.

I don't blame her. It's hard not to worry. Until that man is behind bars, none of us will be able to relax. I get up off the sofa, cross the room to where Hannah's standing by the window, and gently guide her back to the sofa to sit down next to her mum. 'Listen to me, Hannah. He won't be hurting anyone ever again, okay?'

Hannah nods several times, but her eyes still have that wide, shocked look. Not surprising really. She's been suffering in silence for years, and now, finally, something is being done to put a stop to it. It must feel strange. Surreal. She gets up again and heads straight back to the window, like she's attached to a piece of elastic. 'What time did the police say they'd get here?' Hannah asks, a tremor in her voice.

'Any minute,' Lorna replies.

'What if they get here before Stephen?' Hannah asks. 'He might see their cars and drive away?'

'He won't know they've come for him,' I say, drifting to her side once more. 'He'll probably think it's something to do with me again.'

Hannah nods several times, still chewing her nails, her blonde hair tucked behind both ears.

'I know it's hard, but try not to worry,' I say. 'The worst is over.'

I turn at the sound of Lorna gasping, sobbing. Her head is bowed, her face in her hands. Hannah and I rush to her side. 'It's okay, Lorna. It's okay.' What a stupid thing to say. It's obviously not okay, but we always seem to fall back on these platitudes.

'I've been a terrible mother,' she cries.

'No you haven't.' I stroke her hair.

'You're a great mum,' Hannah says. 'The best.'

'You didn't know what was going on,' I say.

'But I *should* have.' Lorna looks up at me, her face a blotchy mess. 'I should have known. She's my daughter, for goodness sake.' She puts a hand to Hannah's cheek. 'You're my baby and I should have protected you.'

'Don't blame yourself,' I say. 'This is not your fault. It's *his* fault, okay? He's the one who should be feeling guilty. Not you.'

'I'm sorry, too,' Hannah says to her mum, tears falling. 'I should have told you. I should never have kept it a secret.'

'Don't you dare apologise,' Lorna cries, pulling her daughter into a hug. 'Kirstie is right. This is *his* fault, not ours.'

At the sound of a car engine, I make my way back to the window and peer out. 'Guys,' I say, my heart speeding up. 'The police are here.'

Mother and daughter get to their feet and come over to the window, wiping away their tears. Lorna's hands are clasped in front of her as though she's praying.

We stare ahead at the entrance to the cul-de-sac, where a police car has just turned in, followed by a second unmarked car. We chart the slow-moving vehicles' progress as they make their way down the road towards us, pulling up outside next door, one behind the other.

'Should I go out there, do you think?' Lorna asks. 'Speak to them?'

'It's up to you,' I reply. 'But you and Hannah have already told them everything you know. They're here for Stephen. You don't need to talk to them or him if you don't want to.'

'Shit,' Hannah murmurs, as a navy BMW turns into the road.

'He's back,' Lorna says, her face blanching.

My stomach lurches in sympathy.

I take Lorna's hand and squeeze it gently. She grips my hand even tighter and then takes hold of Hannah's hand too. The three of us stand together and watch as Stephen Parkfield drives his car past the police vehicles into his driveway and switches off the engine. After a moment or two he gets out, and there's a muffled thud as his car door closes. I can hardly bear to look at the man, my skin crawls with revulsion and rage. If I feel this way, I wonder how Lorna must be feeling.

'He'll go mad when he realises no one's home,' Lorna says. 'He told us that Leo was never to leave the house. Not until we move.'

For a second, Parkfield looks across in our direction at the lounge window. I freeze and the other two shrink back out of sight. *Did he see us?* But he runs a hand through his hair and walks towards his front door.

Behind him, the officers have got out of their cars. DS Callaghan and one of her colleagues have started to walk down the Parkfields' driveway. Parkfield stops and turns around. Callaghan is saying something to him, but I can't make out the words.

'I'm going out there,' Lorna says, letting go of our hands and clenching her fists.

'Are you sure?' I ask.

'Mum!' Hannah cries. 'Don't go!'

'Stay here, Han,' Lorna says. She turns to me on her way out of the room. 'Make sure she stays here.'

I give a brief nod. But as soon as Lorna has left the house, Hannah dashes past me and goes out of the front door after her mother. I hesitate for a moment before deciding that I'd better go after her. I grab the baby monitor from the side table, snatch my keys from the hall and head outside.

Striding up the driveway, I can see that Lorna is already squaring up to her husband, yelling at him, trying to keep Hannah behind her.

'Kirstie!'

I turn my head to see Martin coming across his front lawn towards me. 'Not now, Martin,' I call out. 'I'm busy.'

He doesn't listen. 'I just wanted to say that I didn't see any signs of an intruder yesterday, so maybe you were mistaken.'

It takes me a few seconds to work out what he's referring to.

'Did you see the intruder again?' Martin continues. 'Is that why the police are here?'

I'm not about to answer his questions right now. I jog up the path to see if Hannah is okay, Martin following behind like an annoying shadow.

'How could you?' Lorna is yelling at her husband. 'I trusted you! She's a child! A child!'

I finally reach Hannah. She's pulling at her mother's arm while the police are trying to calm Lorna down.

'Mrs Parkfield, I know you're upset, but this isn't helping anyone,' DS Callaghan says.

'I don't care about helping anyone,' Lorna snarls. 'I just want this bastard to pay for what he's done to my baby girl. To know he will never get away with this.'

'What's happening here?' Martin asks, coming and standing by my side. I take another step closer to Hannah to increase the distance between us, wishing he would leave me alone. I turn away, hoping he'll get the hint.

I notice the Cliffords have also come out of their house next door, and are standing on their driveway gawping at the proceedings with undisguised interest. Rosa catches my eye and gives me an enquiring look, but I don't have the time or inclination to go over and explain. It's not my place to gossip about what's happening here. Mel has now joined them and they carry on talking, pointing, speculating.

Parkfield squares his shoulders and glares at his wife. 'Lorna, what on earth has got into you? Have you gone mad? Get inside now. Take Hannah with you. The police are just here to ask me a few questions, that's all.' He suddenly catches sight of me and his scowl deepens, his top lip now curling in disgust. 'I might have known this is something to do with *you*! What have you been saying to my wife? Spreading vile lies, no doubt.' He turns to Callaghan. 'Officers, I'm so sorry about this, I know how you hate false call-outs, and people wasting police time.'

'Mrs Rawlings,' Callaghan says, 'maybe it would be best if you went back inside your house.'

'Yes, Mrs Rawlings,' Parkfield sneers. 'Run along home.'

While Hannah is still out here, I'm not going anywhere. She and Lorna may still need my support, so I ignore the detective's suggestion and Parkfield's jibes.

He turns back to Callaghan, smoothing his tie. 'I'm the headmaster at St George's, and Kirstie Rawlings is one of my teaching staff. She's on maternity leave, but it seems she may have developed a few mental health issues—'

'Let's not start making unfounded accusations,' Callaghan interjects.

'Hannah!' I turn to see Callum come racing over from the direction of the building site, followed by his dad.

Hannah turns at the sound of her name, but when she sees who it is, she shakes her head and turns back to her mum.

'You okay, Hannah?' Callum arrives out of breath, but his dad puts a hand on his shoulder and stops him coming any closer.

One of the uniformed officers steps forward to usher Callum and his dad away. 'Please can you gentlemen give us some space. This doesn't concern you.' He turns to Martin. 'You too, sir.' Martin mumbles something apologetic and shuffles back to his front garden while Carson guides a reluctant Callum away, but they're still hovering outside number six, watching.

Parkfield stares Detective Callaghan in the eye while pointing his finger at me. 'This woman is the worst kind of troublemaker,' he cries. 'Kirstie Rawlings has accused my family of all kinds of things. She's completely unhinged. You can't trust a word she says. Just this weekend, she was blind drunk at a neighbour's barbecue. So drunk that she fell over and dropped her baby. I'm surprised no one's called social services. There were witnesses. You can ask anyone—'

'Yes,' Callaghan interrupts. 'I'm glad you brought that up. We'll also be questioning you regarding allegations of assault against Mrs Rawlings…'

'What!'

'…following an incident at the same event, where she claims her drink was tampered with at your request.'

'Absolute rubbish!' Parkfield cries, his face colouring. 'Look,' he continues, his newly plastered smile translating as a grimace, a sheen of sweat on his forehead. 'Let me just go inside, have a shower and get changed, then I'll happily come to the police station to set the record straight regarding what Mrs Rawlings has been up to.' He glances at his watch. 'Let's say seven o'clock, yes?' He takes a breath. 'Okay. Thank you, Detective.' He gives a short nod, turns away and begins walking back towards his front door.

Callaghan raises an eyebrow at her colleague. They overtake him and block his path. 'Stephen Parkfield,' Callaghan says, 'I am arresting you on suspicion of rape and sexual activity with a child, and of assault with intent to cause grievous bodily harm. You do not have to say anything, but it may harm your defence if you do not mention when questioned something which you later rely on in court. Anything you do say may be given in evidence.'

'What are you talking about?' he explodes. 'I told you, it's all nonsense. I'll come and talk to you later. Surely you can give me a few hours! This is outrageous. Lorna, tell them!'

But Lorna has fallen silent.

Still protesting, Parkfield is handcuffed and led towards a police car, his face crimson with anger and embarrassment.

Hannah wanted to come out here to see her stepfather arrested, but I notice that she is now shaking uncontrollably. The shock is all too much. I put an arm around her and tell her how brave she is.

The detectives lead Parkfield, ashen-faced, to the marked car, guiding him into the back seat in full view of all the neighbours.

'Are you okay, Hannah?' I ask.

'Yeah,' she says, her voice shaky but clear. 'I am now.'

CHAPTER FORTY

Seven Months Later

The tea tray rattles in my hands as I head out into the garden. It's the first day of the Easter holidays and it's also the first warm day of the year. I went back to work in February, so life has been a bit of a whirlwind these past few months. Mel stands up and takes the tray from me, setting it down on the wooden patio table. I sanded and painted the table and chairs last weekend and I can't stop admiring my handiwork.

Mel and I smoothed over our differences months ago. I decided that life was too fragile to hold grudges. Yes, she's a little flaky and doesn't always think before she acts, but I'm sure there are hundred things that irritate her about me too. That's the thing about Mel and me – since we were kids we were always falling out over something or other, but we always make it up in the end. And Mel hasn't been as lucky. I have a family support network. She lost hers when she was still a child.

Mel cleared up the Tamsin situation for me. Turns out Tamsin lied when she said Dom invited her to the barbecue. Apparently, Tamsin was at Mel's place when the Cliffords popped round to invite Mel to their party, so they ended up inviting Tamsin along, too. Tamsin was just stirring things when she told me it was Dom who had invited her, trying to upset me – it worked.

I'm ashamed to say that I haven't been able to resist a few peeks at Tamsin's Facebook page over the past few months. I noticed that she's training for a triathlon, and I wonder if she's doing it to try to impress Dom. I know I shouldn't even be looking at her page, but I can't help myself. Her updated status says she's "in a relationship", but there are no photos or mentions of her new man.

'That sun is just heaven,' Mel says, smoothing her hair back, closing her eyes and turning her face skywards, looking for all the world like a 1950s movie star.

'It's about time the weather cheered up,' Lorna adds, picking up the teapot. 'It's been a long old winter. Cal! Hannah! Are you having tea or a cold drink?'

'Tea please!' they call back. Callum and Hannah currently have their hands full. They're on the lawn – not only are they keeping an eye on Leo, who is now at the crawling stage, they're also running around after Daisy, who has just started toddling, as well as Mel's two little ones. But there's a lot of squealing and laughter, so I'm not too worried. Hannah doesn't want anything more than friendship from Callum, but he is so besotted with her that he says he'll be with her any way she wants. Lorna now thinks the world of the boy and has apologised many times for treating him so badly before the truth came out.

'So,' Lorna says, pouring the tea, 'have you decided what you're going to do about Dom yet?'

I screw up my nose and sit down, angling my chair so it faces the sun. 'I don't know. He's fine at his mum and dad's for now. I miss him, of course I do, but I can't quite seem to forgive him for not believing me when it when it was all going wrong, you know?'

'He misses you, Kirst,' Mel says. 'And he misses Daisy. He's miserable without you and, you know, if you take him back you can hold this over his head for years. I mean, he owes you big time.' She grins.

'If I did take him back,' I reply, 'I'd want to put all this behind us. I wouldn't use it against him, tempting as it sounds. Trouble is, I don't know if I *can* put it behind us, which is why I can't make up my mind what to do. And I don't want to make the wrong decision because it would be a nightmare to take him back and then end up resenting him every day.'

Dom has tried his hardest to make it up to me – looking after Daisy whenever I ask (although I suspect it's more his mum who's doing the looking after) and ringing me every day to see how I am and checking whether I need anything. He also stopped taking the steroids and pulled out of his triathlon. He said it didn't feel right to compete after everything that had happened. Said his heart wasn't in it any more.

Something else occurs to me. 'So, you're in touch with Dom, then?' I ask Mel.

'Oh, yeah. It's just, you know, he sometimes needs someone to talk to. That's okay, isn't it?' She blows her fringe out of her eyes.

'Of course,' I reply. But actually, I'm not sure that it is okay. I'm not sure why. Is it that I don't trust Dom, or that I don't trust Mel?

'You've got to do what's best for you and Daisy,' Lorna says. 'No offence, Mel, but if Dom's miserable without her, that's not Kirstie's problem. He needs to realise that he wasn't there for his wife when she needed him most.' She doles out our mugs of tea.

Some days I feel like it would be easy to forgive Dom, other days, not so much. But the main thing I've realised is that whatever I decide, it will be fine. *I* will be fine.

Mel and I have become close with Lorna these past few months. We both feel terrible about our earlier judgement of her. We never realised that the reason for Lorna's stand-offishness was firstly because she's always been incredibly shy, and secondly because she was being abused by her husband. It just goes to show how wrong we were to have judged her. She was going through a horrific time and needed our support, not our judgement. I just hope we've gone some way to making things right by being here for her now.

I still can't believe I didn't see what was going on next door – Hannah was my pupil and my neighbour, and I wish I could have put a stop to Parkfield's abuse earlier. But if I feel guilty, Lorna feels utterly wretched. We've told her it's not her fault. He never bullied any of the girls in front of her, so she never suspected a thing. And how could you even begin to accept that the man you once loved was capable of such evil?

Both she and Hannah are getting regular counselling, but I don't think what they've been through is something you can ever get over. Perhaps, one day, you reach a stage where you can learn to live with it, to enjoy those rare moments where you forget it ever happened. Perhaps.

Stephen Parkfield is serving nine years in prison. He will also get life on the sex offender's register and an indefinite restraining order after he gets out. And of course, he can kiss goodbye to his precious career. Parkfield denied the allegations right up to the point where he was presented with the results of the paternity test for Leo. Then he had no choice but to admit his vile behaviour. Personally, I feel that *ninety* years would have been too short a sentence.

'Hey, Lorna, what's the new family next door like?' Mel asks, sipping her tea.

'I haven't met them yet either,' I add, also curious about the family who've moved into number two. 'They've got a baby, haven't they?'

'They seem nice,' Lorna replies, shrugging her shoulders. 'Younger than us. Their little boy is a similar age to Leo. Haven't really spoken to them much. Then again, we never really spoke to the Cliffords either.'

'I wonder what happened to Jimmy and Rosa,' Mel muses. The Cliffords moved out of their house the week Parkfield was arrested, and left no forwarding address. None of us has seen or heard from them since. 'I still can't believe they were selling drugs in our road,' Mel adds, dunking a chocolate-chip cookie into her tea.

I give a vague murmur in response, not mentioning the fact that Dom was getting steroids from them. Although Dom has pissed me off, he's still my husband, still Daisy's father. I don't want people gossiping about him. I discovered that Jimmy also supplied the drug used to spike my drink. I'm glad they've gone.

'I doubt we'll see the Cliffords again,' Lorna says. 'I mean, one day they were there, the next they weren't. I wonder if the police will ever track them down.'

'I always assumed they owned number two.' I run a finger around the rim of my mug. 'Never realised they were renting it. I thought they were loaded.'

'It's funny, isn't it,' Mel says. 'You live next door to these people but you never know what's really going on behind closed doors…' Her voice trails off as she realises the same could be said for the Parkfields. 'Sorry, Lorna. Didn't mean to—'

'It's fine, don't worry about it.' Lorna waves away Mel's apology, but her face tightens, closing down.

'Do we really have to go to this thing this afternoon?' Mel asks, changing the subject quickly.

'Yes,' I reply. 'We really do. Anyway, play your cards right and you might end up in the paper.'

'What?' Lorna and Mel cry in unison.

'Didn't you know?' I say with a smirk. 'Apparently, the local paper is coming to cover the story.'

True to his word, Martin has invited the neighbours to the great unveiling ceremony of his Lego model of Magnolia Close. We've all been issued with strict instructions not to touch anything. Which seems a shame, as Lego is such a lovely tactile toy. But I didn't really expect anything less.

'How did *Martin* manage to get the paper to cover it?' Mel asks.

'I have no idea,' I reply. 'The ways of Martin Lynham are mysterious and strange.'

'Well I won't be going,' Lorna says. 'Not if the media are there. I've had quite enough of that lot over the past few months.' As Parkfield was a prominent figure in the local area, there was a fair amount of media attention over his arrest and conviction. Luckily, Lorna was able to keep Hannah's and Leo's names out of the papers, thanks to a court order. But it didn't stop people speculating.

'You're not getting out of it, Lorna,' Mel says. 'I'll text you once the journos have gone. If *I* have to go to the Lego model of joy, *you* have to go.'

'Fine,' Lorna says, rolling her eyes. But I don't imagine she'll be there.

'He still gives me the creeps,' Mel says.

'He's all right,' I reply. 'Just a bit lonely. He's trying to get the new couple at number six to join the Neighbourhood Watch, but they're not having any of it.'

'Their place is incredible.' Mel's eyes take on a faraway dreamy expression. 'I wonder if I could get the builders to do that to my house.'

'Don't even think about it,' I say. 'One year of building mayhem is quite enough, thank you.'

The work at number six was finally finished the week before Christmas. The new owners are an older couple and they invited all the neighbours over for drinks, so we were able to have a good old nosy around their house which, like Mel just said, is incredible. They've transformed their fifties family home into a contemporary glass and cedar-clad box filled with light.

Martin gave the couple an ear-bashing about the disruption they caused while the builders were there, and they were completely apologetic and lovely, which eventually seemed to mollify him. But, apart from their moving-in party, they keep pretty much to themselves.

And me? What about me? I guess I'm happier now, in my own way. I sleep more soundly and I don't have to check the locks more than a couple of times each night. My emotions were all over the place after everything that happened. Grief and shock at what Hannah went through. Fury at Parkfield. Frustration and anger at my husband.

All those weeks spent worrying for my baby, fearing there were monsters out to get her. But it was never my own child in danger; it was Hannah. She was the one who needed saving, protecting. I may have got it wrong to begin with, but at least I followed my instincts. I knew something wasn't right, and so I hunted down the monster until he finally showed himself.

And right now, I'm doing okay. I have my child, my work, my friends. That's got be worth celebrating, hasn't it?

My mobile phone buzzes on the table. I pick it up. Dom's face shows on the screen. A photo of him holding Daisy just after she was born. Mel's eyes flick from my phone screen to my face. I can't quite discern her expression. My belly flutters. I think about rejecting the call, but then I change my mind at the last minute, sliding my finger across the screen and bringing the phone to my ear. I walk back into the kitchen where it's quieter.

'Dom. How's it going?'

'*Yeah, you know. Still missing you.*'

I don't reply.

He clears his throat. '*I was just wondering if you and Daisy wanted to come to the beach for a picnic next week.*'

I sigh. There was a time when I'd have been thrilled that he wanted to spend quality time with me and Daisy.

'*I love you, Kirst,*' he says. '*I want us to be a family again. Come to the beach.*'

'Let me think about it,' I reply.

But as I end the call, I realise I already know what my answer will be.

EPILOGUE

It's a risk, inviting everyone down here this afternoon. Especially the papers. But what better way to throw everyone off the scent once and for all?

After I realised my neighbour was snooping, I had to do something. It was silly of me to have left those Toy Shack bags at the top of the stairs where she could see them, but I think I managed to divert Kirstie's attention with my hastily put together Lego street. In actual fact, I thoroughly enjoyed creating it. I might even make another one.

But the truth is, I paid the builder an extra twenty thousand cash-in-hand to dig out that additional soundproof room at the end of the basement – couldn't risk it showing up on the plans. And, of course, I couldn't let him live after he'd finished. He's buried under the floorboards. Been down there eight years now, along with a few of my other friends who tried to get away from me.

I suppose some people might be horrified by what I've done. By what I do. But, you see, since my wife died, I get lonely. It's just me and Priddy rattling around in our empty house. We just need someone to talk to... Is that so wrong?

A LETTER FROM SHALINI

Thank you for reading my fifth psychological thriller *The Child Next Door*. I loved writing it and I do so hope you enjoyed reading Kirstie's story.

If you would like to keep up-to-date with my latest releases, just sign up here and I'll let you know when I have a new book coming out.

www.bookouture.com/shalini-boland

I'm always thrilled to get feedback about my books. Hearing your thoughts helps me to become a better writer, so it's very important to me. If you have the time, I'd be really grateful if you'd be kind enough to post a short review online or tell your friends about it. It also helps new readers to discover one of my books for the first time.

When I'm not busy making up conversations with fictional characters, I adore chatting to my real-life readers, so please feel free to get in touch via my Facebook page, through Twitter, Goodreads or my website.

Thanks so much!
Shalini Boland x

ShaliniBolandAuthor

@ShaliniBoland

shaliniboland.co.uk

ACKNOWLEDGEMENTS

Thank you to my incredible publisher Natasha Harding for believing in me and helping to make my stories the best that they can be. It's been an absolute privilege – and also fun! – working with you on my latest novel.

Thanks also to the wonderful team at Bookouture: especially Ellen Gleeson, Lauren Finger, Peta Nightingale and Noelle Holton who are always SO lovely to work with. Thank you Natalie Butlin for your commercial wizardry, and Alex Crow for your voodoo marketing skills – I'm in awe of you both.

A huge thank you to Publicity guru Kim Nash, a truly fabulous person who seems to know everyone in the book world, although I'm beginning to suspect you might also be a vampire as I don't think you ever sleep.

Thanks to my fantastic copy editor Fraser Crichton for your eagle eyes and insightful comments. Also thank you to Emma Graves for such an eye-catching and cleverly designed cover.

I'm very grateful to the ultra-talented Katie Villa for narrating the audiobook and making my novel come to life. Thanks also to Arran Dutton at Audio Factory for your superb direction and innate understanding of exactly how the characters should sound.

Thank you to author and police officer Sammy H.K. Smith for advising on all the police-procedural aspects of my book, especially as you've had your hands full with your beautiful new baby this year. As always, any mistakes and embellishments in procedure are my own.

Thank you to the moon and back Terry Harden and Deanna Finn for beta reading, and to Julie Carey and Amara Gillo for proofreading. I always value your feedback and opinions.

Massive thanks to all my fellow Loungers in the Bookouture Lounge. You really are the best of the best. Special beer-and-chips thank you to Susie Lynes for being such a fab running mate.

Thanks also to Tracy Fenton, Charlie Fenton, Helen Boyce and the rest of the Basement Babes at *TBC on Facebook*. Thanks to David Gilchrist, Sarah Mackins and Caroline Maston at the *UK Crime Book Club* – your support and friendship is always appreciated. Thank you to Wendy Clarke and Mooky at *The Fiction Café Book Club* – such a warm and entertaining spot for bookish types to hang out! And thanks also to Ann Cater at *Book Connectors*, a fabulous place for authors and readers to chat.

Thank you to all my readers who take the time to read, review or recommend my books. I'm awe of your tremendous support and it's been great getting to know some of you. I'm looking forward to chatting about *The Child Next Door*! I always love to hear your thoughts.

I don't think I would even be writing books if it wasn't for my husband Pete Boland. You're my biggest support and the absolute love of my life. Can't wait until your own thriller comes out later this year!!